"Tonight, my primary ~~focus is saving~~ **Danny," Melissa snapped.**

"Be alert," she warned as Troy parked again. "From the pictures, her mother fits the build of the woman who took him."

Troy glanced at Antonio through the rearview mirror. "You good?"

He nodded and climbed out of the car, hoping with everything he had that this would be the last stop of the evening. He needed to see a happy ending for baby and mother, and for his own peace of mind, as well.

Technically, he could walk away. Melissa would surely approve that choice. But he was too invested. Despite the old pain and loss dredged up by the situation, he wouldn't let another parent suffer if he could help it.

* * *

The Coltons of Grave Gulch: Falling in love is the most dangerous thing of all...

* * *

If you're on Twitter, tell us what you think of Harlequin Romantic Suspense! #harlequinromsuspense

Dear Reader,

Welcome to book one of a thrilling new Colton family drama. Set on the shore of Lake Michigan, Grave Gulch is a small city full of heart and bigger-than-life characters, not to mention budding romances and deadly mysteries.

In a luxurious hotel ballroom, police chief Melissa Colton barely has time to toast the newlyweds when her baby cousin is taken from the reception. But the ransom isn't about money. The kidnapper has demanded a review of evidence in a murder investigation.

When hotel owner Antonio Ruiz hears why the child has been taken, he isn't surprised. He has his doubts about the police department, too. Although Melissa protests, he insists on helping with the search so a child doesn't suffer from yet another mistake.

Thanks for loving these Colton family sagas as much as we do, and I hope you'll enjoy the excitement ahead as Melissa and Antonio work together to find lasting love and a future full of hope.

Live the adventure!

Regan

COLTON'S DANGEROUS LIAISON

Regan Black

Special thanks and acknowledgment are given to Regan Black for her contribution to The Coltons of Grave Gulch miniseries.

Recycling programs
for this product may
not exist in your area.

ISBN-13: 978-1-335-62878-7

Colton's Dangerous Liaison

Copyright © 2021 by Harlequin Books S.A.

This edition published by arrangement with Harlequin Books S.A.

For questions and comments about the quality of this book, please contact us at CustomerService@Harlequin.com.

Harlequin Enterprises ULC
22 Adelaide St. West, 40th Floor
Toronto, Ontario M5H 4E3, Canada
www.Harlequin.com

Printed in U.S.A.

Regan Black, a *USA TODAY* bestselling author, writes award-winning action-packed novels featuring kick-butt heroines and the sexy heroes who fall in love with them. Raised in the Midwest and California, she and her family, along with their adopted greyhound, two arrogant cats and a quirky finch, reside in the South Carolina Lowcountry, where the rich blend of legend, romance and history fuels her imagination.

Visit the Author Profile page at Harlequin.com for more titles.

For Mark, my personal hero and partner through everything. Here's to the next thirty years!

Chapter 1

Melissa Colton studied the ebb and flow of hundreds of guests enjoying the lively wedding reception. She recognized nearly every face. Friends and family, most of them local to Grave Gulch, the vast majority tied to the city's police department, of which Melissa was chief. It was refreshing to see the people she cared for so much cut loose and celebrate the occasion.

At twenty-two, Mary, the newly minted Mrs. Edwin Suzuki, made a stunning bride in her winter-white gown that highlighted her petite form perfectly. She wore her long, dark hair down tonight, and it spilled in artful waves over her shoulders. Such a contrast to the dark blue uniform she wore while working as the front-desk clerk at the Grave Gulch Police Department. The entire department was happy for Mary, though they would miss her while she was away on her honeymoon.

Mary and Edwin were practically glowing as they

danced and visited with their guests. And why not? Surrounded by loved ones, today marked the beginning of a bright future for the newlyweds.

She'd confided to Melissa the plan to spend the wedding night here at the bridal suite of the Grave Gulch Hotel. Tomorrow they'd travel to whatever tropical destination Edwin had chosen, well away from the typically bitter cold of Michigan in January.

When—*if*—Melissa married, she envisioned a summertime event. This beautiful historic hotel could work, if they held the ceremony outside in one of the lush courtyards full of summer color. They'd host the reception on the grassy bluff where she and her currently imaginary groom and all their friends would enjoy the extended twilight and stars winking into view over Lake Michigan.

And in pondering that wispy future, she realized suddenly she was missing the magic of this moment. Right here, tonight, the couple radiated pure happiness in the grand ballroom that had been decorated like a winter wonderland. Boughs of sparkling, silver-dusted evergreens and ivy twined with soft blush roses, and pops of deep red berries framed the arched windows and doors, and decorated each table.

Out on the dance floor, Melissa spotted her plus-one, Martin Tate, having a blast with another woman and resisted another little pang of envy. Oh, not of the woman he was with, just the romance of the occasion.

But the timing that was right for Mary and Edwin wasn't right for everyone.

Melissa had been twenty-two during her rookie year as a police officer. A husband and family were the furthest things from her mind then. Fourteen years later, she'd earned her post as the chief of police and took great pride in the accomplishment. Though she had no regrets, a little balance between a fabulous career and what amounted to a pitiful personal life would be nice. Edwin and Mary were utterly lost in each other and the mutual devotion was so beautiful. Had she missed her window for a husband and family entirely?

Martin was a prime illustration. He was a local, successful handyman and she'd been invested in their relationship right up to the day he'd dumped her. She'd thought they were fine, while apparently, he'd grown frustrated with coming in second to her job, weary of her changing plans or bailing on dates due to one emergency or two others. She was thankful they'd salvaged their friendship, though, or she would've arrived to the reception alone.

This was a silly time for a pity party and she had to work to shake it off, find a better distraction. With a mental chuckle, she wished Martin better luck with his new dance partner. Melissa didn't regret the hard work or any of the tough choices that had carried her to her current position as chief of police. Events like this just left the door open for doubts to creep in and push at her from every angle. From the newlyweds to the happily married couples to the children, ranging from toddlers to teens, it seemed every exuberant person served as a reminder of what she didn't have…which she'd recently felt a deep longing to have.

No husband or children. No partner to wake up next to or unwind with at the end of the day. No one willing to share a meal, no round-faced baby to rock to sleep or a little one to chase around the playground. She'd all but given up on finding a man willing to exchange vows and build a family with her. She'd never trade her job for anything—and it came with too much baggage.

She sipped the sparkling punch and smiled as the music changed to a Frank Sinatra ballad. At the center of the dance floor, the bride stepped into her groom's embrace. They shared a sweet kiss and started to sway. All around them, others paired up as Sinatra's voice cast a romantic spell.

Melissa swallowed the lump in her throat, searching for any other place to focus her attention. Would her natural ambition be as all-consuming had she been in any other career? It was a question she'd asked herself more frequently, knowing she didn't want to settle for a solitary life. She wanted it all: the satisfying work *and* the loving, messy family. The self-help books and gurus claimed she could have everything, others said she could have it, but not all at once, and still more experts touted that a definitive choice had to be made. She still wasn't sure which view was right.

A fresh awareness stung the back of her throat. Right here and now, she'd choose family. A surprise, considering her badge was wedged into her tiny purse alongside her cell phone and a lipstick.

In the aisle between a row of tables and the dance floor, her cousin Desiree Colton, and her eighteen-month-old son, Danny, danced with Melissa's older brother, Clarke. The trio was laughing and Melissa grinned as she crossed the room to join them. Seeing her, Danny dashed her way and she scooped up the toddler. Kissing his nose, Melissa spun them in a circle while he giggled. The sound was so addictive, the pure joy on his handsome little face so uplifting. She drank it in, giving him another spin before nudging him back to his mom.

She and Desiree had always been close, but since Danny's birth, they'd spent even more time together.

Though Melissa was aware it wasn't all smooth sailing, Desiree managed single motherhood with such devotion and grace that Melissa often wondered if she couldn't have it all, that maybe she could manage at least one child.

Of course, when she'd confided in Desiree, her cousin had pointed out that she was a part-time sketch artist and had schedule flexibility. Meanwhile, Melissa had a full-time job that was far more demanding. Having a baby on her own would mean leaning heavily on the help of her parents, who had active lives of their own, as well as finding an affordable nanny willing to take over no matter when a call came through.

Enough of the litany of what-ifs, she scolded herself, stepping outside into the winter garden for a moment. She wasn't here to wallow; she was here to celebrate Mary and Edwin.

With the music drifting softly behind her, she walked along the cleared path. White lights were strung overhead, turning the fresh snow to a blanket of diamonds. Heaters had been strategically placed along the walkway to prevent anyone from catching a chill. Silk floral arrangements, in deference to the season, echoed the colors and textures of Mary's bridal bouquet. It almost made Melissa rethink her ideal summer wedding.

Refreshed, she headed back inside, pausing at the beverage station for another glass of punch. Several guests were enjoying the open bar, but Melissa had a rule about drinking in public. Other than a single beer at the annual department picnic, she didn't indulge. She put stock in being ready for anything. A young man, wearing the black shirt, slacks and shoes of the hotel catering uniform, walked up to the station to collect the dirty glassware.

"Victor Hadley?" Melissa asked. When he turned and smiled, her entire mood lifted. "Wow. It's good to see you."

"Look, Chief. No handcuffs," he joked, parting his hands. Tall, bordering on skinny, he hadn't quite outgrown that sharp-elbow-and-knee teenager stage yet.

Victor was the grandson of one of her mother's friends. Melissa had met him when he was fifteen, after he'd been arrested for shoplifting. She'd worked with the store owners, arresting officers and Victor to negotiate a lengthy and strict community-service penalty rather than bring formal charges against him. Once his year of community service had been completed, she'd spoken with several local leaders to get him interviews for various jobs he could work around his high-school schedule. He'd been working here at the hotel quite happily, based on what she heard, ever since his first day.

"Mr. Ruiz," Victor said, referring to the hotel owner, "is amazing. He sat in on my last personnel review."

"You're kidding." The idea of the wealthy hotelier with a reputation for serial dating giving any attention to a kid from the wrong side of the tracks shocked her.

"No. It was cool. Intimidating, but cool," he added. "He asked about my interests here and what I had planned after graduation."

She smothered another wave of surprise. "You want to own hotels?"

Victor laughed. "Not really. Wouldn't mind running a kitchen, though."

"Seriously?"

He nodded. "Someday." Excitement shone in his gaze. "Long way from here to there. I have so much to learn. Mr. Ruiz added me to an apprentice program, though."

"That's wonderful," Melissa said. Though she wanted to catch up further, she didn't want to impede his work. "I can't wait to hear more as you progress. If you ever need a taste-tester, come by the station."

He laughed again as he carted away the dirty glassware, leaving her with a satisfied mood boost. Success stories within the community were one of the high points of her career. Antonio Ruiz was a well-respected businessman and invaluable asset in the city. He seemed to hire talented staffers in every area of his hotel operation. Victor's situation was just one example. Mary, during the wedding planning, had mentioned time and again how professional and streamlined the entire process had been, from the first tour to the final walkthrough before her big day.

Melissa appreciated the business acumen that brought tourists to the hotel, but she never would've guessed that the strikingly handsome owner had a heart inclined to guide teens with a knack for getting into trouble. It was an appealing, heartwarming discovery, though it didn't make Antonio her type. He escorted a new date to every event and she was looking for commitment. When she had time to look at all. "You look pensive."

She turned toward the familiar voice and gave one of her younger brothers, Travis, a warm smile. "In a good way," she promised. "Are you enjoying yourself?"

"I am," he replied. A highly successful businessman, he was the founder and co-CEO of Colton Plastics. Somehow Travis hadn't gravitated to law enforcement, or a profession connected to it, like the rest of them.

"Why aren't you out on the dance floor?" She peered around his shoulder, making it obvious she was looking for his date.

"Up-tempo isn't my thing." He raised a bottle of beer to his lips. "You know it's better if I don't put lives at risk with my two left feet," he said with a wink.

"Left feet or not, you know what Mom would say about making sure everyone is having a good time." Even as she said it, she scanned the reception, impressed that no one seemed to be hovering at the fringes of the action or looking left out. Guests who weren't on the dance floor seemed happily engaged in conversations.

"Why do you think I'm standing with you?" Travis said pointedly.

"Was I really the only one alone?" That brushed up too closely to her earlier melancholy.

"That's how it looked to me, Chief," he teased.

"Stop," she said, chuckling at the tone. She was fortunate to have her family's full support in her career with the GGPD. Aside from the requisite sibling jokes, her parents and brothers made it clear they were proud of her accomplishments. "Don't worry about me," she assured him. "I'm having a great time."

"Glad to hear it. Is that legal?" He tipped his head toward their youngest brother, Stanton, who was doing the twist with a bunch of other guests.

Her laughter was cut short by a shout and frantic movement at the tables on the other side of the room. "Danny!" Desiree yelled urgently, pitching her voice over the music and voices.

Her cousin dropped out of Melissa's sight for a moment, likely looking under a table. When she popped back into view, the color had leached from her face and her panic was clear as Melissa rushed across the room.

"Danny! Where are you?" she shouted again. Her long curly hair was in disarray from her searching and her frantic plea filled the room as people quieted and the music stopped. She hurried toward the long curtains framing the tall windows. "Danny!" she screamed. "Mel!" She grabbed Melissa's arm, her grip brutal with her anguish. "You have to help me. I can't find him. Oh, God. Help me find him."

"I will. We will," Melissa said, sliding seamlessly into her professional role even while her heart hammered in her chest. She raised her hand, signaling for everyone's attention. "Folks, it seems Danny has wandered off. He's only eighteen months old." She described his clothing and directed the officers in attendance to systematically search the garden, the anteroom and the hallways. "Show me where you last saw him," she said to Desiree as everyone joined in the effort to find the little boy.

Desiree guided her to the table where they'd been seated for the reception. All around them guests shook their heads, but kept looking. There was no sign of Danny, other than the stylish tote Desiree carried with his necessities.

The officers Melissa had sent into the courtyard and the hallway returned. "No luck?" she asked.

"None."

Melissa steeled herself for the next step, striving to maintain the stoic appearance of a responding officer when she was breaking apart with panic inside. She quickly assigned officers to comb the streets around the hotel and then she called the station.

She nudged her cousin into a chair while she waited for an answer. "Find something with his scent, please," she said gently. Tears streamed down Desiree's face as she clutched the tote. "We'll find him," Melissa promised again. "Just pull out a shirt or his favorite blanket or something."

The GGPD had two K-9 officers, one specializing in tracking and one in suspect apprehension. She wanted them both on scene immediately. Fortunately, Officer Brett Shea and his tracking specialist partner, a female black Labrador named Ember, were at the station. He promised to call Officer Coleman and his German shepherd partner, Bear, on the way to the hotel.

Although fighting her own emotions, Melissa felt marginally better already. "The K-9 teams are on the way," she said. A flicker of hope flashed across Desiree's face. The officers and their partners had earned excellent reputations in the region for helping on a variety of cases.

With one hand on her cousin's trembling shoulder, all Melissa could do now was hang on and trust in her officers to pick up a lead on Danny.

From his office on the second floor, Antonio Ruiz, owner of the Grave Gulch Hotel, tried to ignore the wedding reception going strong in the main ballroom. Oh, he couldn't hear the music or happy voices, couldn't see the celebration unless he went to the security office and watched through the cameras. But he knew it was happening. It was the first big event of the year and normally by now he would've checked in with the staff to make sure things were running smoothly. Sometimes, depending on the occasion, he dropped in on guests and thanked them for choosing his hotel.

Not tonight.

He had no intention of going anywhere close to that ballroom. He was sure the vast majority of the GGPD was down there. Although he valued their role in the community, the police were not his favorite people these days, not even the intelligent, pretty redhead who served as the chief. As a major property owner, it was smart to maintain a good rapport with law enforcement. Up until six months ago, he would've claimed that bond was as strong and healthy here as it was at his other locations around the country.

Not anymore.

Grave Gulch was home and it stung more than a little that the police department had let him down when he'd needed them to step up and take action. Last summer, he'd reported a harrowing incident involving a fellow businessman he'd considered a new friend, Drew Orr.

Antonio rubbed at his temples. It was done; he should be over it. The situation had been a near miss all around. Thankfully, he'd learned Orr's business values and strategies didn't line up with his *before* he'd signed the proposed contract for a multiproperty deal here in town. Though Orr had been good at hiding his shady nature, Antonio eventually saw through the act. Orr was the type of investor who gave them all a bad name. The man viewed bribes as one more cost of doing business and had a shocking willingness to cut corners on construction.

As if that ever worked.

This time last year, he cut all ties with Orr, never expecting to see him again. But in July, the man had shown up out of the blue with blood on his hand, muttering about having killed his girlfriend. He'd claimed she cheated on him, so he'd attacked her and buried the body in a remote corner of Grave Gulch Park. Claimed a lot of things that sounded like rambling excuses to Antonio's ears. He'd urged Orr to go to the police, but the man had run off. Worried some piece of the story might be true, he'd gone straight over to the GGPD and reported the incident.

What had they done about it?

Not nearly enough. Granted, he wasn't a cop, but from his perspective their investigation had been seriously lacking. In his business experience, weak teams reflected the leadership. Sure, they'd found the body and questioned Orr, but they hadn't seen any sign of blood on him and nothing connected him to the crime.

In fact, Orr had fed them some story about jealousy and reputation that had the police taking a hard look at Antonio for the murder. He was furious but he should have expected it of the man after learning how willing he'd been to blur the lines to serve his own interests.

He had a solid alibi, since he'd been helping out an elderly neighbor with yard work that afternoon, but the entire mess only reinforced Antonio's long-held intention to remain as independent as possible. In business and his personal life.

Although hosting weddings at his hotel was lucrative and a consistent boost to the bottom line, this was one contract he'd been tempted to override with a rejection. Fortunately, his business sense and community spirit trumped his temptation to be petty. Just because the GGPD lacked professionalism didn't mean he had to stoop to their level.

Someone knocked rapidly and the door swung open before he could issue an invitation.

"Mr. Ruiz, there's an emergency," Victor said, breathless.

For a split second, Antonio just stared. He surged up from his chair. "Tell me on the way."

"A little boy is missing from the wedding reception," Victor began as they jogged for the stairs.

Antonio listened, dread mounting, as the situation of the missing toddler was laid out for him. There was nothing worse than losing a child—at any age, in any manner. "How long?"

Victor shrugged. "Maybe fifteen minutes. Chief Colton has a search started. I heard someone mention a tracking dog."

"Good." Approaching the ballroom, he slowed his steps, refusing to add to the chaos and panic. But the expansive room was almost quiet and he found GGPD Chief Melissa Colton at the center, taking reports and giving orders. She wasn't in uniform, but she was definitely in charge.

"Tell security to start looking for anyone leaving this room. Tell them to go back thirty minutes."

"Yes, sir." Victor took off at a run, but Antonio couldn't focus on that lapse right now.

He walked in and her gaze locked on him. Almost as if she'd sensed a newcomer invading her domain. Her department's weak response had disappointed him when he'd reported Orr. Tonight, however, she projected fearless strength, competence and confidence.

He wanted to pause and drink her in. Though he often saw her classic oval face and blue eyes unframed because she wore her hair in a ponytail or bun while working, she looked different tonight. Her beautiful red hair was swept up and back in a sleek, formal twist, with a few curled tendrils softly framing her face. Someone had done her eyes in a way that made them look bigger, and brighter than ever. Or maybe that was the crisis. Her skin looked as silky as fresh cream, her throat and shoulders shown to perfection by the forest-green dress she wore.

He couldn't recall ever seeing her out of uniform before. Certainly never in a dress that emphasized every supple curve of her lovely body. This was probably the worst time to register that she wasn't just pretty, she was an absolute knockout.

"Chief Colton," he said, extending a hand. "Victor told me we have a situation. How can I help you find the boy?"

"I appreciate the offer," she began. "Your security office was my next stop."

"I have them searching for anyone leaving the reception in the past thirty minutes."

Her chin dipped in acknowledgment. For a moment, he could've sworn her eyes filled with tears. He braced for waterworks, then she blinked and her gaze was as clear and steady as her voice.

"We're searching for Danny Colton. Eighteen months old. Last seen right here, approximately fifteen minutes ago." She turned the cell phone in her hands and showed him a picture of the little guy.

"Please send that to the hotel security's email address." He spelled out the address when she was ready and watched her hit Send. "Do you need more searchers?"

"My officers are working the area," she replied. She paused, her nostrils flaring. "Creating a search grid," she continued when she had control again. "Our K-9 officers will be on-site any minute. Most everyone in the room is local or federal law enforcement." Her auburn eyebrows flexed. "I have no idea who managed a kidnapping under our noses."

It seemed the embarrassment was holding her other emotions in check, but there was a deeply personal panic just under that cool exterior.

He considered himself a businessman, but dealing with people was his real specialty. His expansive success in the hospitality industry was due to his gift for reading guests, as well as his teams. Early on he discovered an innate ability to recognize the specific talents of his staff members. He loved matching the right person to a role where they could thrive. Every year, he headed up training sessions to teach his employees how to anticipate guest needs. The consistent rave reviews from guests spoke to their expertise. "I have surveillance cameras all around the property," he said. It was a fact she should remember after he'd shared surveillance footage of Orr's last visit to the hotel six months ago. "We can review all the angles in the security office."

She hesitated, her gaze sliding to the woman seated at the table, the only person not actively searching. "This is my cousin, Desiree Colton, Danny's mother."

Antonio crouched in front of the distraught mother. "We will do everything possible to find your son. You'd be surprised how many fun places there are to hide in a hotel. With your permission, I'll borrow Melissa for a few—"

"Melissa!"

Antonio stood up as two men came barreling across the room. He recognized both Clarke Colton and Ken Maxwell from previous professional visits to the hotel. Clarke, Melissa's brother, was a private investigator. Ken, a wedding videographer, was one of the best around when it came to capturing every priceless moment for the bride and groom.

"Have you found him?" Desiree asked, swiping tears from her cheeks.

Clarke gave Desiree's shoulder a squeeze. "We might have a lead," he said, his hesitant tone indicating extreme caution. "It's progress."

He tipped his head, indicating Melissa should step aside with him. "You need to see this."

Melissa soothed Desiree before joining Clarke and Ken at the next table. Antonio followed so he could see what they'd found, as well.

Melissa gave him a sharp look over her shoulder. "What are you doing?"

"Observing. If there's a face or good angle of exit, I'll know just which cameras to ask my security team to focus on."

"Right." She turned her attention to the other men. "Show me."

With the four of them crowded around his camera, Ken tapped the screen and the video clip played, showing a small face peeking around the side of a woman.

"That's Danny," she whispered.

His little face was visible just long enough to leave no doubt. The abductor's back was to the camera; she wore a navy blue dress, and a fancy hat. The video didn't show her shoes, but it seemed either the weight of the toddler or something else was putting some stress on her stride.

Antonio immediately put the images in context. The videographer had been across the room when he'd inadvertently caught the kidnapper's exit through the side door of the ballroom. He made a mental note of the 6:13 p.m. time stamp in the corner of the screen and then asked, "How many children Danny's age are here tonight?"

"Only Danny," Clarke answered. "He's the youngest."

Melissa directed the videographer to enlarge the images as best he could. "I'm sure that's a woman," she said. "Navy dress, stylish spectator hat. I don't remember seeing that hat at the ceremony. Can't see her hair color. Do you have another angle?" she asked Ken.

The man shook his head. "I'll keep looking for her among the arrivals."

"I have more views," Antonio volunteered. He nearly backed up a step under the combined weight of desperate gazes from Melissa and Clarke. "More tools, too. We might find her face as she entered the hotel or the reception."

"Yes, please," Melissa said. "Clarke, coordinate with Troy and keep searching. He can run point while I'm with Mr. Ruiz."

They all gave a start when her phone chimed with an alert. The color drained from Melissa's face as she read whatever had appeared on her screen.

"What is it?" Clarke asked.

"G-get Troy," she replied, her voice hoarse.

She swayed as Clarke rushed off and Antonio guided her to a chair. "Take a minute," he said. "Just breathe." He sent Desiree a reassuring smile before returning his attention to the chief. "Look at me." He paused, waiting until those blue eyes met his. "The boy's mother is watching your every move."

"I know." Though she whispered, her voice cracked.

"Then stay tough," he said. "Show me the message."

"No." Those soft tendrils swayed as she shook her head. "This is police business."

His gaze scanned the room. People were either searching for the child or on their phones. The place would be overrun with reporters any minute now, thanks to the miracle of social media. The brewing publicity nightmare wasn't ideal, but it paled in comparison to the missing child.

"It's a ransom demand?"

"Not your business," she insisted, clutching the phone tightly in her hands.

Before he could argue, Clarke and the man who must have been Troy arrived. Desiree rose and threw herself into his arms. "Shh," Troy soothed her. "We'll find him, sis. It's going to be all right."

"I—I—" Desiree hiccuped and he eased her back into the chair. "He was just here one minute and gone the next."

Troy offered her a few more assurances and then extricated himself to join Antonio and Melissa. The chief stood up, reclaiming her professional distance and authority. He wished he could so easily dispense with the sympathy twisting his heart. The ache of his own losses, the wife and child taken too soon, never left him completely.

"We have a ransom message." Melissa tapped her phone and a few seconds later, Clarke and Troy checked their devices.

As they lamented the message's untraceable source, Antonio peeked at Clarke's screen.

You'll get the kid back when you figure out how there is indisputable evidence that Everleigh Emerson murdered her husband when she is completely innocent. Her trial is a sham. Exonerate Everleigh, get the boy back. That simple.

Clearly he wasn't the only person in town with opinions and doubts about the GGPD. The kidnapper had to be desperate to cast a spotlight on an injustice if they'd resorted to kidnapping a baby with strong ties to the department.

He looked up from the message to find Melissa glaring at him. "That implies the boy isn't on hotel property any longer," Antonio stated, getting nods of confirmation from the others. "We can verify that no one dressed like that made it to the elevators or stairs or anywhere else inside. My events manager will speak with the bride and groom about how to proceed with the reception, and I can open a conference room for you to work from, if you want to stay on-site."

"We do," Melissa said. "This is our best chance of picking up a lead."

Her laser-blue gaze shifted to the others. "Troy, Clarke, find out more about Everleigh Emerson, anything about her case, where her relatives are. Find a motive. I'll go with Mr. Ruiz. With luck, hotel surveillance will give us more information about the woman in the navy blue dress."

Antonio extended his arm toward the main door. "This way." Her efficiency impressed him and gave him hope that mother and son would be reunited.

He didn't speak, as he was unwilling to risk being overheard as they moved swiftly from the ballroom, through the central lobby and past the registration desk to the security office at the back of the hotel. Her heels clicked on the marble floor and her dress swished softly with every stride. Though he'd interacted with Melissa frequently at various community events, he didn't recall smelling the enticing fragrance she was wearing before tonight. She smelled like lilies and moonlight. Which was a ridiculous distraction while a mother wept for her son.

Pressing his access card to the panel near the door, he greeted the two men on duty in front of the array of monitors. "We've just cued up the wedding and reception arrivals, sir."

"Thank you," Antonio said. "Any sign of the woman or child outside the hotel?"

"Not so far."

"All right. Give us the room," he directed, ushering Melissa to one of the vacated chairs.

He didn't care for this rush of awareness of her as a woman. She was a cop. The head of a department he didn't have much faith in right now. He hoped, for the family's sake, though, that this search ended happily for everyone.

"Don't feel like you have to hold back." She leaned forward, her gaze already scanning the various images. "I know you don't like me," she said.

"That's not how I'd put it," he said, hedging. He found her outrageously attractive this evening. Honestly, he'd *always* found her attractive, and also off-limits, especially after the fiasco over the summer. "I don't care for the recent lapses in your department. Based on that ransom note, it sounds as if others share my view."

Her lips flattened into a stern line. "Is that supposed to be an attempt at diplomacy?"

"Yes." He turned his attention to the monitors, looking for any sign of the woman in the hat leaving the hotel with the boy. "You seem to care a great deal for Danny."

"I love that little guy as if he were my own," she admitted. A frown pleated her auburn eyebrows as she studied the videos cycling. "Desiree is a single mom. He's her entire world." She pointed to a camera in the winter garden they'd created for the wedding. "There."

The woman hurried away, the hat blocking the only potential view of her face. Melissa swore.

He followed the route through his cameras, but the woman had been smart about her exit with the child. She must have visited the hotel before to get a sense of where the cameras were. It gave him something to think about.

"He isn't wailing or trying to get away from her. The little guy falls in love with anyone who smiles at him these days," Melissa murmured. "I can't believe that woman is someone familiar to him."

"Why not?" he queried.

"Off the top of my head, I can't think of anyone familiar to Danny who is also this invested in Everleigh Emerson's innocence."

The Emerson case was all over the news and on the front page of every paper since the trial began. Everleigh, a local barmaid, had allegedly cheated on her estranged husband, Fritz. Then she apparently had killed him with a paperweight during an argument over divorce.

Using the controls like a pro, Melissa rewound the few seconds of video in the winter garden. "I do *not* recognize that outfit at all."

"Here." He switched two monitors in the middle of the setup to show the arrival of wedding guests. "Let's see if we can pinpoint her arrival for the ceremony."

"Reception," Melissa suggested. "The ceremony was a small service. I'm absolutely certain no one with that hat was at the ceremony."

"All right." Antonio adjusted the timing of his search. Within minutes, they found her. "Here," he said, pointing.

Again, Melissa leaned closer to the displays and this time her knee bumped against his. The pleasant simmer from the inadvertent contact surprised him.

"Damn. Between the hat and the other guests, her face is blocked. You'd think the hat would've made it harder to tuck in close," she said. "She knew what she was doing."

"Seems so," Antonio agreed.

She reached for her phone and made swift notes in some app. "Clearly, she cares about Everleigh. That narrows the suspect pool quite a bit." She looked up at him then, her blue eyes deep with a desperate intensity. "Can you show me to the conference room you set up for my team, please?"

"Absolutely." The sooner he got her out of this small space, the better. Those eyes of hers drew him in, tempted him to offer more comfort than practical assistance. That was a dangerous line he didn't dare cross.

The desk phone rang and he checked the monitors instinctively, braced for more trouble. "Ruiz," he answered.

His event manager gave him an update. "Thanks. I'll pass that along," he said, replacing the handset. "The reception is winding down," he told Melissa. "The bride and groom are saying their farewells while the staff creates to-go boxes for everyone with food and cake."

"I'm sure they appreciate that."

"Sounds like a friend is keeping the boy's mother company so you can focus on the search," he added, escorting her from the security surveillance room. "I've also been warned that the media is gathering," he added. "We're keeping them outside and offering no comment."

He'd been tempted to keep the presence of the press to himself, but a child was at risk. This wasn't the time to let her walk into a media circus just to be petty. In the hallway outside the conference room on loan to the GGPD, he paused, giving in to that strange and persistent need to comfort her. "Good luck, Chief Colton."

Then he walked away, hoping they wouldn't cross

paths again anytime soon. She was temptation, pure and simple, and challenged his resolve to steer clear of anything with the potential for an emotional entanglement.

Chapter 2

Melissa took a breath, helpless to keep her gaze off Antonio as he walked away. The man rattled her. Always had. He was only a few years older than her, but she'd always admired his commanding presence in any environment. Oh, he was tall and lean, too, and she found him sinfully handsome with his perfectly styled dark hair and sharp-edged short beard. His unfailing self-confidence only added more depth to his overall appeal. She doubted Antonio Ruiz had ever experienced an insecure moment in his life.

She wasn't sure what cologne he wore and, since its scent was practically addictive, she would never dare ask. The strength in his hand, his voice, when he'd helped her through that terrifying moment when the ransom message had come in... He'd kept her from an embarrassing breakdown. That had been categorically chivalrous. Kind. She hadn't expected kindness, not from the man who made no secret of how little faith he had in the GGPD.

From a layman's perspective, she could understand his frustration with her department. He'd reported a murder and had expected justice, especially after the body had been found. But contrary to Antonio's statement, they didn't have anything tying Orr to the crime. Worse, Antonio had been a suspect himself for a short time as the GGPD worked the case. Good police work meant following every lead, even those that turned out to be bogus.

Although she didn't appreciate his nosing into confidential aspects like the specifics of the ransom note, they definitely needed his resources and assistance. Preparing the initial aspects of the search here on-site saved them valuable time when every second counted.

So why was she out here, musing over Antonio, when they had a baby to find?

She walked into the conference room, hoping her team had a list of suspects started.

Troy—who was a GGPD detective, her cousin and Danny's uncle—gave her a hopeful look from his seat on the far side of the big oval table in the middle of the room. "Tell me you have a face or potential ID to go on."

"I wish." She rubbed at the tension gripping the back of her neck. "We found the woman in the navy blue dress and that hat as she entered tonight, but her face was obscured. She came through the front doors with a crowd of reception guests, but I'm not exactly sure where she waited for her moment. Did anyone in the reception remember seeing her?"

"No," Troy replied. "So far, it doesn't look like she spent any time in the ballroom. I've questioned the guests closest to Desiree's table, based on the wedding videographer's footage."

"Anyone recognize her or the hat?"

"No," Troy repeated. He scrubbed a hand over his short black hair. His hazel eyes were haunted and she knew he wanted to turn the city upside down until they found his nephew. "I'm only guessing, but it makes sense that she might have joined the reception when the dinner buffet opened."

"Lots of movement, more distractions," Melissa agreed, thinking it through. "And less than a half hour later, she scoops up Danny and heads straight for the garden."

"He wasn't crying."

"I know. That worries me," she admitted. As a part-time sketch artist, Desiree was often in the police station. Everyone on the force had probably met Danny at one time or another and he was an outgoing child who didn't seem to have any fear of new faces. Did someone inside the GGPD have an issue with the Fritz Emerson murder case? "Any progress on the ransom message?"

"Nothing beyond the wording of the message. Full words and punctuation strikes me as someone over twenty-five." He pressed the heels of his hands to his eyes, defeated. Looking up, he said, "I'd be surprised if the phone is even in one piece anymore."

That was the trend for criminals. Burner phone, blocked number, disposed of after immediate contact. It didn't narrow the suspect pool at all.

"Chief?"

She turned toward her cousin, Grace Colton, a brand-new cop on the GGPD roster. "You have something?"

"I called Mason County Prison and verified Everleigh is in her cell. No visitors since the start of the trial."

"Good work. Thanks." She looked around the room. "All right. Female and over twenty-five is a starting point. Give me what you have on Everleigh Emerson's relatives. Let's clear them one by one. Female first."

She was tempted to step out of her heels, but she couldn't run around barefoot. "Where's Clarke?" Maybe he could swing by her house and pick up a change of clothes for her.

"He went to find the public defender, following that mention in the ransom note, to dig into the evidence against Everleigh."

"Good." Spotting a stack of notepads with the hotel logo and a pile of matching pens, she chose one of each and sat down with Troy. Making notes as Troy reviewed the list with her, she got a good picture of Everleigh's potential support system.

She felt every second ticking down, and worried that the kidnapper was taking Danny farther out of their reach, or worse. Tapping the pen to her palm, she tried to breathe through the crushing pressure. This wasn't just any case. And when she found the kidnapper, she'd…

"Do you need to go home?" Troy asked.

Melissa went still at the suggestion, remembering she had a responsibility to her officers and the community to be objective. "I should ask you the same thing, seeing that you're a closer relative than I am."

"I'm not leaving this to anyone else."

"Then we work it together."

She looked up when Officer Shea and his black Lab Ember came in. "Chief," Shea began, frustration tightening his features. "Danny's trail goes from the reception straight to the parking lot and ends. We can't pick up anything helpful beyond that." Ember tilted her head, ears perked as she waited for a new command. "We did a sweep of the interior of the hotel, but there's no indication he's here."

Melissa ignored the wrenching pain in her heart—she'd been so hopeful. "You've done plenty." They knew where Danny wasn't, which saved time and angst. "Thank you both." She reminded herself that the kidnapper was female and that likely meant better odds for Danny. When the K-9 team left, she turned back to Troy. "Any chance we're missing a motive?"

He scowled at his notes. "Like what?"

"Do you think the mention of the Emerson case is a diversion tactic?"

He looked at the ransom message someone had printed out while she'd been with Antonio in the security office. "No. The message was too personal, in my opinion. Too emotional."

She agreed, but she needed to avoid any tunnel vision that could mislead them and delay Danny's rescue. They *would* find him; she couldn't entertain any other outcome. Those few minutes skimming video with Antonio had threatened her confidence. His concern that her department wasn't up to the task was palpable. He wasn't the first person to be upset with her department and he wouldn't be the last. People didn't understand that GGPD's investigations were rarely cut-and-dried and cases weren't solved in the convenient span of an hour-long television show.

She had good, devoted people in her department. Having worked her way up the chain of command, she'd known most of them for several years. They were passionate about their work, but still only human. Mistakes happened because people weren't perfect. They needed to be perfect tonight.

"Start sending units out," she told Sergeant Brad Joseph. He'd loosened his tie and unbuttoned the collar of his shirt. His suit coat was draped over the back of a chair. "Park teams of two at each of the addresses that Detective Colton gives you. Report only," she added. "I don't want anyone to engage unless they are sure the child is in imminent danger." The stout man picked up his phone and got to work.

Melissa reminded herself that overall, the GGPD had a superb success rate with most cases, from misdemeanors to felonies.

Then there were cases like the Wendy Paxton murder. Cases that became convoluted and troubling and remained unsolved. Antonio had come into the station and reported that Drew Orr allegedly admitted to having killed his girlfriend, Wendy. The GGPD had found the body a few miles away on a remote hiking trail in the county park just north of his hotel. The case had gone cold, despite Antonio's report and a thorough investigation. The security cameras in the park showed Orr and Wendy entering the park in his car that day, matching his statement, but the light and angle made it impossible to tell if she had been with him when the car exited the park. Naturally, Orr was the prime suspect and they'd tried to punch holes in his alibi, but it had held up. The department had been hoping for something helpful from the forensics team, but when the lab finished the evaluation, none of the DNA evidence at the scene connected Orr to the crime. The whole situation still bothered Melissa.

Please don't let Danny become one of those cases.

The Paxton family still wanted justice for Wendy.

Melissa did, too. It was hard to ignore that a killer had gotten away with the crime. Antonio was right to be frustrated with the GGPD over the lack of results in the Paxton case and with Orr's intentionally misleading allegations. He didn't seem to understand they'd worked it by the book, even following up on Orr's assertion during questioning that Antonio was the killer. The lean, sexy hotelier had a solid alibi, but it seemed he still held a grudge against her and her department. Understanding his point of view didn't make it any easier to be around him. And now her baby cousin had been kidnapped right under her nose.

She wanted the city's trust, and gaining the confidence of community leaders was a big part of that. Ruiz had a great deal of influence, considering the number of people in his employ and countless others who carried out work here. His poor opinion of the police could trickle down as a result of his doubts and fester until she had a real problem.

She returned to the chair next to Troy. "Can you think of anyone else who benefits if Everleigh Emerson is exonerated?" she asked, keeping her voice low.

Troy shot her an incredulous look. "You're serious."

"I am."

"Melissa, all due respect, you're off base. It's too soon. If the logical assumptions—relatives and friends eager to clear her—don't pan out, *then* we can dig deeper. I think it's a waste of our limited time to look at long shots this early."

She gripped the pen in both hands. "Thank you. I needed to hear that. Walk me through the closest relatives first. Who do you like? Who has the ability to pull this off?"

Troy sat up straighter. "We're assuming the kidnapper was in disguise?"

"Safe bet. But disguise or not, it was a woman, not a man dressed as a woman," Melissa said.

"Why are you so sure about that?" Troy challenged.

She reminded herself this was the rhythm of working a case—idea, debate, next idea. "I've seen all the available footage of our kidnapper entering and leaving the hotel. I don't think it was a man's walk or a man's way of carrying a toddler."

"Fair enough."

"As you said," she reminded him, "we can explore secondary options once the first and most obvious suspects have been cleared. As fast as she disappeared, I want to conduct interviews based on the proximity to the hotel."

"Divide and conquer?"

She shook her head. "Just you and me. If we divide and conquer, we'd have to segment the list and then we're stuck wondering if someone got played."

"Understood," Troy said. "I'll get our route planned."

Due to the nature of the ransom note, she hoped they could bring Danny home before she had to issue an Amber Alert. Melissa addressed the officers Sergeant Joseph hadn't sent out yet. They'd been trickling in from the reception and the search, each one of them wanting to help. "No one speaks to the press," she began. "I'll give a statement to the media in just a few minutes." She looked around at her team, most in wedding attire, others in their GGPD uniforms. "Thank you all for stepping up. I'm confident we can bring Danny home safely to his mother. Tonight."

She assigned two officers to stay at the hotel to handle any further developments, and another team to stay with Desiree at her house. "If you see anything, call it in, no matter how trivial it might seem. At this point, everything is a possible lead."

When she had everyone's agreement, she walked out, taking a moment in the restroom to freshen up before she faced the media waiting outside. By some miracle her hair was fine. All credit to her stylist for that. Wishing she could do this in her uniform, she added a bit of color to her lips. She clipped her badge to the sash cinching her waist, just to make it clear she was on duty and in charge.

Taking one last deep breath, she headed for the hotel entrance and walked out alone, to the flash of lights and barrage of questions. It was all she could do not to duck and cringe.

"Your attention, please…" She waited for the voices beyond the extended cell phones and microphones to quiet. "Earlier this evening a child went missing from the hotel. My officers began a search immediately. At this time, the Grave Gulch Police Department is working every possible lead and we are confident the child will be found soon. If we feel that help from the public is warranted, we will distribute more information. Thank you."

A chorus of "Chief!" and "Chief Colton!" nearly knocked her back as everyone vied for her attention.

"Is the child a boy or girl?"

"Where are the parents?"

"How old is the child?"

"Did the search dogs find anything?"

Melissa waited a beat. She had to find the balance that would stem the tide of rash speculation and still protect the integrity of the search, as well as her cousin's privacy.

"The child is eighteen months old," she reported. "A boy. That is all I am willing to share at this time. I'm asking you to give us room to work so we can bring this crisis to a safe and swift conclusion. Thank you for your time."

She ignored questions about ransom demands, time frames and suspects. A question about her attire nearly stopped her in her tracks, but she ignored that, too, relieved to slip back into the warmth and steady lighting of the lobby.

"Nicely done," Troy said as she returned to the conference room. He'd removed his suit coat and tie, and rolled back his shirtsleeves to his elbows. Though the dress shirt was a step above his normal attire, he resembled the expert detective she saw most days at the station. He shot her a quick grin. "Thought you were going to snap at the comment about your dress."

"Me, too," she admitted. Melissa longed for her uniform and the plain pearl-stud earrings she wore to work every day. A hairbrush would be appreciated, too. As much as she'd enjoyed the French twist, she longed for the familiar bun or ponytail.

The uniform was more of a signal to others. Neither her authority nor her confidence was tied to her wardrobe, as the people she intended to question would soon find out.

"Tell me you have an interview plan for the Everleigh Emerson connection."

He tapped the notepad on the table. "All charted out. We can take my car," Troy offered. He stood and put on his suit coat, stuffing the tie into a pocket.

His sedan was more subtle than her official SUV emblazoned with the GGPD shield. "The media will catch up with us, anyway."

"Your call."

She wasn't sure it made any difference. Word was out and whoever had kidnapped Danny and sent that ransom message would surely use the advantage to refine the plan or hiding place. "Your car," she decided. "Let's get rolling."

"One more thing. I asked your mom to drop off a uniform for you." He tilted his head toward a garment bag draped over one of the empty chairs at the table. "Just in case you want to change."

She stared at Troy. "Seriously?" Her cousin was a lifesaver. "Give me five minutes." Grabbing the garment bag, she hurried down the hall to the restroom to change.

In the surveillance office, Antonio's cell phone rang nonstop. Reporters, picking up on the crisis from social media and Melissa's brief statement, continued to crowd the hotel entrance. He gave strict instructions not to allow them inside, and to be clear that any and all information would come from the police department. With luck, they would migrate there as soon as it was clear there was no search happening on the grounds.

The press was as necessary as the police department, but that didn't mean Antonio enjoyed their presence. His guests deserved privacy when they stayed at his properties and he did everything in his power to ensure they got it. The poor bride and groom had been through enough. At least the bridal suite was at the back of the hotel, with a view of the lake.

It would always be a balancing act, and in this particular instance, they might eventually need everyone in town on the lookout to find that little boy. As of right now, though, Melissa had refrained from sharing a picture and asking for community help.

He set his phone to vibrate only and returned to his research while the other two men searched for anyone who had interacted with the kidnapper. He was certain the woman who had carried Danny away from the wedding had been in the hotel before tonight. There was something in the way she moved, the way she carried her head, that struck him as familiar. It wasn't enough to take to the police yet, but he wasn't giving up. Melissa and the department were focused on facial features to make an ID, but Antonio had years of practice and experience in recognizing people by their mannerisms as much as appearance. Reading body language helped him serve a businessman whose deal fell through, or do something special for a couple newly engaged.

He reviewed the few seconds of footage of the woman in the blue dress and hat entering the hotel, comparing her to others in the crowd, assessing her height and slender build. He couldn't be absolutely sure, but he felt as if there was a small hitch in the woman's gait. Maybe one leg was slightly shorter than the other, or maybe she had a knee or hip problem. He rubbed his eyes. Or maybe she'd simply been trying to avoid stepping on the heel of the man in front of her.

Although Antonio didn't have Ken's footage handy, he was certain he'd seen someone with that same uneven stride recently.

On a sigh, he thought about the ransom demand the chief had received. Tonight's wedding had been on the hotel calendar for months and was definitely an event known to the police. In a small city like Grave Gulch, that made it public knowledge, too. There was no way this was a spur-of-the-moment crime; it had gone too smoothly.

The kidnapper knew just where to be to avoid the best camera angles. What she couldn't avoid, the hat blocked. And despite that imperfect stride, she'd gotten away swiftly. He muttered an oath under his breath as he accessed more video from the weeks leading up to the wedding. He focused on the routes they knew the woman in blue had taken, but it was still too many hours for him to review on his own.

His phone sounded off again and he sighed at the text message from his manager on duty that the GGPD chief wanted to speak with him. Smothering a sigh, he headed toward the conference room they'd turned into a staging area.

Looking for Melissa in her deep green dress, he did a double take when he saw she'd changed into her dark blue uniform. Her hair was still the same, and her vivid blue eyes were accentuated with the more intense makeup, but the stern expression indicated she was all business.

"Thank you for the space," she said. "We'll be clearing out and moving all of this to the station. I've assigned two officers to remain here at the hotel, just in case the kidnapper returns Danny here."

"We'll make sure they're accommodated," he said. "Are you planning an arrest?"

She frowned at the query. "In time," she answered. "We're just beginning this investigation. There are several people to question about their possible involvement." She stuck out her hand. "Again, the department appreciates your assistance."

"I'm going with you," he blurted, ignoring her offered hand. "I can recognize the woman who took Danny."

"You found footage of the kidnapper's face?" She glanced at his empty hands. "Where is it? Did you send it by email?"

"Not her face," he admitted. "Her stride, the way she moves. Let me come along. I *will* recognize her. I can help you rule out suspects faster."

"No. Absolutely not."

He paused. "You need my help," he insisted.

"This is *police* business," she stated, her lips as firm as her tone. "If you find anything helpful, please contact the department." She handed him a business card.

Now he was annoyed on top of everything else. Folding his arms over his chest, he blocked her path to the door. "Witnesses can identify perps in the field." He couldn't stop the wave of sarcasm. "I've heard it's something that happens regularly in police business."

"You're not a witness, so there's no cause to ride along. If—*when*—we make an arrest, I'll invite you to the station."

Invite him? What a useless line. "Without me, you will likely arrest the wrong person and waste valuable time." He saw the jab land and he didn't regret it. The GGPD had made mistakes time and again. With a baby's future hanging in the balance, he expected her to be smarter than this. Though his hopes of fatherhood had been dashed, he couldn't help identifying with the distraught mother. He wanted her to have a happy ending.

"I have the means to haul you in for obstruction."

"What's the holdup?" Troy asked, entering the room. "I pulled the car up to the kitchen entrance."

Antonio turned. "You have room for me?"

Troy arched his eyebrows, his gaze moving to his

boss, who was also his cousin. "Yes?" he replied slowly, gauging Melissa's reaction.

She caught Antonio's elbow firmly, holding him in place. "You're staying right here, Mr. Ruiz. Someone will be in touch if you're needed."

Her hand was warm, but the contact sent a bolt of unwelcome awareness through his system. More intense than the shock when they'd been in the surveillance room together. Without her heels, she had to look up at him more. Although, in uniform and wearing that air of authority like a cloak, she didn't seem any shorter.

"You do need me. Right now." He turned to the detective. "I'm riding along to help you identify the kidnapper."

The man's eyebrows climbed higher toward his hairline. "That's—"

"*Not* happening," Melissa interjected. She maneuvered around him, clearly hoping to leave him behind.

"Why fight good help?" he said, but she ignored him. "I should've known the GGPD wouldn't change, not even for one of their own," Antonio said loudly. He didn't care who overheard him.

Melissa stopped short. "What did you say?"

"Should I repeat it?" He wasn't afraid to state his opinion or call out their mistakes. "The GGPD is in no position to turn down any assistance, no matter how small. You don't need facial recognition or an immediate confession with me along. I *will* recognize the kidnapper."

Troy stared at him. "How, exactly?"

"He can't." She shook her head. "This is absurd. Let's go."

"Can you really afford to blow off my help?" he asked. "What does it hurt to take me along?"

Storm clouds moved through her blue eyes, but behind her, he could see Troy relenting. "What we don't have is time to waste arguing," the detective said.

"Fine." She planted her hands on her trim hips, arched an eyebrow in challenge. "Keep quiet and keep up."

He fell into step beside her as they moved down the hall and through the kitchen to the delivery area.

"You're in back," she said, holding the door for him.

She sat up front and let Troy drive. When they were on the move, she swiveled in her seat to face him. "You *will* keep quiet while Troy and I handle the questions. If you recognize something or someone, you speak to me about it, not the suspect."

"Yes, ma'am."

She rolled her eyes. "And if we get into any trouble, you will follow my orders. I don't need civilian injuries complicating this case."

"Do you have a safety waiver you'd like me to sign?" Antonio queried.

"In the glove box," Troy said, shocking him. "Always have them ready for media ride-alongs or school career shadow days."

Melissa found the form and pulled a pen from her pocket. "I suggest you hurry up and sign before we reach our first stop."

"I was joking," he said.

"Well, I'm not," she retorted. "We have the forms and policies for a reason."

And yet somehow they kept messing things up. Orr was surely responsible for Wendy's death, but the man wasn't in jail. Antonio was admittedly biased, but he wouldn't be the least bit surprised if they'd messed up things in the Emerson case, too. Melissa was devoted to her work and the community, but somehow she had to lift the rest of her department up to that same high standard. He felt as though he had an obligation to prevent another blunder with the kidnapping. His stomach churned at the thought of a mother and son being separated forever. He signed the paper and thrust it back at her. She looked at his signature and, apparently satisfied, folded the sheet, then tucked it into her pocket.

Troy turned off Lakeview Drive into an older neighborhood. Streetlights glowed over cleared sidewalks and small, snow-covered lawns. He parked on the street in front of a Tudor-style home and cut the engine. For a moment no one moved. Melissa was reviewing some information on her cell phone.

"This is Janet Carlisle's residence," Melissa said. "She worked with Everleigh at Howlin' Eddie's bar prior to the Fritz Emerson murder. She could possibly be our kidnapper and she wasn't at work earlier this evening."

"You have the still shot?" she asked Troy.

At his affirmative nod, she opened her car door. "Let's go."

Antonio obediently followed, keeping his thoughts and opinions to himself as they approached the house. The woman who answered the door confirmed she was Janet, but she was shorter than the kidnapper and her hips were wider. She left them on the stoop instead of inviting them in and he noticed that roused the suspicions of the cops in front of him. But when she walked away to ask her roommate to come and verify her alibi for the time of the reception and kidnapping, Antonio was sure she wasn't the right woman. Her gait was too even.

Troy showed them the picture of the kidnapper. Neither of them recognized anything about the woman or offered any information that would move the search for Danny forward.

Antonio was surprised when Melissa shifted gears and asked Janet a few additional questions specifically about Everleigh.

"I know she didn't cheat on her husband," the woman said with unwavering confidence. "That girl is loyal to the bone. Fritz probably started the rumors about Everleigh as an excuse to leave her. That man was a class-A jerk."

"How so?" Melissa queried.

The woman rolled her eyes. "Sometimes he'd come in while Everleigh was working. He was a big tipper, especially if the waitresses gave him extra attention. And he would flirt with other women in front of Everleigh all the time."

Sounded like a jerk to Antonio.

"Did you ever see Fritz get physical with Everleigh?" Troy asked.

"No," the woman admitted. "That doesn't make him less of a creep. However it went down, I say the world's better off without him."

Antonio expected Melissa and Troy to blow off the claims in a rush to get back to their search. Instead, they continued to ask intelligent follow-up questions, waiting patiently for the replies and taking notes. The thoroughness earned a bit of his respect.

They repeated the same thorough process at their next stop with an old high-school friend of Everleigh's and he was grudgingly impressed by their steadiness, neither of them jumping to conclusions.

After each interview, Melissa checked in with the teams watching Everleigh's relatives. So far no one was acting strangely. At their visit with Everleigh's aunt,

Antonio realized Melissa deliberately asked for a glass of water to give him a chance to evaluate the woman's stride. But the aunt was far too short to be the kidnapper. On top of that, when asked to send a text, she fumbled through the test. No way she'd sent that ransom message.

"How did you decide the order of interviews?" Antonio asked when they were back in the car on their way to speak with Everleigh's mother.

"Proximity to the hotel," Troy answered.

"Based on the timing of the ransom note and the swift disappearance of the kidnapper," Melissa added. "The scent dog lost the trail at the parking lot. Do you have a suggestion?"

It was the last question he'd expected. "No. Not exactly. I wondered because it appears we're talking to a cross section of Everleigh's associates. A coworker, an aunt, a good friend from high school and so on."

"None of them strike you as the woman under that hat?" Melissa asked.

"Not so far. I think we might be dealing with an older woman."

"Why older?" Troy asked.

Antonio explained the issue he'd noticed with the woman's stride. "I'm not one-hundred-percent convinced it's permanent," he admitted. "But it was too consistent not to be real."

Melissa didn't respond, her gaze on the street in front of them.

"I haven't given you enough credit," he said. "Watching you tonight, you're a solid cop, Melissa. You're both good with the people and the investigation." This peek behind the curtain had given him a better appreciation for the delicate line she walked.

"Thanks. I appreciate that," Melissa said. Troy shrugged.

"But you still don't want me here."

"Not really," she admitted with a faint smile. "This situation has become enough of a circus already."

They'd picked up a bit of an entourage on the way, as reporters caught wind of the questioning and followed them in a grim parade, hoping to be there for the baby's rescue or a big nasty takedown.

"Chief, you want to go out of order and visit Emerson's grandmother?"

"Stick with the plan," Melissa said. She checked in with the team outside the grandmother's home.

Was that doubt in her voice? He was all in to help find the little boy, but the more people they spoke with, the more he wanted some kind of confirmation that the GGPD would take another look at the evidence against Everleigh, who was on trial for murder. If Melissa was open to that, maybe he could eventually convince her to investigate Orr again, too. So far, no one bad-mouthed Everleigh outright and no one exhibited any stress over being questioned.

"Hard to believe a woman this widely adored did something as nasty as kill her husband," he mused into the heavy silence in the car.

"Tonight, my primary focus is finding Danny," Melissa snapped. "Be alert," she warned as Troy parked again. "From the pictures, her mother fits the build of the woman who took him."

Troy glanced at Antonio through the rearview mirror. "You good?"

He nodded and climbed out of the car, hoping with everything he had that this would be the last stop of the evening. He needed to see a happy ending for baby and mother, but for his own peace of mind, as well.

Technically, he could walk away. Melissa would surely approve that choice. But he was too invested. Despite the old pain and loss dredged up by the situation, he wouldn't let another parent suffer if he could help it.

Chapter 3

All of the interviews without results were wearing on Melissa. It was as if the January weather grew colder with every stop. Troy's stoic reserve was in place, but she'd caught him gripping the steering wheel with extra force as they headed to Everleigh's mother's house. They had to find Danny, then they could sort out why the kidnapper resorted to such drastic measures.

Compounding the stress were the consistent denials from the family and friends. Not only about being involved with the kidnapping, but also about Everleigh. No one they'd interviewed so far seemed completely convinced she was a murderer, but they weren't convinced of her innocence either. The DNA evidence and witness statements had resulted in her arrest and anchored the prosecutor's case. Obviously someone with significant doubts had kidnapped Danny to force the department into action. When Melissa found her little cousin, she would take action, but it might not line up with what Everleigh's ally intended.

"Maybe we've gone at this the wrong way," Troy said quietly as they paused on the walk.

Behind them, Antonio snorted. She wished the man was anywhere else right now. Recent compliments aside, he got under her skin, whether he was voicing his opinion or keeping it to himself. So far he hadn't recognized anyone's build or seen a similarity in their movements, and he sure wasn't behaving as if he noticed her efforts to give him a chance.

She knew he wasn't pleased with how GGPD handled his statement about Drew Orr being involved, but she couldn't just toss one man in jail on the word of another. The system wasn't perfect, but it was in place for a reason. Evidence had to back up theory or it would be chaos.

"Want me to get another team started with questions to cover more ground?"

She heard the urgency in his voice and was so tempted to agree. "No," she said after thinking it through. "I'll worry about missing something. And Mr. Ruiz can't be in two places at once." She didn't make a habit of micromanaging her detectives and the investigation had led directly to Everleigh, supported by the evidence reports.

"That's true," Antonio said.

His deep voice rolled over her. In another time and in a better context that voice might make her shiver with anticipation.

Right now, she could barely tolerate him. She sensed his frustration with her methodical approach, yet he'd been the one to forcefully offer his assistance and supposed expertise. His improving opinion of her as a cop shouldn't matter, couldn't impair her own assessment of the situation. He hadn't been pleased with anything about the GGPD for months now. She could practically feel him looking for a chance to contradict or challenge her every decision.

Ignoring his presence as much as possible was her best option until they found Danny. Then she could address his lingering frustration with her, her work and her department.

"We can't abandon a plan because it takes time to execute," she said, reinforcing that fact for her sake as much as for his. "We planned this search in a logical manner. Based on the timing and the tone of the ransom message, the kidnapper doesn't want to hurt Danny."

"You're assuming a female kidnapper will nurture the boy and keep him safe?" Antonio asked.

More like she was praying, but wouldn't admit it to a civilian. "I'm not assuming anything," she stated. "I am working a case with one of my best detectives. If you're not happy tagging along, you're welcome to walk back to the hotel."

"Wouldn't be much of a walk," he said. "Any one of those media outlets would give me a lift."

He was right. Several cars had parked behind Troy on the street. Melissa turned to the porch of the sweet craftsman cottage. It felt a mile away from where they stood, though it was only a few yards. By now word had surely traveled through the family that the GGPD was convinced a relative or friend of Everleigh's had taken Danny, so any element of surprise would be gone. That didn't bother Melissa. All she needed was a clue. One lead or reasonable cause and she could bring in Ember and search until she found her favorite cousin.

Amie McPherson, Everleigh's mother, was waiting

on the porch when Melissa, Troy and Antonio reached the stairs. Amie had a medical boot on her right foot. If it was real, Melissa didn't need Antonio to tell her that she couldn't be the woman involved. Unless she had taken it off for the duration of the kidnapping. The only way to find out was to start the interview.

"I know why you're here," Amie said, dabbing a tissue to the corners of her eyes. "I don't have that little boy."

"We understand," Troy said. "Are you here alone?"

"For the moment," she stated.

"We just have a few questions," Melissa explained. "Would you be more comfortable inside?"

Mrs. McPherson glanced to the media clogging up the sidewalk. "Fine."

"How did you hurt your foot?" Melissa asked as the three of them followed the woman into the house.

"I tripped over the cat and twisted my ankle," Amie said glumly. "Two weeks to go in this contraption."

"Do you have the doctor's report?" Troy asked.

At the woman's indignant gasp, Melissa intervened. "It feels intrusive, but it would speed things along," Melissa said.

Mrs. McPherson muttered under her breath. She flipped on the light over the dining-room table. Thankfully their conversation would be blocked from view by the drawn curtains over the front window. "Wait here. The physical-therapy instructions are on the refrigerator—will that be sufficient?"

"Yes, ma'am," Troy said. He followed, keeping an eye on her, then she returned and they all sat down.

"Mrs. McPherson, we have a photo of the person who did take the baby," Melissa began. Just because Everleigh's mother wasn't the woman under that hat didn't mean she wasn't involved somehow. Melissa imagined it would be torture for a parent to have a child accused of such a violent crime.

Troy showed Mrs. McPherson the picture while Melissa continued. "The only ransom demand for the return of the little boy is for the police to exonerate your daughter." Melissa steered the questions, much as she had with Everleigh's friends and aunts. "Could you please tell me where you've been this evening since five o'clock?"

"Here. My husband and I did the grocery shopping this morning." She sniffled. "I put a stew together when we got back and we sat down to eat around six. I don't know what else to tell you."

"Please take another look. Do you have any idea who this is?" Troy slid his phone closer, urging her to take a good look at the image on the screen. "Do you recognize anything about the outfit?"

Melissa gave the woman credit for studying the picture. Beside her, she could sense Antonio taking in the details of the woman and the home. She wondered what he was thinking now.

"No. I don't recognize anything or anyone," Mrs. McPherson said.

"Where is your husband?" Melissa asked.

"Andrew went out to watch the hockey game with his friends."

When Melissa asked for the information, Amie provided the name, address and phone number.

"On it," Troy said. He stepped away from the table to make the calls to confirm Amie's story.

"Do you have any idea why someone would do something so drastic to help your daughter?"

To Melissa's dismay, Mrs. McPherson broke down

crying. "I'm s-so sorry," she stuttered through the sniffles. "So, so sorry."

Melissa's instincts went on high alert. "Why are you sorry?"

"For my daughter. The family. His, too. I—I can't believe she killed Fritz. She is such a good person. Big heart. Gentle." She lifted her gaze to Melissa, her eyes red and swimming with tears. "I didn't want to believe it. But she must have done it." Her gaze darted between Melissa and Antonio. "Her attorney told me they have her DNA on the murder weapon." She cried into her tissue for another few seconds. "Her DNA," she repeated, shaking her head. "Why did my sweet girl snap and smash her husband over the head with that paperweight? I didn't want to believe it, but the facts…" Whatever else she wanted to say was lost in another crying jag.

Melissa sympathized with the overwhelming grief of a disillusioned parent unable to comprehend a child's actions. Amie McPherson was conflicted and emotionally distraught because she was sure her daughter was guilty.

Standing, she extended a business card to Mrs. McPherson. "If you hear anything about the kidnapping or the people involved, please give me a call." She stopped just short of apologizing.

Out on the porch, they joined Troy. "Husband is with the guys. They say he arrived just before seven. I sent a patrol car to verify. Based on the physical description and the pictures on the dining room wall, no way that man packed himself into the blue dress we saw."

"You're grasping at straws now," Antonio muttered on the way to the car.

"Hush," Melissa ordered. She didn't want any of the

reporters hovering nearby to pick up any dissent between the three of them.

Once they were in the vehicle, though, Antonio started in again. "That poor woman. Her faith in your system has torn apart her family," he said.

"Save it," Troy barked. "We work within the system, or it's chaos. We build a case from evidence and facts, like Mrs. McPherson said."

"After everything we've heard so far, you still think Everleigh's a killer?" Antonio persisted. "You're convinced everyone who knows her well *must* be wrong because the evidence is king."

"Stop," Melissa ordered. "Arguing gets us no closer to Danny. And besides, her mother apparently does believe her to be guilty." She twisted in her seat to glare at Antonio. "If you can't be helpful, you can't stay."

"You need me," he grumbled.

"Doesn't mean I'll tolerate you making matters worse." Melissa took a breath as he quieted, then indicated Troy should head for the next name on their list, Hannah McPherson, Everleigh's grandmother.

The woman was in her eighties, but they couldn't leave any stone unturned. They were running out of people with enough motive to carry out this stunt. Melissa had been so sure they'd have found Danny by now.

In the quiet of the car, her thoughts raced. Antonio made a valid point about Everleigh's friends and family. No one they'd spoken with this evening credited the rumors of her cheating on her husband and no one believed her capable of taking a life.

But the most pertinent question was, who among her friends or relatives might be capable of taking a baby away from his mother? Who could justify causing a mother that much pain? She understood parenthood was a rollercoaster, but this was a low point no one could anticipate. And still, she longed for a family of her own someday. Melissa promised herself that no matter when they found Danny, she would revisit the evidence in the Emerson murder case.

Hannah McPherson lived just over a mile from her son and daughter-in-law and her two-story home was in excellent condition. The walk and steps were clear of snow and the brass light fixtures flanking the front door gleamed. If she handled the maintenance on her own, Melissa and Troy had probably underestimated the widowed grandmother.

"Good evening, Chief," Hannah said when she answered the door. "I just put on a pot of coffee."

Melissa introduced Troy and Antonio. "You were expecting us?"

"Of course." She gave a nod to the media circus arriving on cue. "News travels fast in a town this size. And, of course, the girls called."

Melissa assumed "the girls" referred to Everleigh's mother and her aunts. According to the profile, Hannah was eighty, but she looked much younger in slim jeans and a bulky wool sweater. Her short cap of silver hair framed her face, and behind rimless glasses, her gaze was polite and curious. Not the least bit wary.

"Come in out of the cold," Hannah said. She led them inside and back to a cozy den off the kitchen. A fire was going strong in the fireplace and the television mounted over the mantel was tuned to the news, the volume muted. "Would anyone like coffee?"

"No, thank you," Troy said for all of them. "We have a few questions and we can be out of your hair."

"Of course. I can't imagine how that poor mother is coping. So dreadful."

Hannah settled into what was surely her favorite chair. Troy took the chair closest to her. Antonio and Melissa were stuck with a love seat on the other side of the coffee table. The cushions sagged toward the center and her thigh rubbed against his from knee to hip. Heat flashed through her system. Again, in different circumstances she might enjoy being close to him.

Apparently oblivious to her internal struggle, Troy extended his phone, sharing the picture of the woman in the blue dress and large hat.

Melissa was watching her face for any reaction when Antonio bumped her knee with his own. "It's her," he said as he cleared his throat to cover his words. "I can tell from the way she walked inside just now."

Melissa struggled to accept the revelation, even as Antonio smiled genially when Hannah looked his way as if they were lifelong friends, here to catch up over a plate of lemon bars.

While she answered questions about her whereabouts and her granddaughter's case, Hannah's gaze darted again and again to a dark doorway. That small tell, along with Antonio's certainty, had Melissa's instincts prickling. Did the woman have Danny stashed in that room?

Standing, she moved straight for the doorway, braced for anything. She pushed through the door and found herself in a small room. She turned on the light and looked around.

"What are you doing?" Hannah called after her. "We built that for my husband's hip replacement, rest his soul. These days, I use it when my knees are too sore to get up the stairs at night."

The small bedroom was empty right now, the twin bed neatly made and covered with a beautiful quilt. Melissa checked the big armoire and under the bed, but Danny wasn't here. Discouraged, nearly defeated, she turned around and saw a navy blue dress and spectator hat hanging on the hook on the back of the door. She drew her weapon while she was still out of sight and kept it low as she returned to the den.

"Troy," she said, "cuff her."

Hannah's eyes went round. "What is this?"

Troy was already in motion, snapping handcuffs over the woman's wrists with care.

Melissa called for backup and then turned back to Hannah, summoning every ounce of self-control. "What have you done with Danny Colton?"

"This is outrageous." Hannah's eyes started to tear up. "You've got this all wrong."

"Keep an eye on her, Troy," Melissa ordered. "I'll start the search."

"Wait, please," Hannah begged, interrupting Troy. "The boy is safe, just listen to me. Let me explain. *Please*."

With her weapon trained on the elderly woman, Melissa paused. "Where is he?"

"This isn't necessary." Hannah raised her cuffed hands. "I'll cooperate. The boy is perfectly fine. He's a lamb. I'd never hurt a child."

Troy finished reading Hannah her rights, then Melissa demanded again, "Where is he?"

"Upstairs, first bedroom on the left."

Antonio leaped up from the small sofa and rushed out before Melissa could move. Damn it, he might inadvertently contaminate the scene. She hurried after him, leaving Hannah to Troy.

"I never would've let anything happen to the boy," Hannah insisted, her voice carrying through the house.

"He was tuckered out," she continued, digging a deeper hole for herself. "He fell asleep watching *Tom and Jerry* cartoons."

Melissa felt the space between every heartbeat when she reached the staircase and saw Antonio at the top, his arms full of her little cousin. She returned her weapon to the holster, relief coursing through her. The pressure in her chest eased as Antonio started down the steps. Her arms trembled as she waited to hold the little boy again.

"Got him," he said quietly. Danny was tucked up against his shoulder as if Antonio held children all the time. "Sound asleep." Tenderly, he transferred the sleeping toddler to her.

Tears of gratitude blurred her vision for a moment as she held her cousin, smelled his sweet curly hair. Her hand rose and fell with his steady breaths. "Thank you." When she looked up, Antonio's normally confident, self-possessed expression was gone. His dark eyes were haunted as he stared at the baby. Then he turned and walked away, and Melissa was once again trailing in his wake.

"I had to do it," Hannah said, her voice firm. Troy's phone was out and Melissa saw that he was recording the conversation. "I had to do it to get your attention. Everleigh didn't murder her awful husband. She would never hurt a mosquito."

"I suggest you stop talking," Melissa said, simply as a matter of form. Troy had already read Hannah her rights.

"I'll testify that the detective read her her rights," Antonio said. "That is, if you need me."

Support from the man that had been a thorn in her

side all night was the last thing she expected. With a nod of thanks, she gave her full attention to Danny. The little guy seemed to be in perfect health. "I'll call Desiree while we wait for the CSI team."

It was over. Danny was safe and would be reunited with Desiree within the hour. But as Melissa cuddled him close, it didn't feel over. She couldn't shake the feeling that the worst was still to come.

Antonio surreptitiously checked his hands, expecting to find them shaking, but they were still. So the trembling was only on the inside. That didn't make him feel much better. He kept his gaze away from Melissa and the toddler while she spoke with the boy's mother and listened along with Troy as Mrs. McPherson poured out all of the details and reasoning.

When he'd found the little guy tucked into the bed, his heart had threatened to crack in his chest. Antonio didn't do kids or family. Fate had crushed those dreams twenty years ago. And yet the sight of Melissa holding the toddler in her arms stirred up emotions he had no intention of facing again.

He walked out, aiming for the front door, half tempted to call the hotel car service to come pick him up. The flashing lights of the police responding to the scene and the slew of reporters kept him rooted in place. He'd come along to help and he would see it through.

Besides, this chaos was nothing compared to the night his pregnant wife and their unborn baby had died. He didn't have any stake in this, no real ties to the people most affected, so it shouldn't be this hard to distance himself.

He opened the door for the crime-scene unit and again when Desiree arrived with a police escort. Although he was happy for her, he couldn't bear to watch the reunion. It cut too deep, left him staring at the aching emptiness of happiness he'd been denied because life wasn't fair.

It seemed like a lifetime ago. It was, in fact. He'd been twenty-two when Karen and the baby had died due to a complication with the pregnancy. If life was fair, he'd be headed home to a house filled with love and a busy, happy family. His oldest would be almost twenty now, leading a pack of younger siblings in Antonio's dream world, and Karen would be more beautiful today than the day he'd fallen in love with her.

"I had to do it," the grandmother said again. "You didn't give me a choice."

She hadn't stopped that litany since they'd found out she was the kidnapper.

"Everleigh's own parents gave up on her. I had to do something," Hannah wailed. "She's the sweetest of all my grandchildren and would never hurt a fly. All her life, even crickets or spiders that wander into the house, she scoops them up and carries outside."

Antonio wondered if Melissa and Troy were even listening anymore. Worse, he feared it wouldn't make any difference for Everleigh. With his mind still circling the what-ifs of family dreams long gone, he struggled to sort out his feelings and opinions of the entire mess. He was angry that anyone in this city felt the need to go to such lengths and he was equally angry that Hannah had made an innocent mother suffer.

It was past time for Melissa, as the chief of police, to take a hard look at what was going wrong in her department.

She appeared abruptly, as if his thoughts summoned her. "We're heading back to the station," she said, her gaze moving past him to the swarm of reporters crowding the path to Troy's car. "I can't order you to keep quiet, but I would ask you to please be careful if you choose to give a statement."

"Careful?" Was she serious? "Will you be careful with this case?" She flinched and he almost regretted his hard tone. "That woman is the personification of desperate. What are you going to do to help her?"

Melissa's mouth flattened, her blue gaze going sharp. "The kidnapping is a police matter," she said. "The GGPD is grateful for your help in the rescue of a child." She cleared her throat, her eyes still locked with his. "*I* am grateful for your help, Mr. Ruiz."

"Antonio," he said.

She acknowledged that with a nod. "Would you like us to drop you at the hotel?"

"I'll ride along to the station," he decided. "Someone should make sure Mrs. McPherson is treated fairly until her legal team arrives." He would personally see to it that she didn't have to settle for a public defender. "I have personal experience with not being heard by your officers."

"It's regrettable that you feel that way," she said. After exchanging a look with Troy, they headed out and Antonio followed.

Questions pelted them from all sides behind the lights of cameras and cell phones. Both Melissa and Troy repeated the no-comment line while Antonio just followed, fuming in silence. For now.

In the car, Troy slid his phone toward Melissa. "Worse is waiting," he said.

From the back seat, Antonio had a clear view of the short video clip of local and regional media blocking the front doors of the police station.

"Guess it's a good night to use the back door," he said.

"On the contrary," Melissa replied. "I'll take that mob head-on and make sure they understand the three of us rescued Danny."

"And when they ask if you'll take another look at the Emerson case?" It seemed he'd lost all his normal tact and diplomacy.

"The whole mess is a police matter and will take some time to sort out," she replied. "But, yes, we're already taking steps to verify Hannah's claims. Contrary to your opinion, I *do* care about the people in this city. It disturbs me more than I can say that she resorted to kidnapping because she felt it was the only way to get our attention."

No one spoke the rest of the way to the police station. Troy parked in the space reserved for the chief and cut the engine. The only visible indication of Melissa's state of mind was the quick swipe of her palms across her slacks before she stepped out of the car.

The media were kind enough to give them a path as they climbed the steps to the front door of the station. Antonio didn't know there were so many reporters and cameramen in Grave Gulch. In front of the doors, Melissa paused to give her planned statement about the cooperative effort to rescue Danny.

"Does this mean Everleigh Emerson is innocent?" someone shouted.

"Is it true an elderly grandmother took the toddler?" asked another unseen reporter.

Variations on those two questions rippled through the air as several reporters simultaneously vied for attention and answers.

Troy kept his mouth shut, while Melissa paused at the top of the steps. "At this time, I can only reassure you that the toddler taken from a family event earlier this evening has been reunited with his mother. No injuries were immediately apparent and we expect his pediatrician will give him a clean bill of health."

"Chief! According to the ransom note this kidnapping occurred because the police made some sort of error. Will tonight's events affect the trial of Everleigh Emerson?"

Antonio was close enough to see Melissa's breath catch. Who could've fed the media the details of the ransom note? As far as Antonio knew, not even Desiree had seen it.

"Please…" Melissa held up a hand. "This an active investigation. We will be handling every detail thoroughly and with the utmost care. That's all I have at this time."

"Mr. Ruiz, do you blame yourself for tonight's kidnapping?"

He was so shocked, he replied to the media question without thinking. "No. The hotel is not at fault in this matter."

"What measures will the hotel take to prevent such a tragedy in the future?" another reporter called out, heedless of his first answer.

"The hotel systems and security protocols in place were instrumental in recovering the boy swiftly," Melissa interjected. "If you'll excuse us."

Her praise caught him off guard, but he acknowledged it with a nod. "I was glad to be of help tonight," he said simply. But he had to wonder if he'd helped find a little boy only to wreck a grandmother's life. No, he couldn't take that on. Hannah McPherson had made her own choices. "Please excuse me."

He turned to follow Melissa and Troy into the station. Not his favorite place, but it would be an instant improvement over the media crush. Raised voices chased the trio.

"Do you still believe your partner, Drew Orr, murdered his girlfriend?"

To name Orr and not the victim annoyed him immensely. "Her name was Wendy Paxton," he snapped. "Orr and I were never partners. And yes, I believed he killed her."

"Chief, will you reopen the Paxton case, as well?" The follow-up question was no surprise to any of them.

"You can be sure we'll do everything necessary to see justice served in Grave Gulch."

A chorus of questions about "Granny" McPherson's fate chased them into the station.

Rather than make a beeline for the back door, Antonio followed Melissa straight to her office, pausing in the doorway. After closing the blinds at the window, she tugged the pins from her hair. One by one, they plinked to her desktop, then she finger-combed the deep red mass into loose waves. His fingers tingled with an urge to take over that task, to learn the weight and texture of that fiery hair. He dragged his thoughts to more appropriate territory.

Her eyes rounded when she realized he was still there. "You don't need to stay," she said.

"You defended me out there," he said, and entered her office.

"Of course I did. The hotel didn't make any mistakes and you were instrumental in finding Danny quickly."

Was she trying to flatter him so he'd forget the department's previous errors? A few hours ago that would've been his assumption. Now, after seeing her in action, he wasn't so sure he understood her as well as he'd first thought.

The potential error bothered him. He took great pride in assessing people accurately. If he was wrong about her, that would bring his current tally to two big mistakes in the past year. His skill at reading people should be improving, not faltering.

"Are you okay?" She tilted her head. "You seemed a little…"

"What?" he prompted when she didn't finish.

Her auburn eyebrows flexed. "I don't know. Be careful with the reporters. You know how little it takes to breathe life into an old story."

"But you may not have the right killer on trial for Fritz Emerson. No one was ever even arrested for the Paxton murder, either."

She shook her head, her hair rippling across her shoulders. "You want me to reopen the Paxton case? All because a heartbroken grandmother did something drastic?"

"I saw you out there."

She stared at him, her gaze cold and hard. Here was the unyielding law-enforcement officer he was used to seeing. Although he appreciated confidence, a person had to be open to changing course when necessary. Melissa didn't seem at all that way and it lit his temper.

"You have doubts." He drummed his fingertips against her desk. "If something went wrong in the Emerson case, is it such a stretch to think something was off with the Paxton one? So, yes. I do want you to look at Orr again for that murder."

"Antonio—"

"There was blood on his hand," Antonio said. "The man was frantic, chattering like a loon about what he'd done and what he should do next. And somehow your department can't find any evidence tying him to Wendy? How is that possible? They were in an intimate relationship." He was pressing hard and he didn't care. "That woman's family deserves real justice. Closure." If Melissa couldn't handle the criticism, she shouldn't be the top cop in town.

"I couldn't agree more," she said at last. "Why do you think I got into police work?" She pressed her fingers to her temples for a moment before meeting his gaze again. "I promise you I'll closely review both cases, but Emerson's, being an active trial, takes precedence."

"All right." She'd surprised him again. "I thought I'd have to push harder."

"Harder?" One eyebrow arched and he would've sworn her lips twitched with amusement. "You've made it clear time and again how little you think of me and my department," she said.

"It isn't personal," he said. "I told you seeing you in action changed my perspective on the quality of your work. But I still think something's off, in both cases."

"And you won't stop pressing until you see me personally take some definitive action?" she asked, folding her arms over her chest.

"Something like that." He tucked his hands into his pockets. It rattled him how much he wanted to touch her, to take some of the burden he could practically see piled high on her shoulders. "I'll give you some space."

"And time," she said as he started for the door. "This kind of thing isn't managed instantly, no matter what you see on television."

He smiled. How was that even possible when facing off with her? "I'll keep that in mind."

After walking out of the office, he studied his surroundings with fresh eyes. The classic stone exterior of police headquarters fit in with the age and architecture of the city center. Inside, it was clean and modern. Brighter than he remembered from the days he'd been in here dealing with Orr's mess. From the front desk to the back doors, the desks seemed to be laid out for efficiency, with her office and a few conference rooms in view on the perimeter. He saw the sign for holding cells and wondered if Hannah had been tucked away already.

He would see if there was anything he could do for her before he left. It wouldn't earn him any points with Melissa, though. And why did that matter? He was headed down the hallway to the holding cells when someone called out Melissa's name.

Turning back, he saw Clarke jogging toward her office. "Mel! You need to see this."

"You found something?" she asked, stepping into view.

"Yes." He paused to catch his breath. "Look at these lab reports. I think Everleigh's grandma might be on to something."

Chapter 4

"Show me," Melissa said. She couldn't decide if it was good news or bad that Clarke had found something so quickly. She had to remind herself to breathe. As a private investigator he rarely helped directly with active GGPD cases, but she'd officially authorized his assistance in this instance and was grateful for her brother's skills tonight.

Clarke flipped a couple pages in his notebook. "First off, the CSI report from the scene and the forensic scientist's report are in conflict. Originally no hair and fibers matching Everleigh Emerson, GGPD's prime suspect, were found at the scene. None were processed at the lab. But in a report that was filed the next day, signed by our forensic scientist, Randall Bowe, he states that two hairs and three fibers previously overlooked were a DNA match for Everleigh."

Melissa swore. "Her attorney didn't catch the discrepancy?"

Clarke shook his head. "A poor excuse for a public defender. They had a stack of cases, one of which is also being tried right now. According to the court transcript, didn't even address it on the cross-examination."

"Conflicting evidence? That sounds a lot like what happened in Orr's case."

Melissa followed that unmistakable voice to find Antonio leaning on a nearby desk, his long legs stretched out and crossed at the ankles. Her pulse hummed in a purely feminine reaction that was the epitome of bad timing. She jerked herself back to her senses.

"What are you doing here?" she demanded. This was *her* station and he should've been on his way back to his hotel.

"This is a public building, right?"

"Yes," she said, curbing the urge to snarl at him. She had no real expectation of privacy out here, but even the media respected her boundary within the building.

When would she escape this nasty spiral of a bad day? This was supposed to be a night off, a time to relax and celebrate with friends and family at Mary's wedding. And yet, here she was, back in the station, butting heads again with the one man who simultaneously stirred her senses and infuriated her. "This doesn't concern you," she responded.

"But it does." He advanced, as if daring her to throw him out. An action she might've considered if the media wasn't still flocking outside.

"The witness—*me*—saw one thing and your lab couldn't manage to corroborate it."

She supposed she should be grateful he didn't mention how they'd interviewed him as a suspect based on

Orr's statement. "As I said earlier, I will look into both cases." He didn't seem inclined to leave. "Surely you're needed at your hotel."

"I doubt it." He sent her a slow smile. A hot energy simmered through her system. "My staff is remarkably dependable."

Aggravated by the heat in her cheeks and unwilling to give him any more of her attention tonight, she asked Clarke to step into her office. She turned to Antonio, keeping her voice low. "You said you would give me time and space."

"I've changed my mind," he stated. Another smile.

She barely contained her sigh of exasperation. "About what?"

"Time. I want to speak with you about the Orr case tonight."

No. No, no, no. This unending day was exactly why Martin had given up on their relationship. He hadn't been the only one… "No," she said. "You are keeping me from handling my top priority."

"Threatening to charge me with obstruction?"

She didn't like the way he seemed to see right through her. "If that's what it takes to make it clear." She took a half step closer, regretting it immediately. His masculine scent, a clean, woodsy spice, zipped along her senses. "You are not *qualified* to interject yourself here. I will be in contact when I've reviewed the Orr case. It will *not* be tonight."

"I'll wait." He dropped into the nearest chair.

He wasn't the first man, officer or civilian, to believe merely being present or persistent would change her course.

She was a woman in a typically male-dominated field. While it wasn't quite as much of a boys' club as it had been for her sixteen years ago at the Michigan Police Academy, female officers in general consistently faced uphill battles with sexism, or worse. Antonio couldn't know how the general ribbing between officers, outright sexist jokes and sheer tenacity had focused her on her path to become the chief of police. From her first day on the job, she'd met and overcome every single obstacle with patience, humor and tenacity.

His stubbornness wasn't the same thing, but she was up to the challenge. Doing her best to forget him, she returned to Clarke, closing her office door. She would deal with any complaints from Antonio later. "Continue, please."

"Is he a problem?" her brother asked under his breath.

Yes. To more than just her work… On levels she wasn't about to explain to her older brother tonight. "He believes we mishandled a case he brought to us last summer. I'll address his concerns after we sort this out."

"Mel, if you need something—"

She cut him off with a smile. "We both know I can fight my own battles."

"True. But I'm your big brother. The offer never expires."

"One more reason you're my *favorite* brother," she joked. This wasn't the time or place to get mushy on him. Her emotions were too close to the surface, had been nearly out of control since Danny had disappeared from the wedding reception. And though mother and son had been reunited, she felt edgier than ever about the role her department might have played in this. Mistakes happened, but they were not the norm here. She'd been part of this department from her first day as a rookie cop and working her way up; she had a unique perspective on the strengths of her people. An error like this was unthinkable and she was determined to root out the truth.

She gestured to his notebook. "Getting back to Everleigh. Her grandmother's actions are compelling. Adding in what you found…" Her voice trailed off. "I'll need to speak with the DA. There has been some turnover in the forensics department. It would be maddening if something fell through the cracks with Bowe, because of the personnel changes."

Clarke scowled. "So how will you figure out who made the mistake? Was it the CSI on the scene, or did something get misfiled in Bowe's lab?"

Neither scenario gave her any comfort at this point. "I'll do what we both do well—investigate." She tried to smile.

Overwhelmed didn't begin to cover it. Inside, she felt as if she'd been squeezed too tightly, every emotion twisted up and wrung out from the moment Danny had been taken. Unfortunately, finding him hadn't set everything right. She had no idea how the errors that led to Hannah McPherson's desperate move had happened, but she would not allow a blatant miscarriage of justice to stand. As a department, they would retrace their steps in the Emerson case until they found the answers.

"Who was the CSI at the scene?" she asked, ready to make her own notes.

Clarke pulled a face, looking pained. "A rookie."

That was all the information she needed. "Jillian," they said in unison.

Their younger cousin was new to the department and, as with all rookies in any capacity, she wouldn't have been attending a murder scene alone. From everything that drifted up the grapevine to Melissa, the woman was good at her job and eager to prove herself. Jillian had made some mistakes—nothing on the level of suddenly finding forensics where there'd been none before—but minor errors were part of any learning curve. "Who else?"

"No other name is listed," Clarke said.

Something had truly gone amiss. "That's my starting point," Melissa said, checking the time. "Is Ruiz still out there?" she asked, picking up her phone to call Jillian.

Clarke shifted just enough to peek through the office blinds. "Right where you left him."

She rolled her eyes, waiting for Jillian to answer the call. When it went to voice mail, Melissa left a message and requested a call back as soon as possible.

When she'd told her parents that she'd applied to the police academy, they'd worried about the dangers of her confronting violent offenders. Once on the job, Melissa had discovered that, personally, waiting for a case to develop was a big hurdle. Good investigations required patience for evidence to process and leads to play out.

But the really low points were those instances when justice was elusive.

Melissa carried vivid memories of the overwhelming shock and sadness when Aunt Amanda, mother of her cousins Desiree and Troy, had been shot and killed in a home invasion. She'd been only six years old and remembered those early days as feelings and grieving faces that eventually faded to resignation. The case had gone cold and remained unsolved.

From day one on the job, she worked to bring justice to her community, even knowing it wouldn't always be possible. And right now there was a man waiting outside her office eager to remind her that was becoming a distressing norm within her department.

She rolled her shoulders and took a long, slow breath.

Good cops out there were counting on her to guide them through this crisis. The anger and frustration had to take a back seat to unraveling what had gone wrong and where so justice could prevail. "I'm authorizing you to stay on this," she said. "Keep pressing the public defender for anything else he may have missed. Being overworked isn't a sufficient excuse."

Clarke raised an eyebrow, but agreed to do it.

"Thanks." She felt like a fugitive when she peeked through a slit in the blinds to check on Antonio. Still there, stubborn man. "Do you have any idea how the media got wind about the ransom message?"

Clarke's eyes went round and he swore. "I didn't share it."

"Troy wouldn't, either," Melissa said. She didn't want to accuse Antonio, but it was possible. "Do you think Hannah McPherson could have sent it out?"

Clarke nodded slowly. "It would certainly fit with everything else she's done."

Melissa hoped Hannah McPherson had been working alone, as she'd claimed at the house when they arrested her.

And would the evidence they gathered hold up? Both Antonio and Hannah McPherson insisted the evidence on two different cases was wrong. Was there an issue with her forensics team? She knew her department—her investigators, officers and detectives in particular—was excellent, but she could not afford incompetence at any level.

There was no choice. She had to call in someone at the state level to help her investigate these discrepancies. She reached for her phone when it rang under her hand. "Chief Colton," she answered.

"It's Jillian. I just saw you called."

"Thanks for the quick response," Melissa said. She sank into her chair and pulled a notepad within reach. Not a chance with Antonio lurking nearby.

"Is this about the Everleigh Emerson case?" Jillian asked.

"Yes." Melissa exchanged a glance with Clarke. He'd pulled a chair around to hear as much as possible. "I've always felt awful about missing that evidence," Jillian said. "I'm sure you know that they teach us some hairs and fibers aren't obvious to the naked eye. It's why we bag everything for the lab."

"Right," Melissa said. "So there isn't a mention in your report of any hair visibly different than the victim's hair on the paperweight—the murder weapon—because it wasn't visible to you at the scene?"

"That's right. I took pictures and worked the scene, but obviously I must have missed something big. The goal is to put the right person behind bars."

"I understand what happened," Melissa said. "It takes all of us, especially on a murder case. From this end it seems you did everything right," she assured her cousin.

"I'm glad you think so, Chief. I am trying to be careful out there. And I'm glad I brought in everything for the lab to process."

Melissa appreciated her humility, but she just wasn't convinced this was all on Jillian's shoulders. She made herself a note to check on the new CSI's other cases later this week. Rookie issues like this one rarely needed a chief's attention. The forensics teams had an internal management structure that dealt with scheduling and the day-to-day.

"Did Bowe reprimand you for the oversight?" Melissa asked. Clarke nodded his approval of the question.

"Not officially. But when the final report came in,

I had to do a few hours of coursework review. I didn't mind," she added quickly. "I want to learn from my mistakes. Since then, I've done everything possible to be more diligent."

Her earnestness warmed Melissa's heart, made her want her cousin to get better at her job. "And this was the first crime scene you worked alone?"

"I wasn't alone," Jillian replied. "Billy McClusky was there with me."

Clarke shifted, then pored through his notes and eventually shook his head.

Another discrepancy to add to the growing list. A chill slid down Melissa's spine. "Jillian, you can't share this conversation with anyone," she began. She lowered her voice. "I'm not convinced you or Billy made any errors on this case."

There was a long pause. "What?" her cousin asked, incredulous. "What are you saying?"

"We're just digging in, but we're finding some inconsistencies with the Emerson case as a whole. Until I sort that out, would you please take extra precautions on your cases?"

"How so?"

"Please back up your notes, pictures and copies of your final reports in a separate location. Whatever system you choose, make sure it's somewhere different from the official department database."

"You're serious?" Jillian breathed.

"I am. Again, none of this is for public knowledge."

"Understood," Jillian promised. "If I can help you sort out anything else with this, please call."

"I appreciate that." Melissa ended the conversation and cradled the phone in her hands. She looked up

Billy's personnel record and dialed his cell phone, despite the late hour.

He answered immediately. "Hey, Chief."

"Sorry to bother you so late," she began. "I just have a couple questions about the Emerson case."

"I figured, after the mess at the wedding," he said. "Fire away."

"Were you Jillian Colton's supervisor at the crime scene?"

"Yes, I was. She did a great job, everything by the book. She's a real asset."

His confidence gave Melissa a much-needed boost. "And you filed your report as usual?"

"You bet. We delivered everything to the lab all at once, same as always."

"Just what I needed to hear. Thanks so much, Billy."

She sat there for a moment, dumbfounded. Her cursory search didn't show any evidence logs or reports from Billy at that scene, though there were records from other cases he had worked that same month.

What on earth were they up against here?

"Want me to go back to the defense attorney tonight?" Clarke asked.

"You've done enough tonight," she replied. "Tomorrow is Sunday. They won't be in court and we can use that time to get a better picture. I'll add this as part of our official investigation of the kidnapping case."

"Sure thing," Clarke said, standing. "Be careful."

"Always."

She followed her brother out of her office, pausing to lock the door. It was no shock that Antonio was sitting right where they'd left him. "Closing up without giving me a chance to talk?" he asked.

She bit back a scathing reply. It wasn't entirely his

fault that she was antsy. Picking fights wouldn't help anything. Before she could form a polite response, her stomach rumbled.

"I'll remind you this was supposed to be my day off." It was so strange to be the person complaining about her demanding job. "Since Danny was taken before I got my dinner, I'm willing to hear you out as long as food is involved."

His expression softened the hard angles of his chiseled features as her words registered. "My place or yours?"

"Neither." She couldn't imagine having this striking man, the owner of several opulent hotels around the country, in her very average three-bedroom, two-bath, single-story home. "I was thinking that Paola's Pizza sounded good."

"That works for me," he said.

It dawned on her then that her car was still at the hotel. "Let me just get the keys to a cruiser. Unless you'd rather walk?"

The restaurant was only a few blocks away and the chilly night air might be just the thing for the heat building under her skin when he was near. Her professional distance seemed to evaporate around Antonio.

"For the record, I wasn't just sitting here doing nothing," he said with a heart-melting smile. "I asked one of the hotel drivers to deliver your SUV."

She didn't know what to say to that.

Antonio chuckled. "Is there a law against that kind of peace offering, Chief?"

"Probably. But I'll let you off with a warning tonight."

She'd always found him handsome, but that twinkle in his eyes made him too sexy for any safe association.

It was going to be an interesting conversation, assuming she could concentrate on what he had to say and not all the things he made her feel.

Antonio had to work a little too hard to smother his amusement. Melissa was one surprise after another, starting with the lovely dress she'd had on earlier all the way through the competent search-and-rescue. He didn't want to be attracted to her and yet he didn't want to avoid it, either. Best to chalk it up to bad timing and keep the boundaries clear.

Especially when he wanted her to reopen the Wendy Paxton murder case.

He'd used the time she left him cooling his heels to sort out the bits and pieces of information he'd picked up tonight. He didn't condone Hannah McPherson's actions, but it sounded to him as though someone in the forensics department had made a big mistake on that case. Didn't that make it more plausible that the evidence against Orr had been overlooked or mishandled, too?

"Did you ask the driver to leave the car out front?" she asked, pausing as they approached the back door.

"Nice of you to assume the worst of me," he replied, not the least bit offended. He'd thought about doing just that so she would have to face the press one more time. But after all they'd gone through tonight, the move felt petty, so he'd instructed the car to be parked behind the police station.

"It feels like our pattern."

And there it was, that simmer of attraction, nudging him to shift their pattern toward more amicable terrain. "I double-checked with another officer and had the valet leave the car out back. I can't promise a complete absence of press, but with luck it won't be as bad as earlier."

"I appreciate that." Sincerity shone in her blue eyes.

He shrugged into his coat and then took the coat she had draped over her arm, holding it for her.

"Thanks," she said, clearly surprised by the gesture.

"My dad told me good manners make the man."

"Is that so?"

He watched, mesmerized, as she buttoned the dressy wool coat over her bland uniform. The effect was a strange illustration of the two parts of her life: the hard-nosed chief who worked diligently for her department and her city, and the lovely woman underneath those responsibilities.

"Mom said it lulled her enough to fall for him," he added.

"So after hours of giving me grief tonight, your new plan is to lull me into whatever you want with chivalry? Interesting approach," she quipped as he held the back door of the station for her to walk out ahead of him.

He wasn't accustomed to letting a woman drive on the way to dinner. Then again, he usually spoiled his dates with one of the property cars, sometimes a chauffeur, depending on the occasion. Besides, this wasn't actually a date. The police chief was undeniably beautiful and his perspective about her had shifted since seeing her in that dress and later, with the little boy in her arms.

Didn't matter, though. He wasn't about to let his old memories throw him off. He had two decades of practice keeping his old baggage locked down. Now that he had her full attention, he intended to make the most of it: for Wendy's sake.

"Why did you go into law enforcement?" he asked as she parked the car in the lot behind the restaurant.

She cut the engine and gave him a long look, her face a study of contrasts between the dark car and the glow from the tall parking lot light overhead. "Why did you start buying properties?" she countered.

"Money," he admitted easily. "Security and profit." *To support my new family*, he thought, pleased he'd stopped himself before that slipped out. "I doubt that's why you joined the police."

"Well, no, I'm not in it for the big payday."

Her smile was slow and edged on exhaustion. For a moment, he considered giving her a break and putting off this conversation. The search for her young cousin had taken a toll. On both of them.

She pulled the key from the ignition, tracing the jagged edge with her fingertip. He was mesmerized by the movement and too curious about how those long, slender fingers would feel against his skin.

"My aunt was murdered," she said, capturing his full attention. "The case was never closed. I guess the effects lingered."

"I'm so sorry for your loss."

Another faint smile. "You don't have to say that."

"It was sincere," he assured her.

"Thanks," she said. "The loss and all of the unknowns rippled through the family in different ways. I wanted to catch the person responsible, to learn why they decided to hurt her. You might say an initial morbid fascination matured into a hard line about the meanings of justice and fairness."

And yet a killer was walking around free. Orr should be in jail, but he wasn't. Antonio supposed the count was actually two killers on the loose, if Hannah McPherson was right about her granddaughter's innocence. If the buck didn't stop with Melissa, then who could the city count on to handle the problem?

Her stomach rumbled again. "Let's take care of that." He got out of the car and rounded the hood, not quite in time to open her door for her. Instead, he offered his hand.

"I'm good," she said, avoiding his touch.

"Habit," he explained. But he had to wonder if he would've helped her with her coat, held the door or shown her any such manners prior to this evening.

The answer was a resounding "no" and for some reason that annoyed him. The sidewalk from the parking lot to the entrance had been cleared and salted, and she was in sturdy shoes now with thick treads. He was the one more likely to slip on an icy patch than she was.

"While I was waiting, the wedding coordinator called and told me the newlyweds were settled into the bridal suite. I thought you'd be happy to hear they took the abbreviated reception in stride."

"I'm glad." Melissa tucked her hands into her pockets. "I should've checked in with her when we got back to the station."

"Plenty of people around to handle the bride. You had other priorities."

Melissa's lips were moving, but the whine of a car engine blotted out her words. They both turned into the glaring headlights of a small dark car, fishtailing through the slushy side street.

Antonio barely registered that the window was down as the car came closer. Was the driver not paying attention at all? The streetlight illuminated the person's face at the same time Melissa shouted, "Gun!"

On reflex, he dragged her to the ground and blocked her body with his. He heard the pops of gunfire, expected pain to follow any second. Instead, there were only sounds. Bullets ricocheting, the engine revving, the tires spinning as the driver fought the conditions and sped away. Antonio jerked around to look, but snow blocked the license plate.

His pulse slowed and he picked out details, one by one. Freezing cold wetness seeped through his slacks and his leather gloves. A line of bullet holes marched along the wall of the building. Fine dust and bits of paint from the wall had landed on her coat, in her hair. Her hands fluttered up and down his arms, across his chest, even over his hair, but her voice was calm.

"Are you hit?" She helped him sit back and lean against the wall of the restaurant. "Antonio, answer me."

"I'm not hurt," he said. It felt like he was shouting with the echo of gunfire ringing in his ears. "Are you?"

"I'm good."

He listened to her make a phone call. Could hardly believe it when she said the words *drive-by shooting*.

"What?" He tried to stand, but she held firm. "What the hell was that?" Her eyes were so big and her cheeks pale. She looked almost as scared now as she'd been when the ransom message had come through. Only this time, she hadn't melted—she'd taken charge.

"Thanks for the cover," she said, as the sounds of emergency sirens grew closer. "Keep breathing."

He followed her gaze back to the wall. He counted seven holes before he gave up and closed his eyes. It was too much. Too close. "No promises," he said, rubbing his chest. He would never just stand back and do nothing when a woman or child was in danger. "It was Orr."

"I beg your pardon?"

"The driver. I couldn't make out the license plate on

the car, but I saw his face." He pointed up at the street-light. "It was Drew Orr."

"You're sure?"

"Absolutely." And he had inadvertently put Melissa at risk with his comments to the press. Unacceptable. His throat was tight, his hands curled into fists. He had to fix this.

"All right," she said, standing. "Glad one of us got a good look."

GGPD patrol cars already blocked both ends of the block. He hauled himself up out of the wet snow to stand with her. The shooting had brought out a few bystand-ers, too, searching for the source of the noise.

"Why would Orr show up now?" he wondered aloud.

She rubbed his shoulder and even through the layers of his coat, he felt the comfort she offered. How many new facets of her personality would she show him to-night? "We'll talk about it in a minute."

He was ready to argue when he spotted the blood. A thin line of red trickling from behind her ear and down her neck, disappearing into her collar. Not seri-ous, but enough to make his stomach cramp. "You…" He pulled himself together, away from the memories of Karen's body, lifeless… This was hardly the same thing. "You. There's blood." He gingerly turned her chin to the side so he could see how bad it was. He reached inside his coat, pulled out a handkerchief and folded it, then pressed it to the small wound, while holding her face still. So fair and fragile. "I pushed you down." Too hard, clearly.

Her fingers curled around his hands for a moment and her lips parted. He wanted to kiss her, to breathe her in and know they were both okay.

"You saved my life," she said. "Thank you." Easing back, she kept the cloth in place, her gaze intent on his.

He didn't have time to respond as the officers descended on them. At her encouragement, he gave his statement first while she and another officer and the CSI team examined the damage to the wall, then started collecting evidence.

He watched, detached from it all as the cops moved like a well-oiled machine around him. "Maybe this should wait until tomorrow," Melissa said when she was done with her official role as chief and as a witness. A paramedic had cleaned the small wound behind her ear, declaring it a scratch that didn't need stitches.

"You still haven't eaten," he replied. He felt weak and shaky as old losses and near misses twisted and tangled up in his gut. Fortunately, after two decades of practice, he hid his emotions well.

"I'll grab a sandwich at home," she said. "Come by—"

"You can't go home!"

He didn't realize he'd shouted it. Her vivid blue eyes had gone cool under arched eyebrows. The other officers turned toward them, clearly ready to leap to her defense. Later he might admire that devotion. "Pardon me," he said, scrubbing at his face. "I'm more rattled than I care to admit."

"It happens," she said in the way that professionals dealing with a volatile, inexperienced public did.

Her steady calm scraped against his jangled nerves. The doctor had used that carefully modulated tone when reporting the death of Antonio's wife and baby...

"I'll take you home," she began. "And then—"

He shook his head. "You can't be alone." He leaned closer. "It isn't safe. That was *Drew Orr*." He was certain of it. Who else would have the audacity to take a shot at the chief of police?

"So you've said."

"He's already killed one woman," Antonio said, struggling to match her cool detachment.

"We'll handle it." She opened her coat and tapped the emblem on her uniform shirt. "If you're worried for my safety, you should be worried for yourself, as well."

He might be pushing his agenda to make sure Orr paid for killing Wendy, but Melissa was the real threat to Orr's freedom now. Antonio might be a thorn in the man's side, but his statement was already public record. Only Melissa had the authority to give Orr real trouble. Until she understood the danger, Antonio wouldn't leave her alone and vulnerable. A badge didn't make her invincible. "Come with me to the hotel. I can feed you and explain it all."

"Antonio. We have this under control."

"Do you?" he challenged. "Orr is free to drive around and shoot at people because *you* didn't do your job."

She wrapped herself into her coat, cinching the tie. "Or maybe it wasn't Orr—he's just on your mind. Maybe the shooter is connected to the Emerson case," she snapped. "Either way, you're leaving now so I can do my job without any distractions."

"I'm not leaving without you. You were nearly a victim. Aren't there rules about that?"

"Spare me." She rolled her eyes. "Am I driving you home or is someone else?"

"You, please. And the hotel instead of my house."

If he could get her to join him inside, he might have a chance at making her understand the risks of underestimating his former associate.

Chapter 5

Melissa had never been more grateful for silence or the distracting task of driving. Neither of them spoke on the short drive to the hotel. She'd promised him a conversation, but she needed space. When Antonio was close, she nearly forgot herself, her focus. And they'd never been closer than during those moments on the sidewalk, his long body sheltering hers.

That hum of awareness whenever he was around had been pervasive long before tonight. It went back further than the day he'd walked into the police station last summer to file a report against a business associate.

It was as if the sight of him sent her back to the days of her awkward high-school crush on the star basketball player. Antonio was a walking sexual fantasy. One of the most desirable bachelors in the state, if not the country. She'd seen the splashy photos and gossip columns that proved how many women succumbed to that sharp smile and smoldering gaze. Galas, charity events, local and around the world. In addition to his powerful presence, each picture had one thing in common: a different, beyond-beautiful woman on his arm every time.

The man was an expert at dating and clearly averse to commitment.

Although she couldn't argue the appeal of a no-strings, blow-off-some-steam kind of fling, for her, in her position, the gossip that would light up the city wasn't worth it. As attracted as she was to Antonio, she was really after more than a one-night stand. She was in the market for a partner who wanted to be there for the long haul, even with the hours she worked. A husband, kids and the kind of happily-ever-after bliss usually reserved for fairy tales…

Big dreams? Sure, but she wasn't quite ready to settle for less.

She followed Antonio's directions around the hotel and parked in a small paved strip that must have been reserved for his personal use. "Take care of yourself," she said.

He turned, frowning. "You need to come in."

"I think it's best—"

But he was already out of the car and rounding the hood. Resigned, she stared him down as he opened her door.

"You need to eat," he said. "I have kitchens full of food. And I need to talk."

"Fine." She cut the engine. It wasn't as if she had a better offer at home. He guided her up the short walkway, tapped a card to the security panel and then held the door for her.

This man didn't quit. She couldn't recall the last time a date had held the door for her…although this *wasn't* a romantic encounter. For that matter, she'd be hard-pressed to remember her last real date. Attending the wedding with Martin didn't count. For the most part, her boyfriends had been few and far between. Unending days like today made it easy to understand why they usually gave up on her. No one wanted to feel ignored in their personal life.

"This is my job," she murmured, thinking aloud. "My life is one interruption after another."

Antonio didn't break stride as they continued down the hallway. "You were quite focused this evening while we searched for Danny."

"Crisis of the moment," she said. "You were a big help," she added. She had to admit his actions at Hannah McPherson's home were downright heroic. She and Troy had picked up on the older woman's nerves, but having that confirmation from Antonio allowed her to take swift, decisive action.

He used the card again and she found herself in a commercial kitchen. It felt way too small to manage the demands of his hotel. And it was empty even though she knew the restaurant was still open. "Where are we?"

"One of the events kitchens," he explained. "We allow caterers to stage from here. It's also available if we need to accommodate a guest with severe allergies."

"Wow." The kitchen was still and the air cool. The stainless steel gleamed from every angle. Counters, coolers, racks with empty trays ready to be put to use.

Antonio opened a refrigerator and pulled out two platters covered in plastic wrap. After setting them on the nearest counter, he paused. "Would you like coffee, plain water, infused water, or lemonade?"

"Water, please. Plain," she clarified.

He returned with a tall glass pitcher filled with clear

water and ice. "Can you carry those?" He dipped his head to the platters.

"Of course." What was he up to? "Is feeding people your thing?" His eyebrows arched. "Does it settle you down? My mom is like that," Melissa rambled on. "She cooks when she's upset, delivers food when she knows others are hurting."

"Are you hurting?"

"The question was about you," she said, picking up the platters as he started toward the door.

"I won't deny being shot at shook me up," he admitted. "And I wouldn't be in the hotel business if I didn't enjoy people."

"Enjoy caring for people?" Why was she pushing? They didn't need to be friends. She wasn't sure she even wanted a more in-depth understanding of the man who sent her body into overdrive with just a look.

"Sure."

So much for an in-depth answer. She told herself she was relieved. "Where are we going?"

"My office," he said. "It's the best I can do to guarantee your safety and privacy."

He'd relaxed bit by bit the farther they went into his hotel. "You're confident about your security," she observed.

"I am." He glanced at her, his gaze serious and sincere. "And I'm sorry that they failed to see the threat Mrs. McPherson posed before she took Danny."

Melissa shrugged that off. "She was determined. If not here, she would've managed it somewhere else."

"Because she's desperate."

"True," she agreed as they entered his second-floor private office. She'd never been up here and yet she immediately recognized his personality and standards in every feature and fixture. The decor was sleek and masculine without being stark, thanks to a neutral color palette offset with pops of deep colors. Accents were placed with care and she'd bet most of the pieces were personal, either family heirlooms or from his travels.

She noticed a blue-and-white ball vase on the corner of his massive desk with a smaller arrangement of the fresh flowers from the lobby. A live-edge coffee table anchored a conversation area; the contrasting color of the wood grain gave the pretty piece the suggestion of movement like a river.

This was a luxury condo compared to the chief's office at the station. The gap between his work and hers, his life and hers, felt as big as the dark expanse of Lake Michigan outside his windows.

"We can eat here." He set the water on the glass-top table centered in the bay window. He turned and relieved her of the platters, then set them down on the table.

She unbelted her coat and discovered Antonio was right behind her, ready to ease it from her shoulders. For a split second she wished she was back in the dress she'd worn to the wedding instead of her uniform. The reaction was so unexpected she shook her head. Clothes did not make the woman.

"Something wrong?" He'd moved off to a tall cabinet built into the wall near the table, and was taking out glasses, plates, utensils and napkins.

"Just a little awestruck." She watched him fill each glass with water, admiring his steady hands. His world was so different from hers. "Our, *um*, *offices* are night and day."

"As they should be. If you had Baccarat crystal in

your break room at the station, I imagine taxpayers would come after you with torches and pitchforks."

"And they'd be right to do so," she said with a laugh.

"Please, sit down," he suggested. "Be comfortable." His smooth baritone slid over her skin and she had to suppress the urge to lean in to him.

Ridiculous reactions. This was not a date. Not even a prelude to a fling. She was here because of the case he thought she'd screwed up. There might even be a new case if that had been Orr behind the gun.

It was the sobering reminder she needed as he took the seat across from her. She sipped her water while he unwrapped the platters of cheeses, fruits and various meats and cold vegetables. "Beats a plain sandwich, right?"

Her stomach growled again and they both laughed. "This is a thousand times better. Thank you."

He smiled and she was glad to be sitting down when her knees went all weak. Again, it would be nice to blame her fascination and attraction on stress, but it was all him. They dug into the food, the silence companionable, and she enjoyed the peaceful reprieve while it lasted.

He seemed to fill up faster than she did, reclining and stretching an arm out across the back of the banquette, peering at his water glass as if wishing for something stronger. But he didn't speak until she pushed away her plate.

"That was delicious," she said. "Thank you again."

"You're welcome." Now he sat forward and despite the table between them she felt crowded. "That *was* Orr in the car."

She blotted her lips with the napkin and shifted into

the cop she was. "All right. Let's start with that. Was he shooting at you or me, do you think?"

"I've been giving that some thought," he admitted, a troubled expression brewing in his dark eyes. "I think he must have been after you."

"What?" She was too tired to completely hide her surprise. "Why?"

"Because I reported him over six months ago. He was furious, but he managed to turn the police on me and eventually go on with his life as a free man. He's aware I've given the police all the information I have. I think he's afraid you really will start digging into the Paxton case."

"You were never a serious suspect," she said.

"Apparently neither was he."

The words cut deep and she struggled to stay professional. "We recovered the body and evaluated the evidence, Antonio. I'm sorry it didn't line up with what you saw and what he told you."

He opened his mouth and snapped it shut again. "He killed her. I know it."

It bothered her, deeply, that he might be right, despite the fact she'd gone by the book. "The timing feels coincidental," she admitted. "Was there a business deal you'd originally planned to discuss this time of year?"

"No, our business ended about a year ago." His gaze drifted to the window as he thought about her question.

"Have you seen him in town again prior to tonight?"

"No," he said with a sigh. "Once he got away with the murder, I never expected to see him again."

Another solid blow, but she held her ground. "Tell me why you're so sure he's a threat to me, rather than you." She studied him as he gathered his thoughts and caught herself leaning forward. He often spoke at city-council meetings and other events around town and she always appreciated his sharp mind and flawless logic.

"Because you said earlier today you'd reopen the Paxton case. He can't let you do that."

"I said that in private," she countered after mentally rewinding the events of the past few hours.

"Not just in private. You said something about justice for Grave Gulch."

He was right. "I wasn't specific. I'm not sure I was even thinking about Orr directly at that moment."

"But you were standing right next to me when I said I believed he was guilty."

"Even so—" she checked her watch "—he must have been close to take action that fast."

"Orr isn't one for patience," Antonio said with aggravating certainty. "I know him better than you do. He had me fooled for a long time."

"I'm listening."

He ran a fingertip around the rim of his glass. "Drew started as a casual acquaintance. Looking back, I'd say he worked me over systematically. He stayed at the hotel a few times. Introductions were made and we found common ground as property owners. He asked my opinion on a couple of developments he was kicking around." He finally raised the glass and took a sip of water.

She was nearly distracted by what should've been uninteresting motions. With Antonio, even something as mundane as swallowing had her temperature rising. She'd been tucked under his body when the gunfire started and she now knew the scent of his skin near his collar.

"Eventually, he proposed a joint venture." He shifted in his chair. "It looked good at first, nothing out of the ordinary with a serious profit margin. Then I saw the bids and the list of contractors he planned to use."

"Red flags?"

He snorted. "Plenty. But it was the timeline that put a spotlight on the problem. The only way to make his proposed grand-opening date was to take shortcuts on the foundation and swap out the finer details with cheap finishes."

"You balked."

"I tried to talk first. It's not my nature to bail without reason." Another sip of water, followed by the glide of his tongue over his lips. "Fortunately, I hadn't invested any serious money at that point and we hadn't finalized the contract. As his friend, I didn't want to leave him hanging, so I confirmed he had the capital to get started. Told him not to worry about what I'd given. Once he got started, it would be easier to find investors to carry him to the finish line. About the same time, one of my Florida hotels took some serious hurricane damage. I couldn't responsibly spread myself so thin."

"And he understood all of that?" she asked.

"I thought so." He took a deep breath. "I dealt with my projects. Drew dealt with his. We had dinner once in a while or went out for a round of golf. And then another friend in Canada called me, wanting insight on Drew after a questionable interaction they'd had with him. Suffice it to say, either he'd always been shady, stealing from one project to pay off another, or he'd made some significant mistakes after we parted ways."

"Does it matter which?" she queried.

"No to me. I didn't talk to him for several months until the day he turned up with blood on his hand, frantic about what to do now that 'she was dead.'"

"*She* being Wendy Paxton."

He nodded.

"I'll pull the file and read the statement, but can you refresh my memory?"

He drank some water, taking his time. "Drew said, and I quote, 'I killed her. Oh, God. I don't know what to do.' He told me he tossed her body in some area of the city park. When he asked for my advice, I suggested he turn himself in. Repeatedly."

That was concise, but not quite what she was after. She could see he wasn't enjoying the conversation, but she'd never spoken directly with him about the case. "Where were you when he turned up that day?"

"I was helping my elderly neighbor with yard work…"

His voice trailed off as she burst into laughter, too tired from everything else to stifle the automatic reaction.

His gaze narrowed. "That's funny to you?"

She fanned her face. "I'm sorry. Blame it on fatigue or—"

"Being shot at?"

"That, too." The drive-by *had* rattled her. It seemed as if she'd climbed onto a never-ending roller coaster of emotion and drama since the moment Danny had disappeared. She tried to catch her breath and, noticing the amused sparkle in Antonio's eyes, she started sputtering all over again.

"Seriously," she said at last. "Forgive me for having a hard time picturing you up to your elbows in dirt and mulch." She bit her lip. "You're always so…you."

He stared at her and then tapped the table. "I will take that as a compliment. And, yes, I was getting my hands dirty. One more reason I didn't shake Drew's hand when he showed up."

"The blood was on his right hand?"

"Yes," Antonio replied immediately. He turned his own hand palm up and showed her where he'd seen the blood. "My first thought was he must have been in an accident. He had that frantic, shocked energy."

She knew exactly what he meant, having been on scene for emergencies ranging from fender benders to domestic violence. Adrenaline was a powerful chemical reaction and the rush manifested in many ways, depending on the person and the situation.

A prime example was that moment on the street when she thought Antonio was going to kiss her. When she would've kissed him back.

"The more he talked," Antonio continued, "the clearer it became that he'd done something terrible."

"You didn't offer to help him?" she queried.

"How? By covering it up? Not a chance, even if I had still considered him a friend. He showed up, distraught and close to a panic, and I told him to go to the police."

"No one else overheard this conversation or recognized him?" she persisted.

He shook his head. "He wore a hoodie, pulled up and shading his face. He called me over to him near the curb. Looking back, it becomes clear he was avoiding as much contact as possible."

She had to give him credit for delivering details without embellishment or speculation. "You didn't tell him to get a lawyer?"

"The man was not my friend." He leaned back, propping an ankle on the opposite knee. "I have no idea why he even came to me. I went straight to the police after he came to me and your department let it go."

She bristled at that—they hadn't let it go, but had investigated and not found sufficient evidence to charge

Orr—but contained her reaction. "Did he tell you why he killed her?"

"He told me she'd been cheating on him. He was a wreck," Antonio replied. "I'd met her a few times, over dinner. They weren't what I'd call a stable couple."

"How so?"

"They argued over dumb, irrelevant things. He kept tabs on her phone location, checked her messages. They fought once in front of me when she and my date bonded over their latest sexy celebrity crush."

"So he was the jealous type." It shamed her to feel a pang of envy for the woman who had been his care-free date that night. She couldn't imagine thinking of another man, celebrity or not, while spending time with Antonio.

"He was the unstable, criminally negligent, fiscally dangerous, murderous type." Antonio leaned forward. "I don't have psych evaluations or a rap sheet to show you, but Drew Orr is as shady as they come in business. He takes shortcuts, makes payoffs to smooth his way."

"In other words, he's nothing like you."

"That's right." The cool, slightly aloof mask she recognized from city-council meetings dropped over his face. "I'm confident you were his target, not me. I can't do anything more to him. You can. His past ac-tions prove to me there is no limit to how low he'll go. He wants to prevent you from taking another look at Wendy's case."

It was a logical argument. If Orr wanted to get to Antonio, he could've been more aggressive at any time in recent months. Still, the timing of tonight's attack bothered her. "Are you aware of any other connections between Orr and the police department?" She assumed his arched eyebrow meant no. "Never hurts to ask." It was something she'd have to dig into as soon as the Everleigh situation was handled. "Any idea where Orr spends his time when he's not shooting up Grave Gulch?"

"You aren't taking me seriously," Antonio accused, pushing to his feet and pacing away from the table before turning around. "I underestimated him once and nearly lost a fortune. I won't repeat that mistake. Lives—yours, mine, Wendy's—are invaluable."

Fortune. She briefly wondered how a man like Antonio defined that term. She didn't ask, as that detail was irrelevant to the case and wouldn't advance the situation with Orr.

"Thanks for the meal," she said, standing. "Can I help you clean up?"

"I can manage. If I get stuck, I'll just call Housekeeping."

She really had offended him with the laughter over him working outside. "All right." She went to the coatrack for her coat and folded it over her arm. "I'll let you know when I have news."

"Haven't you been listening?" He scowled and stalked closer. "You can't go home. Stay here. At the hotel," he added in a hurry.

"No, thank you." The city would never approve that kind of expense and she wasn't in the mood to toss away money on a pricey room when she had a perfectly good house a few miles away.

"Melissa." There was an ache in his voice that struck a chord deep inside her. She caught the flash of pain in his eyes, the clenched jaw. "Tell me you're taking precautions. Please. This man is dangerous."

"I'll be careful. I can defend myself, you know."

"I've had more contact with him than you. He won't

hesitate to hurt people close to you." He stepped closer. "Wasn't the trouble with Danny enough of a scare?"

"Any trouble is always too much," she said. He was pleading with her. "I'm on high alert. You might not trust my department, but we are good people. Smart and reliable, too, though I understand why you would doubt me." She managed to get her coat on by herself this time.

He scrubbed at his face, then shoved his hands into his pockets. "There's a penthouse suite with private access and impenetrable security right upstairs."

She gripped the ties of her coat. "You have a safe house."

"Yes. I build at least one into every hotel. It's yours," he said. "No charge. You'll have everything you need and Orr can't get to you."

The urgent worry was a wave crashing over her. Where was this coming from? "That's very kind." And *definitely* too much. "*You* should use it."

"But he's after you."

She tried to smile. "Your opinion. The smart cop in me says we're both at risk."

He blew out a breath, muttering something in a mix of languages she couldn't decipher. "There's room for both of us in the secure suite."

"Stop." She held up a hand. The idea of hiding from her responsibilities was bad enough. But sharing a private suite with Antonio was far too tempting. She needed a clear head if she was going to bring her department thought the problems with the Emerson and Paxton cases.

With deliberate steps, she moved to the door. "Thank you again for your assistance tonight with Danny and…" It was suddenly difficult to mention the drive-by shooting. "I will keep you updated on the Orr case as things develop."

"Nothing I can do will change your mind?"

"No." She wanted to touch that whisker-shadowed jaw, to smooth away the worry creasing his forehead. She couldn't recall another man outside of her family ever being so concerned for her safety.

"Then I'll have to settle for walking you to your car," he said.

Ever the gentleman, she thought as he stuck by her side from the office to her vehicle. He waited for her to get in, buckle up and start the engine. But it was the tilt of his mouth, a little sad, a lot frustrated, that left her second-guessing her decision.

Back upstairs in his office, Antonio finished clearing the table but he couldn't relax. Tension gripped his shoulders in an unrelenting hold. Had she made it home? He should've insisted that she call one of her officers to escort her. Why hadn't he asked her to call him when she got to her house?

He knew she could keep herself safe… But Melissa was out there alone with a killer on the loose and there wasn't a damn thing he could do about it. His supposedly legendary charm and influence had no effect on one stubborn police chief. Who would help her if Orr struck again?

He tried work, his preferred method of distraction, but he couldn't concentrate on the work that had been interrupted when Victor stormed in with news of Danny's abduction. More than once, he caught himself with one hand on his cell phone, determined to let Orr know he'd been seen driving that car.

Firing that gun.

That would pull the jerk's focus off Melissa.

Well, to be fair, he hadn't seen Orr's finger on the trigger. And now he was thinking like Melissa. Facts only, no guessing allowed. In Antonio's mind it was the only logical conclusion. They'd been shot at by the driver of that black car and the driver had been Drew Orr.

He went back to the table and discovered the lingering scent of Melissa. She'd worn a soft, unforgettably feminine fragrance tonight. Instantly, he was back on that sidewalk, wishing he'd kissed her.

His gloves had been torn, but his slacks had survived. They were nearly dry now. His heart worried him more. The feel of her hands skimming over him, searching for any injury...well, he wouldn't be forgetting that anytime soon, either.

He enjoyed dating and was always clear about his short-term philosophy. It was a rare woman who gave him enough sparks to remind him of the joy and affection he'd shared with his wife.

Melissa had done that, and they didn't even like each other.

Maybe he liked her a *little*. She was undeniably attractive. He'd definitely gained more respect for her while she'd worked the rescue operation, too. Her sense of justice needing to prevail resonated with him, too. A normal man might enjoy that connection, but it only made Antonio twitchy.

He shouldn't be looking for common ground. Not with her. Nothing could erase the mistakes made by someone in her department. Where and why those errors occurred wasn't his concern. Orr should be held accountable for his crimes.

Antonio stretched his neck and stared out across the

dark lake. Yesterday, he might not have cared if that pursuit put Melissa at risk. Somehow, tonight, he couldn't stop worrying for her safety.

Aggravated with himself, he walked to the closet he kept stocked with a few key items and changed into worn jeans, a thermal shirt and a thick flannel. Melissa would probably laugh all over again if she got a look at him now. Well, if everything went well, she wouldn't.

He donned thick socks and a pair of boots in case he had to keep watch for any length of time and then grabbed his heavy coat and another pair of gloves. If she had a patrol team posted, watching her back, he could go home with a clear conscience. If not, he'd stay until morning just to make sure she didn't get hurt by Orr's violent tenacity.

Melissa's home address was a matter of public record. And even if it hadn't been, she kept her official car parked in the driveway in an understated attempt to deter crime in the neighborhood. That kind of subtlety would hardly stop a man who'd opened fire on her once already.

As he waited for his car to warm up, he told himself he should just head to one of his southern hotels for a few weeks. He could let winter blow itself out without any more frigid nights or worrisome drama. Then he recalled the stark relief on Melissa's face when he'd come down those stairs with her little cousin in his arms.

Who was he kidding? He'd stay the course, do everything possible to protect her from whatever Orr had planned.

Maybe if he'd told her the whole story she would've stayed in the secure suite. He really shouldn't have held anything back. Once she finished the urgent matter of the Emerson case, he trusted her to dig into the Paxton case.

Based on comments and conversations with his friends in the last few months, it seemed Orr had moved on, leaving Antonio and Grave Gulch behind. It made him twitchy to think of Orr returning to this area, being close enough to react so swiftly to a throwaway comment during a media crush.

Antonio drove slowly down Melissa's street. She lived in a neat cottage with craftsman details and a wide front porch. It was similar to the house he'd grown up in just a few blocks away. When his dad retired, his parents had sold the house to him and moved back to Florida. He'd lived there and made some updates while he built his home on the lakefront. A home big enough for his parents, siblings and their families to visit anytime.

It was a double-edged sword to see Melissa's official SUV in the driveway. At least there was a GGPD cruiser parked at the curb across the street. He took a deep breath, inordinately relieved that she wasn't taking anything for granted. She'd pegged him when she observed that he enjoyed caring for people. With her, though, he didn't *want* to feel anything except professional courtesy. Unfortunately, he couldn't put a lid on the emotions surging through him and the streak of overprotectiveness that reared up in him.

Maybe it was the kidnapping that brought back all of the grief and angst with such a vengeance. Much as he wanted to blame that situation, he knew there was more to it. She was more.

Melissa Colton threatened his peace of mind. Even when all he'd known was her quiet, calm professionalism, something about her tempted him. Now that he'd seen her in action, that tough competence broken up by the flashes of vulnerability when she'd seen the ransom message or worried he'd been shot, he was utterly fascinated.

It wasn't good news.

At the end of the block, he turned and made his way back toward the hotel. He'd spent more time in this neighborhood of the city tonight than he had in years. It pressed in on him, and he gripped the wheel. At one time, this was the very heart of his biggest goals and dreams.

"I can't do this, Karen," he said, addressing his dead wife. "Not with *her*."

She and the baby she'd carried had been gone for two decades, both of them dead in a complication during delivery. Every so often he felt as if she was still by his side. A breeze would brush his cheek and he'd be right back in those days, reaching for her. They'd been inseparable from the first moment they'd met, happily married before they could legally drink and worrying both of their families in the process.

"She's smart, but she takes risks. I'll never be able to protect her," he continued. "I can't get close to a woman like that."

She could make you happy.

The words echoed in his head, so clear he wanted to believe the light of his life was right here in the car, listening to him vent about another woman.

"I'm happy enough," he told himself. He had more than enough money. As a property owner, he held substantial influence in this city and others. The only thing missing was his wife and the half-dozen kids they'd dreamed of raising. But he'd lost her and the baby in one dreadful afternoon. They'd gone to the hospital together, full of hope and wonder, and he'd left a shell of a man, lost and haunted.

"I'm happy enough," he repeated with more determination this time. Widowed at twenty-two, overcome with loss and grief, he funneled all of his energy into business as a property developer, working day and night to reach a substantial net worth by a young age.

And you keep pushing.

For the first time ever, he was annoyed with the memory of his wife's voice.

"How could I quit?" He parked in his reserved space at the rear of the hotel and rested his head on the steering wheel.

In those early days, if he stopped for more than a few minutes the loss caught up with him, knocked him down and threatened to keep him there. So, hell yes, he kept going. He let the media dub him an eligible bachelor and took hold of that moniker with both hands.

By the third year of grieving, his mother tried to set him up, urging his siblings to bring female friends to family events. He put up with it, knowing they loved him, but he wouldn't let anyone close again. The day he'd buried Karen and the baby, he'd buried his broken heart with them.

He stared up at the Grave Gulch Hotel. This was the first major undertaking in his real-estate venture, his only true passion now. His joy. He poured everything he would've given his wife and children into the businesses. Life had given him another shot at happiness. It just looked a whole lot different.

Back in his office, his cell phone chimed with a text message from an unknown number. Not unheard of, but at this hour it usually meant some kind of emergency. He was tempted to ignore it, and then realized he couldn't.

Antonio looked at the screen and the text in the preview sent a chill across the back of his neck.

Call her off or else.

Should he respond or ignore it? He took a screenshot. Antonio wanted something solid to add to the police file tomorrow.

Annoyed and in a contrary mood, Antonio texted back.

Or else what?

For several long minutes he waited for a reply that never came. He gave up on Orr and stretched out on the couch to get some sleep when his phone started ringing. Seeing the caller ID for the alarm company that monitored his home, he picked up and gave his security code.

"Mr. Ruiz, we have two alerts at your home. An open back door and the smoke detector in your kitchen. The fire department is on the way. Are you in the house, sir?"

"No," Antonio replied, his blood thundering in his ears. "Is there video footage?"

"No, sir, not at this time."

That was zero comfort. "I'm at the office, but I'll head over and meet the fire department."

"Just stay clear of the house, sir."

With a promise to cooperate, he ended the call and headed back out into the freezing January night. When he reached his home he could see smoke rising into the night from the rear corner of the house. Exactly where his kitchen windows overlooked the lake.

Antonio parked as close as he could and jogged the rest of the way to join the first responders. The fire department seemed to have everything under control and there wasn't anything he could do about it, anyway.

He recognized one of the police officers who'd responded to the drive-by shooting. "Busy night, Officer Warren."

"Mr. Ruiz, I'm glad you're not in there. Your security company informed us the house was empty at the time of the fire."

Antonio glanced around, but most of the homes on this street were nestled back into wooded lots. His nearest neighbor probably wouldn't notice anything amiss until tomorrow.

"Is there anything we can do for you?" Officer Warren offered. "Anyone we should call?"

The generosity surprised him. "Me? No, thanks. I was planning to stay at the hotel tonight, anyway, to catch up on work."

"That's good, that you have a place to stay. I meant to say thank you earlier. Everyone in the department is grateful for your help finding Danny."

That explained the new heights of friendliness. The GGPD officers who responded to calls at the hotel were always polite, but not always this warm. "You're welcome." It came out more like a question that it should have. "I was happy to help."

"That little guy means the world to all of us."

They both turned as the firefighters emerged from the house, sparing Antonio from further praise or conversation.

"Wait here," Officer Warren said, then jogged over to converse with the firefighters. When he returned, he was shaking his head. "The fire's out, Mr. Ruiz, but please don't enter the premises until further notice. We'll need some time to investigate."

"Do you suspect arson?" If that was the case, he had a good alibi, right up until the point when Melissa went home. Then again, swiping in and out of the various areas within the hotel would confirm his whereabouts. Not to mention he'd have no motive to burn down his own house… "What concerns you?"

"The damage around the sidelight at the back door," Warren explained. "As I said, we'll look into it and co-ordinate with your security company."

After leaving details of where and how to reach him, he drove back to the hotel. This time, he stopped by the security office to let them know he was moving to the secure penthouse. "Unless this particular building is coming down, I am not to be disturbed before nine o'clock tomorrow morning."

That gave him time to get some sleep before he took Orr's text message to Melissa…or before she came looking for him once she heard about the fire.

Apparently, Melissa was right. It seemed he was the target after all.

Chapter 6

Sunday morning came far sooner than Melissa had hoped for. On top of her derailed Saturday night, she wasn't in the best of moods when she rolled out of bed the next day. She set a cup of coffee to brew and walked to the front window. The patrol car was still in place. When she sent the officers a text to check in, they confirmed they were fine, and coffee and breakfast had been dropped off by another team.

Satisfied, she checked for any new messages while she let the caffeine kick her brain into full function. A run would be nice, so she could breathe out the last of the tension from the chaos of last night, but she changed her mind when she saw a voice mail from Desiree.

Her cousin had called and left a whispered message that she couldn't stop watching Danny sleep. All of the sincere thank-yous and I-love-yous held a sharp edge that sliced through her frazzled nerves. It was wonderful to hear the love, to know two of her favorite people in the world were content and safe. But it was tough to swallow that the GGPD was the reason they'd been subjected to the trauma and nightmare to begin with. She needed to track down the forensics reports in question today and set up a face-to-face with the CSI on the Orr case.

She sent a text message reply to Desiree, just in case mother and baby were sleeping in. Her phone rang immediately when Desiree called her right back.

"Good morning," Melissa greeted her cousin.

"It's a *fabulous* morning," Desiree gushed. "Say hi, baby. Say hi to Mel."

"Hi." It was Danny's sweet voice.

Her heart swelled to bursting with love and relief all over again. That bright greeting intensified her longing for children of her own, despite all of the chaos with her career as chief of police. If most of her department could juggle family and work, surely she could figure it out.

"Hi," Melissa said through the guilt that chased the happier emotions.

Desiree came back on the line and talked about the weekend plans and the newlyweds for a few minutes. "Do I have to press charges?" she asked abruptly.

At last, the crux of the call. "We've already charged her," Melissa replied. "Right now, it's out of your hands. First-degree kidnapping is the tip of the iceberg. I'm not sure what else the DA will pile on."

Desiree sniffled. "Forgive the waterworks. I just want it to go away, Mel. I saw her face on the news this morning. She looks like the sweetest grandma. And she did it to help her own granddaughter."

More guilt wound around Melissa's heart, although she knew she had to hold firm. "Hannah McPherson struck me the same way. Caring and devoted. I know you can relate to that. Although I don't believe she ever would have hurt a single hair on Danny's head, she did steal him."

"To get your attention."

"Trust me, that's clear," Melissa said. "I'm following up on everything we learned last night."

"I just want it on record that I forgive her. And then I want to forget it all happened."

Melissa understood completely. "We'll sort it out," Melissa promised. "No guarantees, because the DA is in control, but I will let you know if there's anything you can do for Mrs. McPherson."

"Thanks. Swing by anytime if you want some fresh air and sunshine with a handsome guy today."

Antonio's face flashed into her mind before Danny's and she felt the heat rise in her cheeks. Good thing she was alone. "I'll call first," she promised. "One more thing." She took a deep breath. "There was some additional trouble last night."

She explained the drive-by shooting with the fewest details possible. Calming Desiree's initial concerns about her well-being, Melissa continued, "As much as I'd like to believe it was random, chances are high that this is a problem. We don't have a definite ID on the shooter, but if our best guess is correct, it's *possible*— not likely, just possible—that the person involved will try to manipulate me by going after my family. So please take extra care in general. I'll let the rest of our relatives know, too."

"Mel, it's me," Desiree said. "Do you think this is connected to Everleigh Emerson?"

"No. This is about a different case, but it is the potential indicator of another GGPD error and that worries me."

"Oh."

There was a wealth of meaning in that single syllable. "Just be careful," Melissa said. "If you see or feel anything that makes you uncomfortable, report it or tell me right away."

"I will," Desiree promised.

One down, Melissa thought, ending the call. What a way to start a Sunday. She dialed her parents next. They were the most vulnerable, not just because she enjoyed a close relationship with them, but because they weren't tied in any way to the GGPD themselves. Travis, as a businessman, had a good handle on his surroundings at all times. Clarke, as a private investigator, and Stanton, owner of a protective detail agency, were always ready for anything. Not invincible, but sharp. Still, she had to call each of them about this new risk. While she spoke with her immediate family one by one, she finished her second cup of coffee of the morning.

It was past ten and bright sunlight made a run irresistible. She pulled on layers to ward off the cold and laced up her running shoes. Stepping outside and breathing in the bracing winter air was an immediate improvement.

Striding to the police car, she made sure they could track her phone and gave them her planned route. "Just keep an eye on the house," she said. "I've got pepper spray and a whistle with me, too, if something happens."

"Are you wearing any headphones, chief?"

"Not today," she assured him with a smile. "I promise, I'll stay alert. It's just a two-mile loop."

Broad daylight and a Sunday morning when most people would be home made it a bad time for Orr to take another swipe at her. Didn't mean he wouldn't, but it did increase his chances that he'd be seen or caught in the act.

She'd be okay with that. And maybe, in the back of her mind, she was silently daring Orr to take another shot. As she found a good pace, her mind wandered while her ears and eyes were aware of every detail. No, she wasn't impervious to bullets or fear. Though she didn't relish being shot at again, the fact remained that they had to get the man off the street. And that meant doing whatever it would take—even putting herself in the line of fire—to bring in a bad guy.

And she felt an obligation to her officers to behave with confidence despite the sudden onset of problems. She absolutely believed that as a team, the GGPD could get to the bottom of these issues together.

Antonio was certain his former associate had killed a woman last summer and equally certain he'd fired at them last night. She needed a last known address for Drew Orr and then to get eyes on him. Thanks to Antonio's statement at the scene, one of her officers would be working on that already, making time to speak with Orr and confirm his whereabouts.

As a near-victim of the incident the night before, she had to allow the responding officers to handle it. She was fine with that, too. That freed her up to dig deeper on the Emerson and Paxton cases.

Wrapping up her run, she waved to the officers in the car, just as she'd done with the neighbors she'd seen, and headed inside. Her cheeks were cold and her body felt rejuvenated and loose. She took the time to stretch out the last of the aches before her shower.

Feeling warm and edging toward starving, she wrapped herself in a towel and walked into her bedroom. She tensed up at the realization that someone was in the house and reached for her phone. Relief followed immediately as she recognized the voices drifting from the kitchen. Her parents were here.

Mildly exasperated that they'd enter when she was already on high alert, she quickly dressed in her favorite jeans, fuzzy socks and a cozy half-zip fleece with the GGPD logo embroidered on the shoulder. In the kitchen, her mother whipped up eggs at the counter while her father sipped coffee at the breakfast table, a travel magazine in his hands.

It was always a joy to see them, although she had no idea why they'd chosen to surprise her today. "What are you doing?" she asked. "We just talked about keeping your distance for a few days." Hadn't they heard a word she'd said? "This… I didn't even hear the door chimes."

Last night, she'd adjusted her security-system settings so she'd hear the chime if a door was opened.

"You were in the shower. We called out and sent a text," her mother said, as if she showed up to cook every Sunday.

"And then she just got to it," her father explained. That was the way it had been for as far back as Melissa could remember. Either Frank Colton or Italia Vespucci Colton would start a sentence or a thought and the other would finish it. Frank had met his wife during a vacation to Italy. When asked, they both claimed it had been love at first sight and Italia swore there had never been a moment's regret making the move to Michigan.

They were so adorable and content she didn't have the heart to kick them out. Shoving her concerns down deep, she kissed her mom's cheek. "Can I help?"

"Go talk to your dad," she said. "I've got this."

Filling a glass with water, she did as she was told. Thirty-six and still a child, even in her own home.

"Desiree and Danny doing all right?" Frank asked.

"They are. I, *um*, put her on notice, too, that she should be alert and careful of the person I mentioned to the two of you."

"We're fine," her mother said. Forty-one years in America hadn't dulled her Italian accent. "Obviously." She dipped slices of bread into the egg wash and placed them on the skillet. "Get the plates out, sweetie," she directed. "This will be ready soon."

French toast was Melissa's favorite. She couldn't stay upset when her parents were going to such lengths to offer their support.

"Sounds like quite a bit of drama in the department," Frank said.

"Unfortunately true," Melissa confirmed. "We'll sort it out," she replied. And if there were errors, they would find a way to put the right killers behind bars.

"Will any of these unpleasant things jeopardize your position?" her mother asked. "You are a good chief of police."

"Thanks, Mom." She appreciated the love and the faith. "As I said, we'll sort it out." She carefully filled a small dish with powdered sugar for her dad and set out butter and syrup for her and her mom.

"Is that fire last night connected to any of this?" Italia asked, bringing over a plate piled high with piping hot slices of French toast.

"What fire?" Melissa looked from her dad to her mom and back again. "I haven't heard anything about it."

Her dad speared two slices of the bread with a fork and dropped them on his plate, adding butter and powdered sugar. "The news reported it as Ruiz's place. Said no one was home at the time and there were no injuries."

Melissa's pulse thundered. Was Antonio okay? Had she missed a message? She popped up from the table to grab the cell phone she'd left on the table behind the sofa in the front room. She scrolled through the local news sites for more information as she returned to her seat. Someone should have told her about this.

Irritation prickled like a rash over her skin at the lack of messages. This wasn't the time for her department to get protective. She needed all the information to do her job to her best ability.

"So you and Mr. Ruiz *are* close," Italia asked.

Her mind on the fire and Antonio, Melissa couldn't make sense of the comment. Her mother could not be matchmaking. She looked to her dad for an explanation.

"She saw the two of you during the search for Danny," he said. "Thought you looked like a good team."

"Mom," she scolded gently. Melissa took a bite of her breakfast to smother her annoyance. Not every man she spoke to was a prospective suitor. Her mother never pressured Melissa, but she was fully aware of her daughter's dreams of motherhood. "We're not a team or together or anything. Danny was taken from his hotel. Mr. Ruiz felt obligated. And he had skills that helped us," she explained.

"He's single."

"Mom."

"And handsome and wealthy, too." She reached over and patted her husband's hand. "Never discount that winning combination."

Melissa diverted the conversation to happier topics to get through breakfast.

Before her parents headed out, she pulled her mom into tight hug. "I love you," she murmured. "Love you both." At her dad's quizzical expression she forced a confident smile. "Please be careful. I can't go into detail…"

"That's all you need to say." He gave her shoulders a squeeze. "We'll stay sharp."

"Thanks, Dad."

It was one thing when she took risks for her job and something altogether different when her job threatened her family. She wouldn't use the department as her personal security, but she could ask them to help her be vigilant.

Her mother sensed her lingering distress simmering under the surface and wrapped her into another hug. "We'll be fine, my love. You and your siblings are the ones we worry over."

"Thanks, Mom." She embraced them as they left. She would always be the only girl. That fact wouldn't change. It didn't matter that she could hold her own with any of her three brothers, or all of them at once. Of course, her parents were frequently concerned about her brothers, too, but there was that inherent assumption that they were a little less fragile. Fifteen years ago she would've argued or been snarky about it. Today, with some life experience under her belt, she knew she didn't have to prove a thing. Not to her mom and dad, not to her brothers.

Only to her department. Critical mistakes had been made on her watch and it was up to her to sort it out and restore confidence in the community.

She waved from the porch as they drove off and then stepped back inside, locking the door. With moms and children on her mind, maybe she should go over to

Desiree's place. She could see Danny in his element, no worse for last night's excitement. It might make her feel better, might even be worth the inevitable longing for a baby of her own that resulted from every visit.

But if she did visit, she might lead Orr straight to someone she loved. Better if she went to the station and got some work done. There was no guarantee that the judge would grant any delay in the Emerson trial based solely on the discrepancies Clarke uncovered.

With fresh determination, she swapped the cozy socks for practical footwear and prepared to leave for the station. Officially off duty, she didn't change into her uniform today. Her plan was to lock herself in her office and study the evidence reports in the Emerson and Paxton cases.

And she wanted details on the fire at Antonio's house. Why hadn't anyone called her? She supposed it technically wasn't her business. And she should *not* be curious about where he'd spent the night. After pulling on her coat, she dropped her phone into her purse and pulled out her car keys. She was just setting the alarm at the side door that opened onto her driveway when she heard the doorbell out front.

Not her parents then, she thought with a rueful smile. She paused at the SUV to put her purse on the front seat and then continued around to the front of the house. Antonio suddenly appeared on her front steps.

He was safe. Here. Everything inside her seemed to go loose and bubble to the surface. She clamped her lips together before a ridiculous giggle could escape. "Should I be worried you know where I live?"

"Yes. I mean, it's public record." He seemed to lose his train of thought and then his lips tilted to one side. "Hi."

"Hello." She gave a thumbs-up to the patrol across

the street. He'd shaved, the stylish scruff neatly trimmed this morning. But there were shadows under his eyes that implied he'd had a short or stressful night. "Are you okay?"

"Okay enough," he replied. "You look…refreshed."

"Thanks. I had a good run and then Mom's French toast."

He frowned, opened his mouth and then clamped his lips shut again. "Sounds nice."

"I have leftovers that will reheat easily enough if you're interested." She hadn't planned on making that offer, but something indefinable inspired her to reach out. Loneliness, she realized. The man who was always polished and quick with the charming smile seemed uncharacteristically isolated today.

Oh, it was hard to see under the overall presentation. His hair was perfectly styled and he managed to make basic blue jeans, boots and a puffy jacket the height of fashion, but she could see he felt off. She wanted to gather him into her arms in a big hug, but sharing food was a safer choice. "I heard about the fire," she said. "How bad is it?"

"Bad enough." He rocked back on his heels. "They found signs of a break-in and are investigating for arson." His gaze darted from her to something behind her and across the street.

"Come on inside," she said. Whether or not he was hungry, he obviously didn't want to have this conversation out here.

Her mouth went dry. She'd invited him inside and it was too late to back out. She loved everything about her house. Though it was more space than she needed right now… She'd bought it with that potential family in mind.

"Where were you headed?" he asked.

"To the station. It can wait." The files weren't going anywhere, and perhaps she could glean more information from him in this conversation. She motioned for him to follow her around to the back door. It was easier than trying to maneuver around him on the narrow front walk. She could see it now, making the wrong step on a slippery patch and ending up in his arms. It was too appealing to take the risk.

"I take it they haven't found Orr," he said when they stepped inside. "Or whoever was driving the car last night," he added hastily at her sharp look.

She disarmed her security system and was struck again by the vast differences between them. He'd shared a meal with her in his posh office with furnishings that had probably cost more than her entire house. Here she was, about to offer him leftovers on a table she'd picked up at a summer flea market and refurbished herself.

The hotel offered a Sunday brunch buffet with mimosas and prime rib every week, along with a made-to-order omelet station, a waffle bar and anything else a person could think of. Melissa had been several times through the years with family and girlfriends. Her mom's leftovers were bound to be a disappointment for Antonio, but it was too late to back out.

She draped her coat on a hook in the utility room and did the same with Antonio's. He wore a light brown sweater that brought out the golden hues in his skin and eyes. As if the man needed another layer of sex appeal.

"Coffee?" she offered as he ran a hand across the top of one of her ladder-back chairs. She'd collected them two at a time, so while the basic style and new cushions were the same, the six chairs were slightly mismatched.

"Did you inherit this set?"

To her surprise his tone was friendly and the little knot in her belly loosened. "No. Flea-market finds."

"And you refurbished them on your own?"

She nodded. "Coffee?" she asked, hoping to shift the focus from her secondhand breakfast table.

"I've had my share today," he said. "This is excellent work, Melissa."

How did he manage to make her name sound like a caress? "Just time and elbow grease," she said. "And video tutorials online."

That earned her a genuine smile and her stomach tightened for an entirely new reason. She really needed to get a handle on this persistent attraction to this man. "Have a seat," she said as her pulse skipped, "and tell me why you came by."

Antonio knew he shouldn't have come here. Driving by last night was silly enough. He'd meant to do the same thing today. Cruise by, make sure someone had her back and keep right on going.

Instead, he'd parked and walked right up to her front door. Damn the ghosts in his head.

She wasn't family that he needed to worry about or an employee he felt obligated to keep an eye on. She wasn't *his* at all. She was the chief of police, clearly capable of taking care of herself. No one had handed her the job, which he'd learned by watching her; she'd worked hard to earn that office and the weighty responsibilities that came along with it.

Still, if there was any chance to keep Orr's attention on him and away from her, he had to try. His reckless comments to the press last night had made her a target and the ache that left in his gut was unbearable. He waited until she joined him and pulled out a chair for her. When they were seated, he didn't waste any time. "I think you should leave the Orr case alone. I'm sorry I brought it up last night."

Her body went still and she stared at him with those big blue eyes. "Did you hit your head last night? Inhale too much smoke at the fire?"

"That was mostly out when I arrived. You can check with Officer Warren to confirm."

"Count on it," she said.

He didn't think she was kidding. "I think Orr set the fire." She had to understand the gravity of the threat his former associate posed. He pulled out his phone and turned it so she could see the screen shots.

"Unknown number," she noted as she studied the screenshot. "Doesn't explain your sudden change of heart."

"It does if you accept Orr sent the message. I asked 'or else' and within fifteen minutes my house was on fire."

"All right. We'll add this to the case file for last night. Help me out a minute. Did your security company get a visual good enough for facial recognition?"

He shook his head. "Too dark. The security company only has a vague image of a man…*person*," he amended at her slight scowl. "Someone in dark clothing, further blurred by shadows. There is a motion-activated light that didn't work for some reason. I've hired a couple of people from the hotel security team to keep an eye on my place around the clock in case this *person* comes back."

"Smart," she said. "It would be helpful if they coordinated with the GGPD."

He started to protest, but that was pretty much the reason he was here. "I'll make sure and set that up."

"Good." She sipped her coffee. "Thank you."

"Am I wasting my breath asking you to stop looking into the Paxton case?"

"Yes." Her eyes narrowed. "But you had to know I wouldn't back down. I don't even believe you want me to do that."

"It kept me up all night," he admitted. Dropping his head back, he rubbed his temples. He faced her again. "I've made no secret about my displeasure with your department in that situation, but the idea of you or one of your officers getting hurt because of me—"

"Him," she said.

"He's only here because of *me*, even if he also had you in his crosshairs last night." He couldn't let her forget that. He didn't know exactly why Orr had gone on the attack, but it was clear he was furious with Antonio.

"Now this text is threatening you, specifically. Wendy's parents have waited this long," he said. "So why not hold off on the Paxton review until he leaves?"

"Because if he is behind the drive-by and the fire, I intend to catch him. Then we can work on holding him accountable for the murder, too, if he is, in fact, the killer."

"He is." Antonio sighed. "That day, when he showed up with blood on his hand, he said it was an accident, but he often went hunting and I think he was too good for that kind of mistake."

"You didn't say that last night."

"It's in the first report I gave at the station, though." He didn't know why he'd held back. "Makes me queasy to think about it."

"For the sake of debate, if he's that good with a gun, I have to consider someone else could have been shooting at us last night."

And that was the other reason. "I know I'm asking a lot, but please drop this," he said. "Focus on the Emerson trouble until he goes away again."

"You're frustrated and hurt and overtired," she said. "He tried to use you and took advantage of your good nature. Every conflicted thought and feeling you're having is understandable, Antonio."

"I don't need you to soothe me like I'm some shaky victim." He shoved back from the table, too restless to sit and handle this politely. It stung that his behavior only proved her point. Taking a deep breath, he pulled himself together. "He's a risk. I *don't* want you to drop it. Not really. But I can't let you get hurt, either."

"I know how to do my job."

"And still, you went for a run. Are you trying to bait him?"

"The officers sitting outside knew my route and were tracking my phone the entire time. I had pepper spray and a whistle with me. I didn't have my earbuds in. And today is a day when most of my neighbors are home."

"So that's a solid 'yes.' He shot at you yesterday."

She looked at him as if he'd sprouted horns. Maybe he had. "You were there, too," she said. "If he set the fire at your house, then I'm inclined to think you're the real target."

"Did you know about the fire when you went for a run?" he demanded, arms folded over his chest. Recognizing his defensive posture didn't help him correct it.

"I did not."

The admission made it all worse. "I just don't want you taking chances."

"How I do my job isn't your concern," she stated.

He wished he could be okay with leaving her to do her job her way. "He asked me to call you off. I've tried. Be careful. This city would suffer if something happens to you."

She stared at him, incredulous, her lips parted. He ran a hand through his hair. No horns. But that expression made him want a taste of her. He *was* overtired. Kissing Melissa was the worst idea, especially after flipping out.

"Thanks for your concern," she said stiffly. "I understand it. But I won't let a man I suspect is responsible for three violent crimes dictate my caseload."

He couldn't put everything rolling through him into words. Not in a way that would make any kind of sense. "Can you assign the case to someone else?"

"No. I'm taking the lead on this. It's my job to figure out where the Paxton case broke down and find a solution."

"I knew this was pointless," he grumbled. "I didn't even want to come over."

"Then why did you?"

He slumped into the chair he'd vacated. Probably not a good idea to tell her the memories of his dead wife were pushing him into actions he would normally avoid. "Doing my civic duty for Grave Gulch," he said, lamely. "That man's a snake and whatever he's been doing since he was last here, it doesn't seem to have made him a better person."

"Does it help to know I'm more concerned about *you*?"

"No." He cleared his throat, uneasy with her statement. He didn't need her or anyone else worrying over him. Too many expectations went along with worry and concern. Managing that with his parents and siblings was enough.

"I'm a grown man…" He left that sentence unfinished as her blue eyes sparked with a challenge. "I'm not being sexist. I only meant that I value my independence."

"Same." She sat back, crossing her arms over her chest. "Go on and keep digging."

"I have a security team."

Her toe started tapping. "Same."

"You can't blame me or anyone else for worrying if you are the real target," he said in a desperate attempt to drag himself out of the verbal pit he'd created.

She froze, as if time had come to a screeching halt, and then burst out laughing. After she caught her breath, then dried the tears gathered at the corners of her amazing eyes, she said, "The fire implies *you* are the target. Just as I told you before."

"Maybe he just couldn't get to you."

"A fact which only underscores that my precautions are enough."

But how long would those precautions hold up? "He can't get to me now. I'm in the penthouse. Join me there." He caught himself before he reached across the table for her hands. "Please, Melissa. Orr must be coming unhinged if he's back in town and raising hell."

"No. Thank you." Her answer, delivered in that cool, calm tone, only aggravated him more. "And you're still assuming Orr is behind all of this. I can't make assumptions."

"Once again, one eyewitness isn't enough?"

"Your account from last night is a good start. Reliable. Valued. And you will need to give a formal statement at the station, preferably today. Many eyewitnesses are not as reliable as you, which is why the justice system relies on evidence. I have to operate within that system."

"And if the evidence in the system is compromised, like Hannah McPherson claims?"

"Again, I am working on it. For both of you. I can't give you details—"

"The news reported that the DA dumped Hannah in the county jail. That's pretty rough for a woman her age."

"It is," she agreed. "My cousin, Troy, wrote up the report, took her statement and handled the transfer. You don't like it, talk to the DA."

He shook his head. "Seems extreme for such a sweet old lady."

"Sweet old *kidnapper*, you mean." She held up a hand and he had a ridiculous urge to draw those long fingers to his lips. "The case is out of my hands. I just had the same conversation with Desiree," she added.

"Danny's mom is furious, I bet."

"You'd lose that bet," Melissa mused. "She's far more relieved. Maybe it's motherhood."

He waited, but her gaze drifted somewhere he couldn't follow. "How so?" he prompted.

She shifted in her seat. "I won't explain it well."

"Try," he urged.

"Desiree almost condones the grandmother's actions. It's bizarre. As if she can't cast stones because there's no end to how far she'd go for Danny."

"And you can't relate?"

Melissa's nose wrinkled. "I think I'm more worried that I can." She looked up at the ceiling, her hair, long and loose today, falling back in a river of red fire. "When we were talking to Everleigh's mom, my heart cracked at her loss of faith in her daughter. And when we were at Hannah McPherson's place, the desperation was palpable.

"Three moms last night facing the darkest times in parenthood. And…I don't know. My heart ached for all of them in turn."

Not the darkest times, he thought. They each still had the child they loved. Maybe out of reach for a time, possibly in danger or in trouble, but alive. Where there was life, there was hope. Death was irreversible. Insurmountable. No going back, no hope for a brighter tomorrow.

"All of them heartbroken, if only in the short term," he said quietly.

"What do you mean?"

He avoided a direct answer. "I believe your ability to relate to each of them last night and today is part of what makes you a good cop."

Whatever he expected, it wasn't another laugh. "Since when? The rumors eventually get back to me, Antonio. The entirety of the GGPD is aware that you believe we're incompetent and that it starts at the top."

"Surely you have to agree letting Drew Orr roam free isn't a shining moment. Maybe if *you* had taken my statement, it would've been handled properly."

"You're unbelievable," she said. "Just when I think I've figured you out, you change gears. That kind of comment is as much of an insult to me as it to the detective who led the case. It's six months now, right?"

"Pretty much."

"The statements and reports wouldn't change anything unless the evidence backed it up. I don't tell you how to be hospitable. How about you stop judging my work until you have a degree and more than a decade of experience in law enforcement?"

"You're right," he said, stung. He rubbed the spot where his chest ached, standing again. "Forgive me."

He would not burden her with the ghosts of his past. They were irrelevant, anyway. "I really didn't come to argue, only to report the text messages and that's done. I need to get over to the house to meet with the insurance adjuster."

"Would it be a problem for me to join you?"

Until she mentioned it, he hadn't realized how much he wanted her there. "Two cars or one?" he asked, reaching for her coat.

She didn't even roll her eyes this time as he held it for her. She did pull her keys from her pocket. "Two cars."

"I thought there was safety in numbers," he teased.

"Call it an experiment," she replied with a grin that set his pulse skipping. "This way if someone opens fire, we might be able to sort out the real target."

But Antonio was starting to believe neither one of them was safe with Orr on the loose. He had to let her handle things her way, but he struggled with the overwhelming urge to protect her. His fingers tingled and he shoved his hands deep into his coat pockets. The last woman he'd been willing to slay dragons for was his wife. He swallowed an oath. What if Orr won? What if the worst happened and Antonio lost Melissa too?

Chapter 7

The fire damage was worse than Melissa had anticipated. She'd called the station on the drive over and according to the report the officer on duty read to her, the fire hadn't had much time to grow. The officer also told her the firefighters now suspected arson. Antonio's kitchen told a far more graphic story.

The sidelight at the door that connected the deck to the kitchen had been smashed. She agreed that the broken glass allowed the arsonist to reach through and unlock the door, tripping the first alarm. Glass fragments had been trampled by firefighter boots, crushed against the beautiful travertine tiles. Scorch marks bloomed from two corners of the cabinetry. Two accelerant devices had been placed and ignited, according to the fire chief.

He was lucky he hadn't lost the house, she thought for the umpteenth time since walking into the scene.

She didn't bother to say it; she was sure he'd heard the words enough from the others.

There was no sign that the intruder had moved beyond the kitchen, though the insurance adjuster and Antonio had walked the entire residence, inside and out, to be sure all the damage had been documented.

"Your security system did the trick," she said when they stood side by side on his deck that overlooked the lake. "The alarm must have rushed him."

"I don't believe he wanted the whole house to go," Antonio said. "Yes, I'm *assuming* it was Orr, and based on that assumption, I can tell you that he has a good idea how I'd react if he burned down the house."

"Maybe you shouldn't share those details with the chief of police." She smiled, softening the reminder of her position. "Tell me why the house is so important and how it is Orr knows you so well."

He pushed his gloved hands through the snow on the deck rail. The man was always in motion. "He knows it's my pride and joy even if I spend most hours at the hotel. I told him how I designed the house from the front door all the way to this deck. How I wanted it to sit on the site so I'd have the best views of the lake from the right rooms."

"The right rooms?"

"Sure. The most inspiring views shouldn't be visible only from the master bathroom or whatever."

"Got it," she said, amused. "Is there an architecture degree in your long list of accomplishments?"

"No. And the list isn't all that long. I just knew the end result and worked backward. Once I decided Grave Gulch would be my primary base, the land came first. After that I found the right architect, had the plans drawn up properly."

"Well, the kitchen was beautiful." That had been obvious despite the glaring damage.

He rolled his shoulders, tucked his hands into his pockets. "It was."

"It will be again," she assured him. "Do you enjoy cooking?"

"A man must eat. Once I left home I quickly realized how smart my mother was to insist that I learn how to cook for myself and the family."

"My mother is Italian. Same philosophy. Sounds like the two of them would get along."

"Or possibly fight over the counter space," he joked. "Do you think *this* crime will stick to Orr?"

"I'll do my best to find out who did it," she promised. There was no point in debating the accusation. Antonio was convinced and although she'd manage the investigation with impartiality, she had a hunch he was right.

Frankly, she was hoping to break their current pattern of being almost friendly only to wind up arguing again. There were people in town she adored, more people she got along with and a few people she avoided because, like oil and water, they didn't mix.

Antonio had been in the last category before now, a man she was happier avoiding. Oh, he was handsome as sin, but they didn't agree on anything… Until last night. The look on his face when he held her baby cousin had convinced her there was more to him than luxury hotels, increasing his net worth and his next gorgeous date.

"Why this particular piece of land?" she asked as she stared out toward the lake. Deep snow pressed up against the waterline, stretching out in white sheets over the water. Icicles dripped from the trees, jagged beauty that transformed the view. If she lived here, she might never be persuaded to leave.

"You're making my point for me," he said, bumping her shoulder with his. "It's the view. You should see it from the loft. You'll have to come back for the full tour."

The unexpected affection made her skin tingle all over. "I'd like that," she said without thinking. It was too easy to imagine waking up to these views after a night in his bed. Now she'd have to create an excuse if he ever did offer.

Seeing more of his house would wreck the happy little fantasy she'd spun up last night. The one where she was his date to some gala, leaning close enough to breathe in his cologne. The woman within his reach, able to stroke his arm or accept a caress in return... Would that woman ever be *her*?

"Melissa?"

She snapped back to the present, feeling the color rising in her face. If she was lucky, he'd blame it on the cold wind blowing off the lake. "Tell me more about Orr. You've told me he can shoot and I'd imagine he enjoys it. For now, we'll assume he isn't afraid to start a fire."

"He can kill," Antonio said, his voice grim. "And get away with it."

She wouldn't argue that, either, right now. "Any other dangerous skills I should know about?"

"He believes he can outthink and outmaneuver anyone," Antonio said.

"We have a know-it-all like that on the CSI team. He annoys everyone, but he's almost always right. Which is good, but adds to the annoyance." She turned her back on the lake, leaning against the rail while she studied Antonio. Not her smartest move. He wore dark sunglasses against the glare of sunlight on the snow. Unable to enjoy that gaze, her eyes focused on his mouth.

Big mistake. His somber expression didn't dull the appeal of his sensual, firm lips. The temptation to kiss him was overwhelming. Desire pooled low in her belly, sweeter than the syrup she'd poured over her French toast.

"That's not what I mean," Antonio said. "He craves knowledge. At first I thought it was to compensate for a lack of formal education, but he has a master's degree in political science, of all things."

"And he's a real-estate developer?"

"In name only. He's a con man. Always has an angle in play using other people's money. He makes big promises backed only by creative excuses to keep investors from cashing in before he has the next mark lined up. From what I could tell, his education is the only legit thing about him."

"Unless it's fake, too."

"No, I looked him up. He went to Northwestern. The pictures in the yearbook match up. The longer we were associates, the more convinced I was that he lied about everything *but* that."

"So he's proud of his education." How would that change her approach when they found him? "Is he arrogant about it?"

"He wasn't with me and I only have a bachelor's in business."

Only? He had a bachelor's and a mind that turned one hotel redesign into a massive net worth and portfolio. "I should let you have your Sunday," she said, straightening. "I have a full plate and several interviews to prepare for."

"You have a master's in criminal justice, right?" he asked.

"Yes." It wasn't a secret and it was actually preferred

for advancement. "I wish that and determination was enough to solve every case."

His mouth curled into a sexy grin. "If it was, then your work might be as easy as I've implied. I am sorry for my bad attitude."

"Hardly the first time. I've felt the same way," she admitted. The wind caught her hair and she shook it out of her face, wishing for a hair tie. "Way back when I was a kid and my aunt was murdered, I couldn't comprehend why the police couldn't find the killer. Learning it all, working my way up to chief, I think the only silver lining in that entire mess was my ability to empathize with victims."

"I think your empathy is rooted deeper than an unsolved crime." He tugged off his glove and tucked her wayward hair behind her ear. "Not that my opinion matters much."

Her ear and cheek blazed at that light touch, then he put his glove back on. For a long, awkward moment she was speechless. Tenderness and Antonio didn't go together in her mind. Until recently.

She licked her lips and, before she made a colossal mistake and followed her urge to kiss him, she repeated something about how busy she was and scooted around him.

"Be careful!" he called after her.

She urged him to do the same as she hurried to the safety of her car. But his voice and the conversation lingered in the back of her head. It turned out his opinion mattered to her more than she expected.

That was completely new. And the worst possible timing.

In front of the station, she passed protestors braving the cold, waving signs and chanting "Free Granny."

They weren't blocking the street or access to the station, so she decided to let the cold dictate how long they stayed out there.

She closed herself in her office and forced her full attention on the Emerson case. If there was a chance the DA had an incomplete or inaccurate picture of the evidence, Melissa needed to find the truth as soon as possible.

She pulled up the case file on her computer, then read through all of the notes on the Fritz Emerson murder from transcript of the first emergency call to Everleigh's arrest and arraignment. The investigation looked textbook, right down to the witness who put Everleigh near the scene. Things started falling apart with the evidence. As Melissa read the final forensics report, she could understand the logical conclusion that Everleigh had struck that fatal blow.

Wanting to discuss it with an objective person, she stuck her head out of her office to look for Troy, but he wasn't in. She wasn't about to call him after last night. He deserved some rest. Her next visit was to the forensics lab downstairs, but Randall Bowe wasn't in and neither were Jillian or Billy, who had worked the case.

So she returned to her office, took a deep breath and called the district attorney, Arielle Parks. The DA would not be pleased with what Melissa wanted to discuss. After bringing the lawyer up to speed, she waited for the reaction, pen tapping against her palm.

"Her defense attorney should have found this," Parks said.

Melissa agreed. "I wish there wasn't anything for her attorney to find. Can you ask for a continuance?"

Parks sighed heavily. "How much time do you need?"

"I need time to speak with Bowe," she said. "He's

not in the lab today, but I'll track him down at home if necessary. I'm hopeful he can shed some light on this when we talk."

"Be quick," Parks said, her voice stern. "After all the press last night, I spoke with the judge. Neither of us wants a mistrial or hung jury due to public sympathy for Hannah McPherson. I'll call him back. He won't want to risk having a conviction overturned on appeal for a technicality you should have caught. At the same time, Emerson has a right to a speedy trial. I expect he will only grant a continuance through Monday and we'll be back in court on Tuesday."

Just about thirty-six hours. With the clock ticking in her head, Melissa ended the call. At least she'd bought a little time. Next, she dialed Bowe's home number, but it went to voice mail and she left a message. She tried his cell phone too, but he didn't answer. She left another message, hoping her frustration wasn't too obvious. The last thing she wanted was to be here spinning her wheels when time was short.

As a rookie, her training officer had taught her that when she bumped up against a brick wall, sometimes it was best to take a step back and look for a window or a way around. She wasn't making progress on the Emerson case, so she shifted focus and pulled up the Paxton files.

The pictures of the area in the park where the body had been found were comprehensive and she remembered Ian Elward had been the CSI on the scene. The man always documented everything in excessive detail. The body had been located off a remote section of the hiking trail, hidden by natural underbrush. The photos were a bright green contrast to the weather outside today; the trees' foliage would've given the killer excellent cover, even if someone else had been around.

She studied the crime-scene photos, specifically those showing any blood, but nothing at the scene gave her a close enough view to independently corroborate Antonio's story about Orr's bloodstained hand. The victim had been shot, and it had been messy, but what she had here wasn't enough to take action.

She switched over to researching the county park website, identifying the placement for any wildlife trail cameras, but it seemed that section of the park was completely blind. The detective on the case had noted the same thing at the time of the investigation. Being thorough, she called the Parks Department, verifying that no other cameras were in that area.

Had Orr known about the lack of cameras on that trail? Antonio said the man believed he could outthink anyone. If not, it had been awfully good luck to have chosen that particular section of the trail.

The questions plagued her as she left the station, planning to drive out to Grave Gulch Park. She changed her plan, going by Bowe's house first. If he was home, he didn't come to the door. Frustrated, she left another message on his cell phone and then drove out to the park. Walking back to the site where Wendy's body had been found didn't lead to any new revelations and she eventually climbed back in her car for a long drive to think through the troubling situation.

Time was of the essence, and it bothered her immensely that Bowe had not returned her calls. When the sunny day faded to twilight, she turned for home. She'd fix something to eat and, as the best option, study the original Paxton and Emerson files in preparation for the Monday meetings. Contrary to Antonio's opinion, she was not ready to hang herself out like bait for Orr.

She rose with the sun on Monday morning. Rolling into the station early, she was surprised to see Free Granny signs in store windows all along the central boulevard. She knew those store owners and wouldn't have expected them to become protestors, but the media was drumming up community sympathy for the elderly Hannah McPherson.

She doubted most of the people behind the movement had even heard of Hannah McPherson before Saturday night, though. They were simply upset over an apparent injustice. Those who did know Hannah were likely even more upset because the woman was kind, thoughtful and clearly determined to defend her granddaughter.

Melissa went in through the back door and greeted the officers on duty. In her office, she set her travel mug of coffee on her desk and reached over to boot up her computer. While she waited for the machine to come online, she called down to the lab and left a message for Ian Elward, the CSI on the Paxton case to come to her office first thing. She wanted his take on that scene before she spoke with Bowe about it.

She couldn't say that she'd made any real progress or found a glaring error, but she felt confident about the entire case file from Antonio's initial report to the recovery of the body. She went to the break room to top off her coffee and saw Ian striding in.

"Good morning, Chief," he said.

She'd often wondered if he used that clipped tone all the time. That perfect diction made everything out of his mouth sound like he was reciting an academic paper to people who had no hope of understanding the findings. Ian wasn't the most popular of people in the

GGPD, due to his constant need to prove he knew everything, from the science behind a blue sky to the newest method of processing evidence.

"Thanks for coming in," she said, and they went to her office.

"Of course." Ian sat in one of the visitor chairs in front of her desk. "How can I assist you with the Emerson case?"

The query caught her off guard. After closing the door, she took her time settling into her chair. "I actually wanted to discuss a different case. One you processed last summer."

His thin eyebrows snapped together over his nose and she could almost see gears turning in his head.

She clarified quickly, before he could toss out details on every crime scene he'd worked. "It's a cold case. Wendy Paxton. The body was recover—"

"Recovered in Grave Gulch Park. Early July. The second or third. Everyone was gearing up for the Fourth of July, but it was definitely before the barbecue contest."

Melissa pressed her lips together, then said, "That's the one. The victim—"

"Midtwenties. Female. Blond hair, slender," Ian interrupted. "Two gunshot wounds, one in the shoulder. Fatal bullet entered back to front at close range and went through the heart. Do we have more evidence to reopen the case?"

She ignored his question. "That's right. I've read your field report. There were light scratches on her arms and legs consistent—" She held up a finger to prevent another interruption. "Consistent with walking through that part of the park. No defensive wounds."

"Correct. She really should have worn more appropriate clothing for hiking."

And this sort of tunnel vision was why she was glad Ian worked on the scientific side of criminal justice. He wasn't suited to a public-facing role where a careless comment could alienate a grieving family.

"Reading your report from the scene, you made note of scratches that might also have occurred postmortem." She tapped her pen to her palm.

"That's right. Skin damage, but no blood. Not many, but they were consistent with the victim being moved through that environment."

Which led her to believe that Wendy's killer might have wrapped the body before moving it. She checked her computer monitor, where she glanced at the final forensics report signed by Randall Bowe, complete with pictures of the body.

"Anything else you can recall about the case?" she asked Ian.

"Yes, Chief." Ian took a breath and she settled in for a long monologue. "At the scene we were all agreed that the body had been moved to the position in which we found it. A small amount of the victim's blood was discovered less than one hundred yards away. Not enough for it to be the location of the fatal shooting, by my assessment."

He paused, a frown on his face. "Feel free to speak your mind," she prompted. As if anything would stop him.

"I work the scenes I'm sent to. I file my reports, and most of the time, I hear that the officers take that information to close cases. In this case, no arrests were made."

"That's correct."

"Chief, there was a clear thumbprint on the body." He pointed to the corresponding area on his throat. "Right about here. A print in the blood and based on the position and bruising around her neck. It appeared the person, presumably the shooter, had started to strangle her before shooting her a second time. I took pictures of that print and documented the findings in my report. That should've been enough to compare to any suspects questioned in the case."

She shot him a look, enough to have him blanch and back down from doubting the work of her officers. Ian loved to overstep, believing he alone was responsible for finding the evidence to help them do their jobs efficiently. Most of the time he was right, but because he was so snobby about it, no one wanted to listen.

On the other hand, more amiable CSIs, like her cousin Jillian, were easier to work with and were always better received because they maintained confidence balanced by a dose of humility. There were layers to police work and, as Hannah McPherson so vehemently pointed out, evidence wasn't always the whole picture.

Especially if mistakes had been made.

Melissa knew her own triggers after years of experience as a police officer and testifying in various cases from traffic court to felonies. The attorneys didn't like to call Ian to testify because juries never warmed up to him, no matter what he said. She had to fight the same urge to dismiss him now, simply because he was too sure of himself, what he had found.

"The only pictures from the crime scene—"

"You mean the scene where we found the body," he corrected her. "I wasn't aware the actual scene of the shooting had been identified."

"You're right." He was lucky she'd had two cups of

coffee before this conversation. "The pictures in your report from the area where the body was found do not include any clear views of the print."

"That's impossible. I took the pictures. I documented each one and filed it appropriately." Without any invitation, he popped up out of the chair and came around to peer at her computer monitor over her shoulder.

She resisted the urge to shove him back, out of her space. Instead, she slowly clicked through the available photos.

"Where did they go?" Ian was clearly perplexed and his expression indicated he was rushing headlong into being furious. "I know what I saw and how it was documented. There's an error."

"Relax and take a breath," she suggested. "No one is blaming you. Didn't you and Bowe argue about the state of that print?"

"He was wrong." Ian snapped upright, bracing his hands on his hips. "That print was clear at the scene and in transit, and I documented it accurately."

"I believe you," she responded. "However, none of that documentation is with the file. Only a picture of a smudged print in the area you indicated." She pointed to the monitor.

"That's the same case?"

Was he actually accusing *her* of manipulating the file now? "It is."

"That's not at all what I saw then." He started to lean in again, to reach for her keyboard. At her hard look, he backed off. "Check the database."

Each word was delivered with razor-sharp precision, and though she didn't comment, she took note of his lack of a "please."

"I've checked the database," she assured him. "I even

pulled the hard copies, but the photos you describe are not part of the digital or physical case file. Please take a seat."

"You're going to tell me I've confused facts, mixed up this case with another. That simply isn't true."

In fact, she wasn't going to tell him that, because she didn't want to deal with the fit she knew he would throw at hearing it. "No." She sipped her coffee, holding the mug in both hands, doing her best to put him at ease. "I was going to ask if you kept a backup of your files anywhere." At his blank stare, she continued. "The cloud, a private computer, anything?"

"No." He blinked slowly. "Police business stays here, on the official servers. Any other precaution would be a breach of security."

An answer she appreciated as it implied he had the same confidence in the GGPD database as he had in himself. But if he hadn't misfiled the photographs, where were they? His written report referenced a clear print, but in the lab, Bowe contradicted that finding, claiming the print was smudged, useless. This put Bowe at the crux of two questionable findings in two different murder cases.

"Did you know Wendy Paxton?" she asked.

"Of course not. If I had, I would've recused myself at the scene."

Because Ian followed every protocol to the letter. "Great. Thank you for your time."

"That's it?"

He didn't look any happier than she felt. "One more thing," she said. "Did you review or process any evidence in the Fritz Emerson murder case?"

"No. That was Jillian. In my opinion, a rookie should never be on a murder call." He cleared his throat. "I understand she is a relative, Chief Colton. I still stand by the statement."

She didn't react. Ian would always be arrogant. He'd always believe he was right. There were several people who shared her last name on the GGPD. Nepotism, contrary to Ian's inference, had nothing to do with it. Other than Grace, she hadn't hired any of the Coltons currently on the GGPD.

"You were on the team that processed the evidence for the kidnapping case at the McPherson home Saturday night?"

"Yes, I was. I'm filing my reports this morning."

"Then I'll let you get to it. Please send me a copy directly."

She stopped short of asking Ian to back up his information and photos somewhere other than the GGPD as she had with Jillian. Though Ian had never been a gossip, she wasn't in the mood to listen to his opinion on the security risk of cloud services. Nor did she feel that being candid with him about a potential problem within forensics worked in her favor.

She might not like Ian much personally, but she was confident he wasn't the problem downstairs. Bowe was the common denominator in the Emerson case and the Paxton case and she needed to speak with him immediately.

She scowled at her cell phone. Bowe still hadn't returned her calls and she'd been clear that she expected him to call her back at the earliest opportunity. His silence raised her suspicions, though he was a stickler for keeping to business hours barring his presence at an active crime scene. It seemed as if he was the only person in town who didn't realize they were a department in crisis.

* * *

Antonio set aside his cell phone, having completed another call with his insurance adjuster. He appreciated how quickly they were processing his claim. Now all he needed was confirmation from the police that he could start cleanup and repairs.

That made him think of Melissa and the resulting smile was a pleasant surprise. He could always drop in and check on the progress personally. Her interest in the fire was likely just a courtesy after he'd helped them find Danny. Still, he enjoyed talking with her, watching those blue eyes blaze with humor or intense interest.

He picked up his cell phone, already anticipating her smile for his unexpected arrival, when his desk phone rang. "Antonio Ruiz," he answered.

"Mr. Ruiz, this is the front desk. Desiree Colton is here, requesting to speak with you for a few minutes."

Antonio smiled again. "Is her son with her?"

"Yes, sir."

"Let her know I'll be right down."

Since moving to the secure suite, he'd been borderline paranoid about security, but he was confident his staff could keep Orr away from the hotel. Antonio regretted every tour he'd given Orr, every drink they'd had in his office or meal they'd shared in the main restaurant. He felt like a fool to have called the man a friend at any point in their history.

He reached the wide, sweeping stairs that curved into the lobby and spotted Desiree and her son right away. The little boy was gripping her finger and dragging her around the central fountain, giggling with every step.

Antonio's stomach cramped, his heart in a cold vise as the sadness of what he'd lost washed over him. Karen would've glowed like that, a combination of pride and exasperation, all tangled up with endless love for their child. He'd never even allowed the doctors to tell him if she'd been carrying a boy or a girl.

"Ms. Colton," he said, approaching the pair. "It's a pleasure to see you again."

In a smooth, practiced motion, she scooped Danny up into her arms and settled him on her hip. "Mr. Ruiz." She extended her hand to shake his. "We came over to say thank you."

The little boy stuck out his hands and threw all of his body weight at Antonio.

Desiree rolled her eyes. "And now you see why Mrs. McPherson had no trouble sweeping him out of the wedding reception. He doesn't know the concept of strangers."

"May I?" Antonio asked. He'd been so excited about becoming a father before he'd lost everything. It had taken years for him to be comfortable around children again, knowing he wasn't strong enough to bear the risk of attempting to have a family with another woman.

The sweet hands were already grasping his fingers and the little guy was making it clear he wanted out of his mother's embrace.

She picked up on his intention. "Yes, of course, you can hold Danny," she said clearly.

Her son didn't seem to care that she was trying to send him a message about safety and strangers. Danny beamed and patted his new friend's face before dropping his head to Antonio's shoulder, much as he'd done before he'd gone into Melissa's arms at the McPherson home.

The gesture didn't last as long. The boy wasn't at all sleepy right now. He sat up again and touched Antonio's close-cropped beard.

Touch. Giggle. Touch again.

Desiree started to laugh and Antonio joined in.

"He's a goofball sometimes," Desiree explained.

"All children should be," Antonio agreed. He started to walk, just meandering through the lobby, and pausing when something caught Danny's eye.

It surprised him to feel so relaxed with a child. Sure, he'd had similar experiences with nieces and nephews, but today there seemed to be soft buffer between the past grief and the present moment.

"So, as I said, thank you." Desiree beamed at her son. "I was out of my mind with worry. Melissa said you were instrumental in finding him."

"Instrumental is overstating it." He wasn't comfortable with the high praise. "I'm glad I could help, though I don't believe your son was in any danger."

Her eyes widened for just a moment before she averted her gaze. "Melissa didn't say it in those words, but I think she agrees with you."

He wisely withheld comment on that. "Mrs. McPherson was quite desperate for the chief's attention."

"Clearly," Desiree said. "There's another reason I came by. You were there and, well…" She pressed her lips together. "I'd like the DA to drop the case against Mrs. McPherson."

Antonio stopped moving and the toddler strained against his hold. An orchid, swaying in a nearby floral arrangement, had captured his attention. It was just out of reach, but he was determined to touch it.

Antonio took a step away and the toddler fussed. He tickled his round tummy, effectively distracting him. "Maybe we should discuss this privately," Antonio suggested.

"That's not necessary." Desiree looked around the

mostly empty lobby. "I just wanted your opinion. Do you think that sweet old grandmother should go to jail for taking Danny?"

"She committed a crime. You're part of the GGPD," he pointed out.

"Part-time sketch artist," she said. "Full-time mom. My son's never been accused of a crime and let's hope it stays that way. But if I knew he was innocent? Well…"

"What exactly are you asking?" Antonio queried.

"I thought maybe if we both wrote to the DA she would consider dropping the charges."

Antonio was astounded by this woman's capacity for forgiveness. In her shoes he was sure he would want to throw the book at the kidnapper, no matter how benign the appearances. "That may not be the best precedent," he cautioned. "Or even the right thing for the city as a whole. As I told your cousin, I'm prepared to testify to what I saw and heard at Hannah McPherson's home. The hotel has already received an official request for the security footage of any suspected instances of her on the property."

"You have to turn that over," Desiree said, nodding. "I'm not asking you to impede the investigation or anything." She sighed, then smiled when her son blew her a kiss. "I should be angry."

"I imagine you would be still if we hadn't found him so quickly."

They neared the fountain and the boy wanted to scamper. "So much energy," Desiree said. The three of them walked the circle, Antonio making sure Danny couldn't dash away, and Desiree close enough to be sure he wouldn't find a way into the water.

"Melissa assured me Mrs. McPherson's fate is up to the DA. But," he added when Desiree started to protest,

"I will add my support to your request for leniency. In my opinion, the woman was not happy that she caused you stress."

"She just didn't feel like there was another way," Desiree said. Danny leaned on her legs and she picked him up.

"We could both be wrong," Antonio pointed out. "Melissa is being cautious about looking into the Emerson case. She can't afford to be seen condoning this method of bullying the police department."

"Oh, trust me, I heard it all from my brother," Desiree said. "Part of me feels like a traitor for feeling sorry for Hannah."

"You have a good heart, Ms. Colton. And a beautiful son."

"Thank you." She brushed her nose to Danny's.

The tender moment melted through him, right up to the cold ball of fear that protected his heart. Everything had turned out all right for these two, and though Hannah McPherson was in jail right now, her concerns were being addressed. Someone needed to find justice for all parties involved. Justice beyond the obvious legalities.

"We'll let you get back to work," Desiree said, smiling up at him. "Again, Danny and I will always be grateful."

He gave her a friendly smile and send-off, unable to find a more personal sentiment. The outpouring of gratitude shook him more than he wanted to admit, even to himself. For the better part of two decades he'd focused his energy on building his business. There was nothing else for him after losing Karen and the baby.

Heading back up the stairs, he knew he'd done the right thing on Saturday night. Eventually the emotional upheaval would quiet down again. He caught himself rubbing his sternum as he walked into his office. A man didn't make it to forty-two without a few regrets. There was nothing he could do about the past except allow the painful memories to fade away again.

A distraction was in order, and what better option than helping the police figure out where Orr was hiding?

What could possibly have brought Orr back to the city *now*? Antonio had been sure he was working a new angle on investors in Chicago. The possibilities whipped through his mind. After almost falling for Orr's con, he'd spoken with friends and investors, letting them know his opinion on Orr had changed and why. He refused to let people he trusted and respected be pulled into Orr's shady net.

No way to know how much had that cost him. Could Melissa be right that Orr was targeting him and not her? She had to prioritize the Emerson case since Everleigh Emerson was on trial. But maybe he could give the police something more to go on when she could take another look at the Paxton murder.

The text that had come through just before the fire wouldn't help much. It didn't offer a location or even confirmation that it was actually Orr behind the threat.

Sitting down at his desk, he opened the archived file with the communications and notes he'd taken while planning a project with Orr. There had to be something in here the police could use to show a pattern of behavior.

The old emails creeped him out in hindsight. The golf outings, double dates, regional charity events. Antonio stopped skimming emails and retrieved his journals from those same months. He'd been so focused on the business potential, had he overlooked something worrisome about Orr's personal nature?

Everyone made mistakes, but this was a big one, letting himself be fooled. Well, if there had been anything obvious, he would've parted ways with Orr sooner. Other than an awkward argument between Orr and Wendy during a double date, Antonio hadn't noticed any red flags. He needed to give Melissa something more substantial than an easily dismissed personal account and a few random moments of intuition.

He called the firm that provided security for the hotel and asked them to run down anything they could on Drew Orr, past and present. The company had built a file for him, the same as they did for any person or business he planned to partner with. It hadn't raised any red flags back then. Hopefully, this time around they would find an issue the GGPD could build a case on.

It gave Antonio chills to read through his journal entries of those first meetings with Orr. This time, he saw it as the setup Orr had intended. The man was good, but by killing Wendy, even getting away with it this long, he'd burned his bridges with Antonio and Grave Gulch. It made no sense for him to come back.

Discouraged that he was letting down Melissa, Antonio tossed aside the journals and turned his attention to current news and websites that discussed markets and investors.

When he saw a headline, he swore, having completely forgotten about his call with a friend in San Antonio last month. They'd discussed a joint venture that involved the restoration of a sizeable segment of the River Walk. They'd been approached by a third company, new to both of them, that was eager to jump on board. To make the numbers work, the corporation needed three buildings but had a hard cap on the purchase price. The seller hadn't wanted to accept their offer and the new company had offered to make up the difference just to push the deal through. Orr's name hadn't shown up in the background search Antonio had ordered at the time, only a list of lawyers representing a real-estate group.

It was a stretch, but still possible, that Drew Orr was behind that company. If Antonio had inadvertently botched another deal for Orr, that would certainly explain the man storming back into Grave Gulch for revenge. He sent the real-estate-group information on to the security company. If they could connect the dots, it could put a quick end to this pervasive sense of danger.

The thought of spending time with Melissa without looking over his shoulder for Orr sent a zip of anticipation through his veins. He needed to know she was safe, but more than that, he wanted to see those blue eyes sparkle with curiosity as they worked toward a common goal of justice for Wendy Paxton.

Better yet, he was looking forward to teasing a smile out of her. One that had nothing to with a case and everything to do with just the two of them.

Chapter 8

Following her chat with Ian, Melissa had to put out a few bureaucratic fires that included calls from the mayor and the DA about Hannah McPherson. Since there was nothing concrete to share on the case, she could only listen, and it wasn't fun. With still no response from Bowe, she had no choice but to ask the state police to send her a forensic scientist to review the evidence.

When she finally escaped her office at a quarter past nine, she went straight to Troy's desk, pleased to catch him. "Sun's out. Can you take a walk with me?" She often did better thinking when she was on the move. She'd been stuck in her office all morning and she didn't want to be interrupted again.

He squinted toward the window. "Sure?"

"Thanks." She went back for her coat and gloves, and then caught up with him in the break room. Shrugging into her coat, she was surprised to miss Antonio holding it for her. She had a problem where he was concerned, a problem that had nothing to do with police work. It had taken her all of five minutes to appreciate his thoughtful manners. Less time than that to lose herself in his dark gaze. She wanted to keep thinking of him as oil to her water. They would never mix…and yet she really wanted to try.

"Are we just out here for the sake of frostbite?" Troy asked, dragging her back from the brink of those dangerous thoughts.

"No. I need a fresh viewpoint and some scenery before I tackle a delicate interview."

"All right, I'm listening."

"What do you recall about the body we found in the park in July?"

"Paxton?"

She nodded. "That's the one."

"It was memorable in the lack of details. The crime scene didn't give us much to go on."

"Body location," Melissa muttered.

"What?"

"Oh, I said 'crime scene' when talking to Ian about it this morning."

Troy laughed. "And he corrected you." He chuckled again when she nodded. "He was the first to propose it was only a dump site, but we were all thinking it. Not enough blood for two gunshot wounds."

"Ian told me about processing the scene, finding the victim's blood in another location."

"Right. Blood and nothing else. Nothing much to go on except her tie to the boyfriend, Drew Orr. We cleared him, despite Ruiz's concerns, and then cleared Ruiz, too, after Orr pointed the finger at him."

"And that was okay with you?" she queried.

"Not at all. Orr was squirrely. But the evidence..." His voice trailed off. "Man, do you remember that blowup Ian and Bowe had over the evidence?"

She couldn't recall a fight like that. "What do you mean? Where was I?"

Troy squinted, thinking back. "Probably at Danny's birthday party," Troy said. "I got over there just in time for the cake. And before you get all guilty about it, you don't take enough time off as it is. There was no need to call you in over a personnel dispute. Especially not for those two."

Troy was right. Bowe and Ian had frequently butted heads since Bowe had come to Grave Gulch three years ago. Two know-it-alls in one lab didn't always make for a peaceful environment. Ian hadn't mentioned a fight, though he had been indignant and upset earlier when she'd told him his pictures and report weren't included as he'd filed them.

"What if it was more than the typical fight?"

"Over what?" Troy countered. "Ian and Bowe get on each other's nerves. You know how Ian is."

"Randall Bowe isn't much better," she commented.

"No, but he has the last word since he's in charge."

Melissa prompted Troy for the details on the fight.

"Ian asked about the results on a fingerprint he'd seen in the blood. Bowe said the print was smudged, unusable. Ian yelled about photographs, Bowe showed him the body. There were insults and insinuations about who smudged the print and how the angle of the only photo that had been uploaded rendered it useless for identification. They nearly came to blows."

She had a moment envisioning how that fight might

look. Both men were slim, but Ian was taller, giving him an advantage on reach. "How did you separate them?"

"Carefully," Troy said, joking. "Took two of us to haul Ian out of the lab. He's tougher than he looks when he's having a tantrum."

She turned all of that over in her mind. Would it have changed anything if she'd known this at the time? Probably not. They couldn't process evidence they didn't have. Had the fingerprint been smudged on purpose? If so, why?

"Wait a minute. Ian railed about having photos of the print and told me he'd uploaded all of that properly. Where did those photographs end up?" Her stomach knotted at the mere thought of anyone in her department tampering with evidence. She trusted her people. But something was off in these two murder cases.

"No one found a connection between Paxton and Ian or Randall, right?"

"No," he replied slowly. "I didn't look for a connection to Orr." Troy looked at her as if her brain had frozen. "What are you thinking?"

She stopped, her gaze scanning her town, fully aware that there were eyes on them from every angle. "Clarke found discrepancies in the evidence against Everleigh Emerson. After a man, identified by Mr. Ruiz as Drew Orr, shot at Mr. Ruiz and myself, I think there is reason to believe evidence is off in that case, too."

Her stomach rolled and the chill on the back of her neck had nothing to do with the bitter-cold January wind. No matter how she studied the cases, it came down to serious trouble in the forensics department.

"The fingerprint." He stared at her, horrified. "Melissa, you have to be careful."

"I'm aware." She pressed the toe of her boot to the

snow gathered at the edge of the sidewalk. The grid pattern of the sole reminded her of the mullioned arched windows at Antonio's home. Not where her mind should be. "For the life of me I can't come up with a motive. I don't want to alienate good people, but we have to get to the bottom of this. Will you come with me to talk to Bowe?"

"Absolutely. It won't be fun, but it could be entertaining."

She tried to laugh, but couldn't quite make it work. She might as well be walking across thin ice, but the only way to the truth, to real justice, was to keep going.

"And, of course," she added as they started back, "you can't breathe a word of this to anyone."

He lifted his chin toward the central intersection where a dozen people were milling about in front of the station with Free Granny signs. "Anyone other than them? They were listening when you said you'd take a second look at the Emerson case. They're counting on you to keep them updated until McPherson is free."

He was right. "So let's go find something worth an update."

"You know if we do reveal an error in the evidence, defense attorneys will be filing appeals right and left."

"They do that anyway," she said, wishing she felt as cavalier as her tone implied. "The only way to know if we managed to get it right the first time is to look again."

Melissa and Troy deftly avoided the milling protestors, entering the basement lab directly at the rear of the building. They found Randall Bowe, GGPD forensic scientist, in his office. The slender man was a few inches shorter than Troy, with brown hair brushed back off his forehead and brown eyes currently glowering at his computer monitor.

Maybe he didn't appreciate the email she had sent last night on top of her other calls and voice mail messages, asking him to see her as soon as he came in today.

Or possibly he was aggravated by the media coverage following Saturday night's events and the implications made by Hannah McPherson's new attorney. More than one outlet had picked up the story and #FreeGranny had become the social-media hashtag of the moment. Several writers and bloggers were happily pointing fingers at the ineptitude of the GGPD. It was discouraging to have lost the community's faith, but it only made her more determined to set things right.

"I got your messages. I went upstairs but you were out," Bowe said. "Of course, you'd interrupt me now when I'm in the middle of a new report." He switched off the monitor and tucked his hands into the pockets of his lab coat.

"We won't take much of your time," Troy assured him.

Melissa kept her opinion on the timing to herself, letting Troy's cool demeanor lead the way.

"Could we discuss your report on the Emerson case?" Troy asked. "We need to be sure everything lines up."

"It's all in the database," Bowe snapped. "Go on and dig around. Look all you like. There's nothing to discuss. I processed the evidence delivered to me, no thanks to the rookie CSI."

Melissa swallowed an automatic defense of Jillian. Her cousin hadn't worked the scene alone and Billy had backed up her report, though she had yet to find that record in the database.

His arrogance had always irked her, but she'd done

her best to take the high road. The man had an excellent reputation in his field and she'd put that above the challenges of communicating with him. "We're here because of discrepancies between the reports on the evidence gathered and your findings. The DA wants us to confirm the details before the trial resumes tomorrow."

Bowe pursed his thin lips together until they all but disappeared. "As if I don't see the great Colton family uniting against me. Look in the mirror, Chief. It was one of your precious relatives who screwed up at the Emerson crime scene.

"They bag and tag whatever they like and take hundreds of photos."

"As they're trained to do," Troy interjected.

Bowe's lip curled. "And then I must use my education and experience to sort it into something viable for a case. Give me better field investigators and you'd get better results."

Her jaw nearly cramped, but she clung to her fraying patience. "I don't believe the discrepancy originated at the scene," Melissa stated baldly.

Bowe puffed up his chest. "Are you suggesting *I* made a mistake?"

"Surely everyone makes one now and again," Troy observed.

"Not in *my* lab." His arrogance was appalling. "I take my duty seriously and I am thorough, focused and meticulous about it."

"You're implying any discrepancy happened at the scene," Troy said.

"No. I'm stating it outright," Bowe snapped. "Whether or not you believe it, your precious cousin is a weak link in this department. I could list ten mistakes she's made in the last month that could've been disastrous for your cases." His glare raked across both of them. "This particular police department would benefit from less nepotism and more expertise."

Melissa bit back a retort and Troy tensed up beside her. It seemed there was one thing Ian and Bowe agreed on. Clearly, she needed to do a better job rooting out that misplaced resentment. She would add it to her task list once they had answers for the Emerson case.

"The explanation is simple, Chief," he sneered as he used her title. "As you know, not all fibers are visible to the naked eye, which is why my role in the process is imperative."

She'd had enough lectures for one day. "I understand your role," she said through gritted teeth. "It's past time you understood my role as the chief of this department. A woman went to extremes to get our attention. Please review and process the evidence again and get me a new report as soon as possible."

Bowe sputtered. "That's preposterous! I can't—"

"Noted," she barked, cutting him off. "The state is sending someone to handle it. You will show whomever arrives the utmost professional courtesy."

"You *cannot* do this," Bowe said with startling conviction.

She stared him down. "I can. In this case, with a woman on trial for murder, it seems the prudent move."

"You're afraid of those sign-toting fools on the street." He snorted. "Of all the Coltons in this department, I thought *you* had guts."

Troy whistled low and long, but Melissa refused to sink to Bowe's level. "Mr. Bowe, for the sake of department unity, I'll blame your poor attitude on the Monday blues. I expect your cooperation and compliance on this matter moving forward. Be a leader in your department, Mr. Bowe, before I'm forced to conduct a job search for your replacement."

She walked out, giving him no time to anger her further.

"If he didn't like you before, he hates you now," Troy murmured when they were in the stairwell.

"*Us*, as Coltons," she amended. "He can pull himself together or get out, though."

"You think he's at fault?"

"My opinion isn't the point. We need to be sure," she replied with brutal honesty. She pulled open the door to the main floor, letting Troy go in first. "I need to be able to trust our team," she added fiercely. "Even when their personalities annoy me. This is all about getting justice for victims—not ego."

If she'd been forced to point a finger at who made the error, she'd choose Bowe, but only because she was mad right now. She'd had a similar reaction, if far less intense, when Ian had made his insinuations against Jillian. She would need more information before drawing further conclusions.

What was *happening* in her department? A week ago, she would've said her family included everyone on the force, not just those named Colton. She remembered feeling part of something bigger from her first day as a rookie. There had been so much to learn and so many good, trustworthy people to guide her.

Now, she was chief of police and her unspoken goal was to honor that legacy, to build on that foundation. Everyone tied to her department was her responsibility, even the few who regularly got under her skin like a road rash.

What a nightmare. As the chief it all flowed back to her. Any problems within the department ultimately rested on her shoulders. It was hard to convince anyone, even herself, of the good work they did day in and day out when she didn't have any real answers for this dreadful situation.

She signaled Troy to follow her to her office. By the time she'd closed the door her mind was made up. "I'll call the state lab for another forensic scientist to examine our evidence," she said. "I need you to *quietly* dig into the Emerson investigation. Revisit witness statements. Go see Everleigh at the county prison if you need to. Be fast and accurate. Parks only guaranteed us today. Sift through every detail we have on the deceased. You saw McPherson. Whatever we find will likely affect the kidnapping case, too."

Troy shook his head. "She didn't waver, not once, about taking Danny. She was remorseful about causing the family grief, but she did *not* back down about why it was necessary."

"That's what scares me," Melissa admitted. "Get moving. We both have work to do."

Alone in her office, she draped her coat over the back of her chair, but she was too restless to sit down as she made her phone call. They needed the truth, even if it made things worse. She thought about the protestors on the street and the media milling out front, not wanting to miss another update.

Hannah McPherson had kicked over a hornet's nest and Melissa had no idea how she was going to guide her department through the stinging fury.

With the Emerson case in Troy's hands, she returned to the cold case she wasn't ready to hand off: Paxton.

The woman's family deserved answers. Justice. Melissa understood how it felt when those things never came around. A memorial service might offer closure, but peace was elusive when a killer was still out there somewhere, alive and free.

Thinking about the Paxton case inevitably led her mind to Antonio. It would've been nice to enjoy a simple, brief daydream about the man. She knew he'd keep pressing her for answers and she really shouldn't be looking forward to those exchanges on a personal level. Yes, he made her pulse race and stirred up more than a few fantasies.

But he should have answers, too, and she harbored plenty of guilt and worry that mistakes—or worse—made in her department last summer were coming back to plague him now.

Start-of-the-week meetings, calls and emails kept Antonio engaged through Monday morning, but his mind never wandered far from Melissa. Was she getting anywhere on the Emerson issues that led to the kidnapping? Selfish or not, he had to hope the case was resolved quickly so she could shift gears and focus on how Orr slipped through the cracks.

The anonymous text messages prior to the break-in and fire were still on his phone. Clearly Orr wasn't worried about being caught. Was it simply because Orr didn't care if the police found him? Not the latter. Antonio crossed that off his list. Orr's intention to stay out of prison was the only thing that made sense.

He found himself starting at the "or else" message. There was no way Melissa would drop this, especially not after the drive-by and the fire. She was in serious danger just because she was good at her job. He had to find a way to protect her.

Suddenly, his cell phone rang. The caller identification showed the number had been blocked and the icons on the screen suggested spam. Antonio answered, anyway.

"I told you to back her off." Orr's voice, low and tight.

His grip tightened on the device as adrenaline pulsed through his veins. What new threats would Orr toss out today?

"Hello, Drew." Antonio leaned back in his chair, grateful he'd installed the feature that allowed him to record incoming calls. "I'll say it again, turn yourself in. The cops have you dead to rights for the shooting and the break-in at my place."

"Spreading more lies about me. My attorneys will bury you in slander and libel lawsuits."

"Whatever firm is foolish enough to take you on will cut you loose before that happens," Antonio told him. "I gave the police a positive ID about the shooting."

"That won't hold up."

"Take some advice from an old pal," Antonio said. "Breaking and entering isn't your strong suit, either. My security system caught enough that night for facial recognition." He hoped this lie provoked Orr into a mistake.

"My friends in Grave Gulch told me you've been dragging my name through the mud. I've been in Texas for weeks. Michigan is too damn cold in the winter. Whatever you want, I'm not afraid to tell everyone how *you* backed out of our deal, Ruiz. You broke the promises."

Antonio wasn't buying in to any of this. All he'd done was turn down a business opportunity, and he knew Orr must be in Grave Gulch, looking for revenge or trying to save his skin. Likely both. "I changed my mind before anything was inked," Antonio clarified. "I did nothing illegal. You, on the other hand—turn yourself in. If the cops have to come looking for you, it won't go well."

"You first. Tell the truth," Orr said in a mean hiss. "Go on and tell your pretty cop friend what you did with my girl."

"Nothing." That was a line Antonio had never crossed. He didn't mix business with pleasure and breaking up relationships wasn't his thing. "You and Wendy had issues that didn't require interference from anyone else."

"Shut up. You have no right to speak her name after what you did."

Finally, Antonio understood the real motive for the call. Orr assumed that Antonio would be reporting this call or possibly even have the police listening in after the fire. He'd tried to pin Wendy's murder on Antonio before and here was the next attempt.

"Are you done?" he asked as if he didn't care. As if he wasn't the least bit sickened by Orr.

Shady, reputation-wrecking business deals were more than enough cause to part ways. When they'd met, he'd never imagined this affable, charismatic man was capable of taking the life of someone he'd claimed to love.

"Don't worry. You'll know when I'm done."

The call ended and Antonio shut off the recording app with a quaking finger. It would be nice to blame the unsteadiness solely on his anger, but it was fear, too. The sunlight pouring in the window felt all wrong, completely at odds with the dark tone of the call.

He had to take this to Melissa—whether or not she could use it, she needed to hear Orr's threats for herself.

Maybe then she'd take her safety more seriously. He started for his coat and keys and paused. Orr had urged him to "go" and tell Melissa about the call, implying Antonio and Melissa would be in the same physical space sometime soon. If he invited Melissa to the hotel, it was basically the same thing, with one primary street between the two locations.

All Orr had to do was wait on that route and the police chief would be easy pickings.

He sat down again, forcing himself to think and anticipate what Orr might do. Taking a deep breath, he reached for the phone on his desk, giving a start when it rang under his hand.

"Ruiz," he barked.

"Hello to you, too," Melissa said. "I'm heading your way—"

"No!" he shouted, leaping out of his chair. "Sorry. How close are you?"

"What's going on?"

"Turn around," he pleaded. "Wherever you are, turn around and go back to your office."

"I actually haven't left the office yet." Her voice shifted so that she sounded like the consummate professional she was. "What's the problem?"

"Good. Stay inside. Close your blinds," he said. "Please."

An image of the drive-by shooting flashed through his mind only this time it ended with her lifeless on the sidewalk, not checking him for injuries. He couldn't bear a loss that heavy. It terrified him to care this much.

"Give me a reason why."

He caught his breath and pulled the chair back so he could sit down again. He was jittery from head to toe. "Drew Orr just called. Making threats. I recorded the conversation. I'm not sure which one of us he wants to kill more."

"We can sort it out," she said, her voice cool. "I'll come over."

"No. That's just what he wants—another chance to hurt you. I was going to come to you."

"All right. I'll wait."

"Don't do that, either." He scrubbed at his face, aggravated with his indecisiveness. "I think Orr has set a trap for me. Us."

"Mr. Ruiz—" she began.

Her suddenly formal tone was so absurd he started laughing, though it felt bitter. "Stop it." He took another deep breath. "I'm not paranoid, but he is pushing me in that direction," Antonio allowed. "When you hear the call, you'll understand."

"And when will I hear the call if you won't let me come to you?"

"I can send the audio file as an email attachment," he decided as clearer thinking prevailed. "And you should know I've got my security firm researching Orr's whereabouts over the last six months. On the call he claims he's in Texas, but I'm sure that's another lie. I'll share whatever they find with you."

"Great." She didn't sound too happy. "My department is working the drive-by shooting," she replied evenly.

"And doing a great job, I'm sure. I mean that sincerely," he added, regretting that the clarification was necessary.

"Thank you," she said softly. "I'll keep you in the loop as we make progress."

"You haven't reopened the Paxton case, have you?"

"Not officially. I've spent most of the past twenty-four hours reviewing it, though."

Was that the only reason she sounded tired? "You said it would take a back seat to the Emerson situation?"

She sighed. "This would be a better conversation to have in person."

Not if it meant Orr getting a clear shot at her. Another wave of panic threatened to swamp him. With the hotel situated as it was on the lake, there was one primary drive in and out. Of course, there were access roads for service and deliveries to the property, but Orr could park himself at the main intersection and wait for one or both of them to roll on by.

"Is there a way for you to ride over with someone else?" Once he had her here, they could discuss all of the details and then he could convince her to move into the safe suite.

"Let's start with the easy pieces," she said. "Send me the audio file. Once I listen to it, I'll be in touch about the next steps."

"Just stay alert." He tucked the handset between his shoulder and ear so he could send the file from his cell phone. "He isn't going away."

"You be careful, too."

"I'm taking precautions. His picture has been circulated to all the staff." Melissa should be here, behind the layers of expert protection he'd implemented. "There, the file's sent."

Over the phone he heard a faint ping. "Got it. I'll call when I can."

"Melissa—"

But she'd hung up and the disappointment was sharp and uncomfortable. What was his problem? After losing Karen, he hadn't allowed himself to get this involved, to get close enough to be consumed about anyone's welfare. General kindness and compassion were fine, but this swirling thing growing inside him for Melissa specifically... No. He had to find a way to stop it.

His days of sheltering someone precious were gone. He'd buried all of those tendencies with her and the child she'd carried. Independence was what life had decreed for him. Frequent, lighthearted dates were the ideal situation and he could dote on his nieces and nephews. All the fun, and no real risk of deep heartache.

By rights, Melissa should've stayed on the periphery of his life. She epitomized independence. Just being the chief of police, despite the pitfalls and potholes that must have riddled her path to the office, illustrated her ability to watch out for herself. She wasn't his business, yet he couldn't get her out of his mind. Couldn't stop feeling some responsibility for putting her in danger.

He checked his watch, then his cell phone. He'd sent the email almost five minutes ago. The conversation with Orr hadn't lasted even that long, had it? Maybe the file hadn't gone through or the recording was garbled.

He started to dial the station's phone number and stopped himself. If he'd learned anything the night of Danny's kidnapping, it was that Melissa was thorough. And while he viewed police work as reactive, once she got over the initial shock, she'd never been rash or in a hurry during their search, though they'd been searching for her defenseless nephew. He had to give her time.

Antonio went to brew himself a cup of coffee and realized it would only make him more restless and impatient. He poured a tall glass of water instead, then strolled to the window, determined to be calm. He'd done everything he could do to protect his property. Though he'd tried to protect Melissa, he had to trust her to protect herself *and* the town.

His office, on the second floor, offered good sightlines down the main tree-lined drive. This time of year, with the limbs bare, he could see most of the intersection. Was Orr out there somewhere lying in wait?

A dumb question. He had to be. He'd all but told Antonio he would strike again soon.

He glanced back at his desk. What was taking her so long with the audio? He really should be there to explain some of Orr's comments, give her the whole story about Drew and Wendy.

He realized, belatedly, just how successful Orr had been with his phone call. Antonio's focus was gone, derailing the tasks on his agenda. Plus, the entire mess dredged up his old frustrations and doubts of his dealings with Orr. Not a good place for a man who made decisions involving millions of dollars at a time. If Antonio let worry and fear edge out common sense, Orr had the upper hand. He couldn't live that way. Wouldn't.

If he couldn't convince Melissa to move into the hotel for her own safety and his sanity, he would hire a team to shadow her. This seemed like a situation when it was better to ask forgiveness than permission. He would not stand back and allow Melissa or anyone else he cared about to get hurt or die when he had the power to prevent it.

Chapter 9

In her office, with the blinds still open, Melissa played the recording repeatedly. The first time through, she only listened. On the second pass, she started making notes through the brief phone call, trying to gauge mood and motive from both men.

Antonio had clearly urged him to do the right thing, making it easier to believe he'd done that on the day Orr had shown up with a bloodstained hand. The ploy to point a finger at Antonio was too weak to take seriously. She paused and checked herself. She shouldn't be making assumptions because she found one man warm, helpful and too attractive for her peace of mind.

Yes, Antonio had been an asset in saving Danny quickly. That didn't make him a saint. Far from it. Plenty of criminals inserted themselves into cases for a variety of reasons, all of them self-serving. Just because they didn't get much of that here didn't make the possibility irrelevant. But it was unlikely, since Orr's statement against Antonio had held no weight.

She wanted another opinion of the recording to make sure she wasn't accepting Antonio's side simply because he'd helped find Danny and she liked him. She needed someone objective who could listen to this conversation without any bias. But who?

Officer Warren and his partner came to mind, but they were working on the drive-by shooting and the arson. This recording could skew how they worked the cases, inadvertently point them to Orr at the expense of other suspects.

The department couldn't afford to have another case go awry for any reason.

She didn't want to pull Troy from his review of the Emerson case and she wasn't sure he could be impartial, either. Not after they'd rescued Danny as a team. Should she call Ian? No. He'd worked the Paxton case. Once he identified the men speaking, he'd have opinions that might turn into conjecture or, worse, rumors.

As she gazed out over her department, she realized there was only one person she wanted to speak with about this. She called her older brother, Clarke.

"I'll buy if you'll bring lunch for both of us," she said when he answered.

"Pretty late lunch," he countered. "It's already after two."

"Blame it on a long Monday morning," she explained. "I really need an ear that can be objective on something."

"All right. How about I bring over your usual from Mae's Diner?"

"Yes, please." Her stomach rumbled in anticipation. "Thanks, Clarke."

With help on the way, she opened up every file in the database that involved both Antonio and Drew Orr. She didn't expect any big revelations, but she wanted the full context. She was in the middle of a similar search through local media archives for any articles and interviews involving the men when Clarke walked in.

Her office was graced with the savory aroma of juicy cheeseburgers and salty, thick-cut fries. "Did you bring onion rings?"

"Of course." He set the white paper bag and the drink tray on her desk.

She grinned at him. "Thanks for coming." He hadn't closed her door, so she hopped up and handled that detail herself.

"So it's a working lunch," he observed, unpacking the bag. "No milkshakes on the menu today," he explained. "It's a root-beer float instead."

"Perfect." And it was. For a few minutes they ate in companionable silence. When she finished the last onion ring and he was down to a few fries, she told him why she needed to talk.

Clarke sat back, crossed his ankle over his knee and motioned for her to hit Play on the conversation Antonio had sent. A hard scowl creased his face as he listened.

"Well?" she prompted.

"Still wondering why you called me."

"I need someone objective."

"Then you missed the mark," Clarke said. "He saved Danny and then saved you, too, Saturday night. I'm not inclined to be objective. Why are you?"

She picked up a pen and tapped it rapidly against her palm, searching for the most expedient way to explain. "There's the outright lie about the facial recognition at the house. Plus the hesitation in his voice after Orr makes his vague accusation about Wendy."

Clarke motioned for her to play it again. Reluctantly, he nodded and pointed at the pad of paper on her desk. "You made a note to ask him about that, right?"

She nodded.

"I think he's trying to provoke the man." Clarke bounced his heel. "Did Antonio see the shooter on Saturday night?" Clarke asked.

It took her a half second to recover from the unsettling idea of Antonio provoking a man who had likely already killed a person. "He says he did. Gave a description at the scene. He's sure it was Orr."

"But you can't confirm?"

"No." She drummed the pen on her palm. "Antonio blocked my view of the car."

Clarke leaned forward. "On purpose?"

"No." She forced herself to think it through. "Not even a little bit. He was operating on instinct, I think."

"Brave man."

"Or sure he wouldn't be hit?" she asked, for the sake of argument.

Clarke gave her a knowing look that reminded her too much of their dad. "Now you're just thinking the worst of him to be contrary, instead of just considering both sides to be impartial. What would he gain by scaring you?"

"If Antonio did kill Wendy, blaming Orr for the drive-by raises a whole lot of reasonable doubt," she pointed out.

"Come on, Mel. Your own detectives cleared the man when the crime was fresh last summer."

"I know." She swiveled her chair from side to side. "See why you're here?"

"Yes, I think I do." Now his expression turned sly. "You like him," he accused.

"You sound like a twelve-year-old."

Clarke grinned. "And there's the confirmation," he crowed.

"Exasperation isn't at all the same thing."

"Isn't it?" He held up his hands in surrender. "Before you toss me out on my ear, let me say this." He stood up, bagging the trash. "My take is, Orr called to provoke Ruiz and mess with his head. A solid revenge strategy. Yes, Antonio has voiced disappointment for your department recently, but he isn't sowing discord outright. He could've let us flounder in the search for Danny, but he didn't."

"True," she allowed.

He sank back into the chair. "What's really going on with you and Ruiz?"

"Nothing," she assured him. "The Emerson and Paxton cases just leaped out and tossed him into my path."

Clarke smiled, clearly not convinced that was the whole story. One of the detriments of having a private investigator for a brother. "Good thing from this side of the desk," he said. "I owe him a big thank-you for saving my sister from a random bullet. He did the right thing when it mattered. That puts me on his side until something real proves me wrong."

"All right. Thanks." She dropped her pen to the pad. "That gives me a lot to think about."

"You've always had good instincts, Mel," Clarke said. "Don't undermine yourself or your officers."

"Easy for you to say. I have two cases getting picked apart by vultures."

"From what I saw in Everleigh's case, those discrepancies were in the evidence, not the police work itself."

It was a nice affirmation. Now she just had to find a way to determine if the cause was simple human error or if she had a bigger problem. "Thanks for the insight." She stood to give her brother a goodbye hug.

"When you talk to him, ask your questions and then *listen* to the answers," he suggested, giving her a shoulders a warm squeeze.

"I promise."

Her brother's words hovered in the back of her mind while she continued working, her door open again for anyone who might need to check in. She'd invested in herself and her career from the moment she'd applied to the police academy. The road hadn't been easy, especially as a woman. The digs that bordered on mean, the sexist remarks and the assumptions that her heart was too soft or her body too weak for the job hadn't been easy to overcome.

But she'd done it. Her eye had always remained on the goal of helping her community. That coud be one person at a time or as a whole; she'd always wanted to make a positive difference in the city she loved. It didn't always work out in a courtroom, but until recently, she'd been confident in the police work.

The prosecutors and defense attorneys could theorize all they wanted in front of a jury on a case like Paxton or Emerson. Evidence separated one person's account from another, illuminated the situation and led investigators to the right perpetrator. It was interpretation that was fallible.

Knowing the implications and dreading the fallout of making an announcement, she had to accept that the evidence had been mishandled in those two cases. Whether it was done purposely or not would raise more questions, create more problems. Either way, she would be held accountable. She needed to get Internal Affairs involved. The most important thing was cleaning this up for the victims and families involved as well as the department.

One step at a time. She left her office and asked the dispatcher to send a unit to cycle through the area near the hotel. The only instructions were to look for the black car that matched the description from the drive-by shooting. She didn't give Orr's description. Not yet.

Picking up the phone, she finally called Antonio. This wouldn't be an easy conversation to have over the phone. The man had been right to be frustrated with her department.

He picked up on the first ring, as if he'd been waiting on her call. "Well, did the recording help at all?"

She stifled a sigh. "It possibly shed some light on motive," she allowed. "Before I say anything more, the conversation we are about to have is not official."

"I understand," he said too quickly.

"Drew Orr clearly wants to get under your skin," she said. "It seems like he also anticipated that you'd record the call and hoped to make reporting it a challenge for you."

"That was my thought, too."

She didn't bother to ask about whether Antonio had had any interest in Wendy. It just didn't serve any purpose. Her officers had cleared that potential minefield last summer—Antonio told the cops Orr blamed Wendy for cheating, but denied any involvement with his former associate's girlfriend. And the investigation supported his claims, finding no instances of Antonio and Wendy ever communicating or being together outside of Orr's presence. "Based on the drive-by, the fire, the text messages and now this call, it's obvious that we missed something in the Paxton case. I'm sorry we didn't bring Orr in successfully."

"Melissa—"

"The family will get a public apology later. I hope to reach out when we have her killer in custody."

"Did you find something new?"

This was the tricky part. "Not yet, but we're working on it."

"I figured as much." He swore softly. "What are you going to do?"

"We'll keep working the drive-by, the fire." She wanted to swear now, too, because of how thin the evidence had become in both cases. "It will take some time." And she would be hands-on, working with her team until this was resolved. She would be the active leader her department needed.

"You may not have time. He's not happy with me, but *you* are the bigger threat to him."

The urgency in his voice rattled her. "Antonio, please trust me."

"You can't stick with routine," he insisted. "A woman living alone is an easy target."

She bristled at the incorrect observation. "I'm *not* weak and I know how to take care of myself."

"No one said you were weak." His voice cracked. "He shot at you. *Us.* He set my house on fire." Another muttered oath. "Please move into the hotel. Everyone needs someone to watch their back on occasion."

Melissa felt how her body and mind were at odds when it came to Antonio. The idea of tucking herself safely away from danger went counter to her nature. Her role was to lead by example, to protect and serve. She couldn't do that from his hotel, no matter how her skin warmed when she was near him. That simmer of undeniable attraction wouldn't help her drop a net over Orr and bring justice to the Paxton family.

"It's a generous offer," she began.

"Do you want me to meet you at your house to help pack your things?"

"What? No. I can pack by myself."

"Good. What time should we expect you? The front desk will have instructions, of course, but it's best to give the kitchen a heads-up."

He was steamrolling her. "Antonio, *stop*. I didn't say yes." She understood his inherent need to step in and protect, but he had to respect her boundaries and the demands of her job.

"In fact, my answer is *no*, thank you." The silence went on so long, she thought the call had dropped. "Please, don't worry about me."

It seemed she was always saying those words. First to her parents and brothers, later to boyfriends who lasted more than a few dates.

"I'm frustrated," he said. "And, yes, worried."

She wished she'd closed the door. "Because I'm a woman?" she asked under her breath.

"In part, yes."

The admission was so unexpected she stared at her phone, incredulous until she heard him speaking. "…because you are a woman I care for. Who is important," he said. "To the community."

She should be mad, but she wanted to understand why he kept saying things like that. More that she wanted to dig a little deeper into the man she found so captivating. What would he be like on a normal date? Did he need galas and paparazzi or did he enjoy simpler things?

"Melissa?"

She yanked herself away from an unwise and impossible fantasy of getting involved with a man like Antonio. "Yes. I'm here. I appreciate the kind words."

"Kind words? I asked you to have dinner with me."

"Oh. Pardon me. I, was, *um*, distracted by a message." She couldn't go to dinner with him. Not out where they'd be seen publicly. People would start to speculate and that could blow back unfavorably on the night he'd helped them search for Danny. "Do you trust me?"

"Yes," he replied, wary.

"Then let me cook for you tonight. At my place. There's a security system just like at your hotel."

"Hardly the same."

She refused to be offended. Especially not when she caught what might be amusement in his tone. "And armed police stationed outside the house."

"I can add another security team at any time. In fact, I already have."

That sharpened her focus. "You have?"

"Yes." That lone syllable was packed with intensity. "They'll be on-site within an hour."

"You really should clear that kind of thing with me."

"Why? The hotel is private property. I'm telling you now, Melissa. Orr's call emphasized to me that there's one primary way in and out of the hotel. There are service entrances, but that singular intersection is a prime place for him to lie in wait for us. So I would ask you to come via the back entrance."

"That's why you didn't want me to come to you," she said as the revelation clicked for her. "I sent out a patrol car to keep an eye on the area."

"I noticed. They've been by twice already," he said. "Thank you."

"You're welcome."

"What will it take for you to see reason and move into the hotel until the search for Orr is done? You know I can create a command center for you."

She could hardly admit she was afraid her resolve would fail her if they were in the same building all day long. "Why don't we discuss it over dinner at my place?" she asked.

"Why not cook for me here at the hotel?" he countered. "The suite has a full kitchen, or you can choose one of the catering kitchens."

"Not the same," she replied, hearing the flirtatious tone. "Come by—" Her buzzing intercom interrupted her. "One second."

She cringed, grateful he couldn't see her as she set aside the phone and answered the summons. Hopefully they'd found Orr's car.

"Chief Colton, the patrol team at your house has a situation." The rookie on the front desk filling in for Mary sounded nervous.

Remembering her own days as a rookie, she smiled. "Go on."

"On the last perimeter walk of your house a photo was found on your side door, but the officers didn't see anyone suspicious in the vicinity."

The smile and fond nostalgia vanished at the dangerous implications. Someone would have had to cut through the backyards to reach that door unseen. "I'm on the way."

"Um, no, ma'am. I—I mean, they asked me to tell you to stay here at the station. *Please*."

Not a chance. She looked at her cell phone. Antonio was still on the line. "I'll call you back," she said and then ended the call.

Shrugging into her coat, she grabbed her keys and pocketed her cell phone. She would not allow Orr to have his way in her city.

Having something to look forward to this evening didn't erase the worry over how she'd ended that call. Something was wrong and Antonio knew he'd only caught a snippet. Had Orr made another threat already? The little he'd heard indicated Melissa was taking precautions. He wished she would just give in already and agree to move into the hotel.

In her shoes, he supposed he would be offended if a civilian thought they could do better. He would have to keep that in mind when they talked at dinner.

He had to find a way to illustrate that the hotel was safer due to the additional personnel. Her department couldn't devote as many people to her security because they had a broader mission of maintaining the peace. Antonio struggled to believe that would be sufficient against Orr's threats.

Control issues were the root of his worry for her, but understanding that was only half the battle. Maybe less. He'd been unable to help his wife and baby. He couldn't see a way to steer Orr off this violent course. And, apparently, he had no influence over Melissa, either. It was humbling and awful and completely unacceptable.

And yet he eagerly anticipated their next meeting.

She was making him dinner. With a different woman, he might consider it an overture. With Melissa, he felt she was merely trying to prove a point. There had been interest in her voice, almost a teasing tone when she refused his offer to cook in the hotel. It had sparked a warmth under his skin he should resist. With so much chaos and danger swirling around them, this was the worst time to be thinking of Melissa in a personal way. Her focus should be on the needs of the community, not him. And yet, he didn't just want her attention; he also wanted to help, to be her safe haven when things were difficult. Dangerous territory.

As the patrol car she'd sent out cruised by again, he wondered what had drawn her away from the station in such a hurry. He called her, but the call went to voice mail. Picking up the house phone, he called his security office.

"Hotel security, Charles speaking."

Charles had been with him for several years. "It's Antonio. Have you heard about any sort of crisis or emergency in the area?"

"Not near the hotel, sir. But several units were dispatched to a neighborhood in regards to a disturbance."

"The address?" Charles rattled it off and Antonio's breath backed up in his lungs. That was Melissa's home. "Thank you," he said before he hung up the phone.

Antonio paced his office and then went upstairs to the suite. He should let her handle it. She'd call if she needed him. Then again, she would likely downplay any crisis to prevent worry or protect him.

No. That wouldn't fly. He was going over to see what had happened for himself. If the incident wasn't related to Orr, he'd back off. If it was... Well, she couldn't expect him to sit back and let his former associate run roughshod over everyone in his quest for revenge. Though caring for her had blindsided him, he was invested in her safety and would do anything possible to protect her.

Chapter 10

"Chief, you need to think about moving out." Sergeant Joseph drummed his fingers on the clear plastic evidence envelope he held. Inside was an eight-by-ten collage of candid photos of Melissa. All taken within the past forty-eight hours.

Melissa stared across her kitchen at the sergeant, momentarily speechless. She'd trusted him for the entirety of her career and now he was suggesting she hide?

Joseph seemed to take her silence as consent to press his case. "Just until we find this bastard. Those boys out there feel terrible."

"They didn't do anything wrong," she said, finding her voice. "Whoever put that on my door was careful about it." *Whoever*. As if it this wasn't Drew Orr's handiwork.

The man was sneaky. The door on the side of her house was hard to see from the street, which was why the team on guard walked the perimeter at regular intervals. Orr had taped the collage to the glass, timing it perfectly so he wouldn't be caught.

When word got out about the images in the collage, nearly everyone on duty had come to help look for clues. Most of them had already left, or were widening the search through her neighborhood, but she didn't expect any helpful results. She braced against a telltale shiver as she looked at the collection of images.

The photographer had snapped a picture of her with Antonio on his deck the day after the fire. There was an image of her at her office window, another in her car. And whoever it was worked quickly, since there was also a picture of her out on her walk with Troy this morning.

"He didn't get inside," Melissa stated.

"Not yet," Joseph said. "Come on, Chief. It's the smart thing to do."

Joseph was right. Adding patrols only put more people in the way if—when—Orr escalated. But where could she go that wouldn't create the same trouble for civilians or cost the taxpayer a fortune? Antonio's suite was *not* a good option, especially when he needed it himself.

Her best bet was to reach out to her youngest brother, Stanton. He owned Colton Protection, a small protective-detail agency that catered to high-end clients. While she didn't expect him to part with one of his bodyguards, he surely had a safe house she could use for a few days.

Resigned, she picked up her phone to make the call when a scuffle broke out on the front porch. Melissa turned toward the raised voices, peering through the front window.

"What now?" she muttered. Striding toward the door,

the sergeant cut her off, blocking her path. "This is my home," she reminded him. It took a few seconds longer than it should have, but he finally stepped back. The chime sounded as she opened the door to see Antonio arguing with the two officers standing guard. Warmth spread through her system, a burst of summer sunshine in the heart of winter. She worked to suppress a smile and maintain her professional demeanor.

"Mr. Ruiz? Is everything okay?" Why was Antonio here? Granted, she'd been interrupted before she'd given him a time for dinner and she'd ignored his calls, but she hadn't expected him to just show up. Twice in two days, she realized.

"I could ask you the same question." His gaze was sharp, impatient, his mouth tight with worry as he studied her. "I didn't realize dinner was a group event."

She appreciated the attempt at levity. "Come in." She turned to the sergeant. "Thanks for handling this mess, but I've got it from here."

"You'll call Stanton for extra security?" Joseph asked.

Melissa gritted her teeth. "Yes. Please keep one unit on the street. I'll let them know when I'm leaving."

Joseph faced Antonio. "She isn't to be left alone, Mr. Ruiz."

"I understand," he promised.

"That's enough," Melissa guided Joseph to the front door. "We all have things to do, right?" She aimed a meaningful look at the evidence envelope. "I'm counting on you."

With a nod, Joseph walked out and she locked up behind him. A few words were exchanged and then the officers vacated her porch. She'd just taken a breath when Antonio began demanding answers.

"What happened?"

"You get your wish," she said, walking around him to secure the side door as well. "I'm being forced out of my home for the sake of security."

"Why do you think that's my wish?" he queried.

Again, she was speechless. "You've been pushing me to hide out in your hotel. What would the city have to pay for that?"

"Melissa, charging you would be absurd. I've been pushing you to protect yourself," he corrected.

Exasperated, she picked up her phone to call Stanton, but suddenly she was wrapped in Antonio's arms. "What are you doing?" No one was shooting at them; there was no reason for him to shelter her here in her kitchen.

"Making myself feel better."

"Oh." She wasn't sure what to do with this abrupt show of caring. But it felt so good to be held, as if she was a treasure, that she gave herself up to the gesture. She wound her arms around his lean waist, resting her head on his shoulder.

He sighed, as if something settled perfectly into place. Her pulse quickened imagining the pleasure of tipping her head up for his kiss. She wouldn't linger, but she wasn't about to reject the moment, either.

"Tell me what happened," he said into her hair.

"I don't want to." Under her cheek, she felt his body stiffen. She sighed. "You'll only get mad and spoil this." And she needed this respite, needed him, more than she wanted to admit. She wanted a sexy, fascinating and interested man in her life. Not just any man. *This* man. Her persistent attraction to Antonio was growing into something deeper with this constant exposure. She had to pull herself together.

She released him on that disquieting revelation and stepped back so she could watch his expression as she explained. "Yes, Orr was probably behind this stunt. No one was hurt, unless you count the pride of my officers. He, or someone, got close enough to put a collage photo on the side door."

His hands dipped into his coat pockets, but she could tell his fingers had balled into fists. "Where is this collage?" The soft menace in his tone was worse than shouting.

"Sergeant Joseph took it into evidence." Seeing his jaw tighten, she relented. "I took a picture of it."

He swore as he enlarged the image on her phone, studying each candid picture in the collage. "We'll move you into the suite tonight. Let's get you packed."

"Not so fast." He was acting as if they were a couple and he had a vote in her decision. "I was about to call my brother."

"The private investigator?" His eyebrows flexed into a frown.

"Don't be obtuse. I'm well aware that Colton Protection has done business with your hotel guests through the years. Stanton can get me into whatever safe house he has in town."

"So you'll go between this safe house and the station just as you've done from here?" Antonio rubbed his temples, as if she was the simpleminded one. "How is that better? At the hotel, the suite is one-hundred-percent secure and if you won't let me set up a new command center for you, I have the cars and staff to escort you between the residence and the station."

"I can't just move in with *you*!" She threw up her hands. "The optics would undermine my position." She'd never dated anyone as recognizable as the wealthy hotelier. Well, she wasn't actually *dating* Antonio. In one night he'd become a hero to her family and saved her life, but they weren't a real couple.

They'd had exactly one hug. About one minute ago.

She couldn't deny wanting more. Her lips felt feverish whenever she thought of the times they'd been close enough to kiss. The hug was a perfect example of another missed opportunity, but the way they'd been thrown together in the midst of the cases she was juggling wasn't a healthy start for any potential relationship. Definitely not a good start for two prominent figures in the city.

If she moved into his hotel, word was bound to get out, assumptions would be made and her reputation would take a worse beating when the relationship fizzled.

Except Antonio wasn't a relationship man. Recalling that detail cooled her down in an instant.

"Melissa."

She glared at him, willing herself not to melt into a puddle at his feet at that sultry tone. "No."

He spread his hands. "Explain a better option."

She didn't have one. "Your way could cost me my job."

"Orr has shown he's willing to take your life," Antonio said. "Don't put your family through that worry. Don't force me to bear that guilt. I'm the one who brought the bastard into our city."

His gaze was haunted. She'd seen that look time and again. Through interviews and town gossip, she'd heard his wife had died when they were barely more than kids themselves, but she didn't know the details. He was a man who'd taken on significant responsibility in his career choices. Did he carry survivor's guilt or feel responsible for losing his wife, too?

The notion turned her soft and, sensing it somehow, he pounced. "A move to the hotel limits Orr's options. Plus, my security team and your officers are close. It's a sensible decision."

Sensible, sure. Right up to the moment when she was surrounded by everything Antonio. That was the more personal, imminent danger. Unfortunately, it was logical. Combining forces, along with the potential of bringing down Orr with less risk to the community, held tremendous appeal.

"Fine." She scooted around him and down the hall to her bedroom. She wrestled a suitcase from the back of her closet and unzipped it. She reached for extra uniforms first, then paused, wondering what else to take. Did she pack the oversized T-shirt she slept in most nights or something more feminine? Ruthlessly, she popped the bubble of hopeful lust and threw the T-shirt into the suitcase.

All she knew was there was *one* secure suite at the Grave Gulch Hotel. With a kitchen. She could assume it was luxurious, but that was about it. Was there one bedroom or two? Did they have a rollaway option or a sleeper sofa?

She closed her eyes. She should *not* move in with Antonio.

"We have an excellent laundry service." Antonio displayed an appealing confidence as he leaned a shoulder on the door frame. "Along with every other amenity or item you might need. And we can come back anytime."

"*We* again," she murmured.

"Yes." His voice took on an edge she could relate to.

"Would you advise anyone else in your shoes to handle this situation alone?"

"No." More logic. She opened the dresser drawer where she kept her workout gear. "Would you be standing here if I were a man?"

"But you're not," he said.

She tossed the leggings and layers for winter running into the suitcase. "That's a cop-out."

"I disagree."

Her entire body went on alert as he entered her room. This bedroom would surely fit in the suite with room to spare. Possibly the entirety of her house. They were so different and she was getting tangled up in thoughts and feelings that could never come to pass. Stress, adrenaline, whatever it was, she needed some space, but he kept closing the distance. One deliberate step at a time.

The sensual heat in his eyes sent her heart rate into overdrive. Like a cornered rabbit, she looked around for an escape even as her traitorous body quivered, eager for contact.

"Melissa."

Her knees went weak and her gaze locked with his.

"You are the chief of police, and man or woman, I would offer my assistance either way. Especially since a former associate of mine is the one causing trouble." His hands skimmed up from her fingertips to rest at her elbows. "However, if you were a man, I would not be here." He gave her arms a light squeeze, then stroked higher to her shoulders. His thumbs brushed the sensitive skin of her throat. "I fear, even if you were any other woman, I would not do this."

Slowly, he leaned in, giving her plenty of time to say no. She shifted into him, touching her lips to his, her hands resting at his hips as if they did this every day.

Sensation rocketed through her, taking something simple into uncharted territory from one heartbeat to the next. His hands moved into her hair, then he changed the angle and deepened the kiss.

He tasted of heat and dark, enticing promises, and her mind blanked. They were the only two people in the world in this moment. She moaned, her fingers clutching the fine fabric of his shirt as she hung on for dear life. His mouth moved along her jaw, his breath at her lips casting a spell. Her head fell back, caught safely in his hand, as he trailed kisses along her throat.

When he eased back, she rested a hand on his chest, delighted to find his breathing was as rapid as hers. She didn't know what to say, only what she wanted to do next, starting with more kisses.

But his gaze dropped to her suitcase and he frowned. "There's a full gym at the hotel. You don't need outdoor layers."

The momentary intimacy broken, she had to agree. As much as she loved running outside, it wasn't smart while Orr was tracking her. She reluctantly moved away from Antonio's touch, removing the outer gear and choosing other pieces instead.

"I promise you I won't be in the suite for long," she said, striving for her professional voice of calm command. "The GGPD will capture Orr and make sure he's sent away for a long time for the crimes he's committed in this city."

"I appreciate that," Antonio said. "And I believe you."

Why did those words strike her as far more important than a hot kiss or the size of his suite? She should keep packing, should definitely not be hanging on his every word like an awestruck teenager face-to-face with her crush.

"I'd like to be clear," he said. "You're very good at your job and passionate about safeguarding this community. I apologize for ever questioning your commitment."

"Thank you," she whispered.

Heat flared in his eyes as his gaze dropped to her mouth, fanning the flames deep inside her that lingered from that kiss. She ducked into the bathroom to pack her toiletries or they'd never get out of here.

The moment she added the small tote to the suitcase, he caught her hands with his. "I want you to be comfortable at the hotel. *Safe* and comfortable. But, also, I want *you*. Those two facts stand independent of each other."

That was definitely crystal clear.

She laced her fingers through his, tipping up her face. She thought she was ready for the next kiss, but when their mouths met, something exploded. Need. Longing. A promise of satisfaction right here, literally within her grasp.

Pressing her body to his, she gave in to the roar of desire. Shoving his coat off his shoulders, she protested when he released her to shake it off, sighing as his arms came around her again.

But the embrace lasted only for a moment. He untucked her uniform shirt with an urgency that matched the pounding in her bloodstream. His hands trailed up and over her ribs, higher, to her breasts, and she arched into the touch, wanting more. Craving everything he was willing to give.

His hands dropped to her belt and she nudged him aside to deal with her service weapon properly. Once her gun was secured properly in the portable safe, she turned back, shocked and delighted by the stark desire in his dark eyes.

Were they really doing this? Here? The questions went up in smoke as he dragged his sweater up and over his head, then tossed it over her open suitcase.

He was mouthwateringly fit, his skin hot under her hands, the crisp hair on his chest adding more texture to those deftly carved muscles. She stroked his chest and he caught her hand under his, right over his thundering heart.

"You do this to me," he said, not sounding pleased about it.

He cupped her backside and brought her flush to him. Body to body, she flexed her hips instinctively against his arousal. It was too fast and yet somehow not fast enough as they fell to the bed, tangled in each other. His kisses blazed across her skin as he dispensed with the rest of her uniform and boots. And the wicked grin on his face as he stripped away the last of his clothing filled her with an ache only he could soothe.

She reached for the nightstand and pulled a condom from the drawer. Rising up on her knees, she kissed him where he stood, letting her hands wander and finding joy in his reactions. On an oath, he put a halt to her explorations. Grabbing the condom, he covered himself and then prowled over her, leaving a trail of blazing kisses until his mouth met hers again.

At last, they were joined and the world seemed to stop, giving her time to savor every sensation, every pulse arcing between them. Through them. Her next breath, her very existence, was summed up here and now with him.

His every touch amplified her pleasure, as if he knew all her secret desires. She breathed him in, already addicted to his masculine scent. Joy sparkled through her like stars over the lake when he purred his approval as she stroked his arms and back. His body was a masterpiece and she couldn't get enough. When the release crashed over her, his body went taut a moment later, her name on his lips.

As he shifted to stretch out beside her, she stroked his hair back from his face. Though she tried, she couldn't come up with adequate words to express this wonderful blend of physical satisfaction and inner contentment. Sex had never felt this…involved. It was as if he'd answered a question she didn't know her soul had been asking.

He got up to dispose of the condom, pausing at the edge of the bed. "Your pants are glowing," he said with a wink as he reached toward the floor.

Her whole body felt aglow after Antonio's thorough attention and she appreciated that he didn't mention it if he could see that, too. She covered herself with the sheet, taking her cell phone from his hand. Their fingers brushed, but the soft sizzle disappeared when she saw Troy's name and personal number on the display.

Braced for the worst, she answered.

"Bowe is gone," Troy said without preamble.

"I beg your pardon?" She scooped her hair back.

"Randall Bowe didn't go out for a long lunch after we talked with him," Troy explained. "He took at least a year's worth of files and his hard drive, too."

Shocked and furious, Melissa dropped the sheet, modesty forgotten along with Antonio's presence as she dressed. "Tell me everything you know."

The implications struck like hammer blows, one after another, as Troy listed the details he had. The hard copies for both the Paxton and Emerson cases were missing.

No surprise since those were currently under a microscope. Bowe had vacated the lab and it seemed he'd fled town, as Troy couldn't get an answer at the man's house.

"Cell phone goes straight to voice mail. And nothing is showing up on tracking so far."

"Keep trying," she said. "Is Ellie around?"

"Yes." She heard the squeak of Troy's desk chair.

Ellie Bloomberg was the technology expert at the GGPD. If anyone could help them find a way to restore or recover the files Bowe had stolen, it was her.

"You're on speaker," Troy said. "Ellie's here."

"Hi, Chief," Ellie said.

"Hi, Ellie. Troy will give you the details." How to say it with Antonio hovering nearby? "We need you to start a recovery operation. When files are uploaded to our system, we back them up, right?"

"Yes, ma'am."

Her instant confirmation gave Melissa hope that they hadn't lost everything. She wouldn't know how to tell Antonio they'd been pushed back to zero on the Orr case. "As I said, Troy will fill you in and I'll be in as soon as possible."

She ended the call and scrambled for clean socks, avoiding Antonio's gaze. From her peripheral vision she knew he was dressed, but that was about it.

"Trouble?"

"Always." She aimed a smile at him without really making contact. "Just a technology glitch," she fibbed as she tied her boots. "We'll sort it out, but I do need to go back in."

"All right. I'll drop you off and take your things on to the hotel."

"Oh." She hadn't thought about that. "I'll need my car." She looked up and his cool, assessing gaze was such a contrast to the earlier open warmth, she shivered. Once more, her career was taking precedence over her personal life. "I guess dinner will have to be another time."

"No worries, I'll handle it." His smile seemed sincere as he knelt in front of her. "Have your patrol car follow you to the station. My security team is out there waiting for me."

Embarrassment flooded her face as she imagined what his people and hers might be assuming, but Antonio didn't seem flustered at all. He kissed her and helped her to her feet, pulling her close. If they kept this up, she'd never get to the station.

Would that be so bad? Tonight, yes. She removed her gun from the safe and blushed again. "This has to go, too."

"Sure."

He was taking this too well. In the past, when she changed plans or hurried away from a boyfriend, there'd been friction and bruised egos. Antonio, unfazed, carried her suitcase and the empty gun safe while she picked up her purse and coat and then set her alarm system.

On the porch, he hesitated, standing just a little too close. "Call me when you're on the way to the hotel. Please."

"I will," she promised.

He gave her fingers a squeeze and then carried her things down the steps to the waiting car.

She felt effervescent and hoped the bliss coursing through her veins wasn't too obvious on her face to the patrol team as she explained her plans. Worry was a lingering storm cloud in her mind, but not even Orr's threats and antics could blot out the glory of being with

Antonio. She watched him leave and mentally doubled down on her determination. The sooner she sorted out the current crisis, the sooner she could get back to Antonio and start defining whatever was blooming between them.

If anyone had asked, Antonio wouldn't have been able to explain what was going on in his head when it came to Melissa. When she'd let him hold her and finally wrapped her arms around him, he'd felt an electrifying connection he'd assumed he'd lost forever. Melissa's kiss had been fresh and exhilarating, and it scared him more than a little how perfectly they fit together.

One big perk about being the boss was no one questioned where or how he spent his time. As he took her things straight up to the suite, he hoped her officers extended her the same courtesy.

Something about her just struck a chord deep inside him, dredging up thoughts and feelings he preferred to avoid altogether. Did lust count as a feeling? There was plenty of that when he was around her and that scared him. At the taste of her lips, he'd forgotten all about Orr's threats.

Not smart for either of them, and even more proof they needed the security his suite provided. If they lost focus when Orr could reach them, it could be a disaster.

Antonio had had enough disaster for a lifetime.

Surely it was the unexpected attraction and the constant togetherness that was throwing him off. Seeing her in that dress at the wedding had cast her in a different light, moving her out of the professional-associate category. He understood Melissa the Cop, or thought he had. Until the wedding that's how he'd always seen her, whether she was on duty or just around town.

He smiled, imagining her reaction if he told her any of this. The clothing didn't make the woman, but apparently, he was just primitive enough that the clothing changed his perception. Now that he knew what was underneath those clothes, he couldn't wait to have her in his arms again.

Restless and hungry, he headed downstairs to his office. Waiting for her to call wasn't going to bring her back any faster. He thought he'd demonstrated admirable restraint not asking about the call she'd received, but he couldn't help wondering if it had something to do with Orr.

The man was planning something. That collage was a message and he hoped Melissa and her department were up to the task.

Antonio scrolled through digital media for any local news and checked his phone and email messages. Everything seemed quiet this evening, but he couldn't shake this impatience simmering inside him. He wasn't exactly worried about Melissa, but he needed an outlet, a more effective distraction.

No one in his employ had found Orr and no one in the local media mentioned his name. Was that good or bad? There was a brief story on the trouble at the chief's house, but no real details. That was good news in his book. If he was going to protect her, or attempt a relationship with her, he wanted to make sure no one could criticize her choices.

Was he after a relationship?

The answer had been "no" since the day he'd lost his family. The answer had to remain "no" until he understood why Melissa stirred up those long-buried emotions. Until he could say "yes" without any doubts, he wouldn't open himself to that kind of pain again.

Chapter 11

Melissa was running out of time and the DA needed answers about the Emerson case. She'd missed two calls from DA Parks and one from the mayor while she'd been in bed with Antonio. Not that she had any real regrets about that.

Unfortunately, the trial would resume tomorrow, based on the current reports. If Emerson's defense attorney tried to call Bowe, that would be another black eye since he'd fallen off the radar. Naturally the man who processed evidence knew how to avoid leaving a trail. She didn't want to believe the worst about Bowe, but his abrupt disappearance on top of the discrepancies made it nearly impossible to remain neutral. It stung to have relied so heavily on a man apparently capable of manipulating cases.

She'd spoken with Ellie and Troy upon her return, but they didn't have anything to share yet. She'd skimmed through the initial reports of the officers who'd responded to the incident at her home. None of her neighbors had seen Orr or anyone else approach her side door.

Something had to give, and soon, or an innocent woman might go to jail and a presumed-guilty man would continue raising hell. She'd known the job would be a challenge, but this had to be a low point for anyone in her shoes.

Her stomach rumbled, reminding her she was supposed to be fixing a meal for Antonio right about now. He'd been so accepting of her running out, she wanted to make it up to him somehow. It had to be more than infatuation that made her want to go the extra mile for him. Although, maybe he wasn't offended by the change of plans because they didn't really have anything deep going between them beyond a common interest in catching Orr.

She bit her lip, impatient with her own uncertainty. It wasn't like her to get swept away in a moment. She worried that talking about it would only make her look clingy. As resistant as she was to a conversation about feelings, it would help if she understood the expectations while hiding in his secure suite.

When her cell phone hummed against the desk, she rushed over, grinning like a girl in the throes of her first crush, hoping it was Antonio. No luck. Clarke's face filled the screen. She answered, eager for some good news on any front.

"Melissa," he said, his voice low. "I'm in the rear parking lot. I found someone who would like to speak with you. If your office is clear, I can bring my friend in through the back and avoid the media."

"What's this about?"

"We just need to have a casual conversation, that's all," he said.

That cleared up nothing. She glanced out her window, but Clarke wasn't parked where she could see his car. Wary, Melissa thought of the protestors and media camped outside the station. It would be nice to give them some kind of positive update. Her brother rarely asked for favors, and when he did, he had good reason. "I'll be waiting in my office."

Clarke ended the call without another word. Melissa wondered what she was in for and found herself wishing it was news on Bowe. Hard to believe Troy would've reached out for Clarke's help at this point. Whomever he was bringing in, if this casual conversation helped her put any open case into the solved column, she'd take it.

Clarke walked in with a woman that struck Melissa as being vaguely familiar. She appeared to be in her mid-to-late twenties. Petite, with a short cap of dark hair and light brown eyes in a round face. "Come on in," she said, standing as Clarke ushered the woman into the office.

He closed the door. "You might want Troy to join us."

That set off more warning bells, but she called in her cousin and they waited in an awkward silence until he joined them. Troy's eyes widened in recognition when he saw the woman with Clarke. "Stephanie Dunn." His gaze locked with Clarke's, then shifted to her, questions in his hazel eyes.

The name finally clicked for Melissa and she faced their guest. "You were the eyewitness in the Emerson case," she said to Dunn.

"Yes," the younger woman replied. "I was supposed to testify today, but court was delayed."

Thanks to Hannah McPherson, Melissa thought.

"Mr. Colton…" Dunn's eyes darted nervously between both men. "This Mr. Colton," she clarified with a nod to Clarke. "He called me this morning about the case."

"Why?" Melissa asked the room at large. She had a sinking feeling that no matter who replied, she wasn't going to enjoy this conversation.

"Stephanie, just tell the chief and the detective what you told me," Clarke encouraged her. "It'll be all right."

He really shouldn't be making any promises on behalf of the department, but she held her tongue until she learned what they were dealing with.

"When Mrs. Emerson was accused of killing her husband, I told police that I saw her near the crime scene around the time of the murder," Dunn began.

"I took your statement," Troy said leaning against the wall, arms folded over his chest.

"Yes. I'm sorry. Th-that wasn't true. I'm so sorry."

Melissa's stomach cramped and she swallowed hard as her gaze dropped to her desk. The apology was practically useless. How had she let this happen on her watch? Anger slowly burned through her disappointment and her chin came up. She pinned Dunn with the hard gaze that left her most-seasoned officers quaking. "What *is* true?"

"I did *not* see anyone around the Emerson home that night. I lied. I wasn't even outside." She squeezed her hands together tightly in her lap. "I'm really sorry."

"Why did you give a false statement?" Melissa snapped.

"Someone gave me a thousand dollars. I needed the cash. He said I wouldn't have to lie in court."

"Who?" Melissa demanded.

"I don't know. A man…" Dunn looked at Clarke. "I gave Clarke a description of the man a-and the transaction."

Melissa handed Dunn a box of tissues as she started weeping. "Sum it up for me," she said to Clarke.

He jumped in. "She was approached, *after* Everleigh's arrest, by a man she's never seen before or since. No names were exchanged. Payment was handled online and she used the money to cover expenses on a recent fender bender. The man who approached her, however, was *not* the same man driving the car she bumped in a grocery-store parking lot."

During Clarke's recitation, Melissa watched Dunn nod along while blotting tears from her eyes.

"A setup?" She looked to Troy and Clarke. "From the fender bender on."

Both men murmured in agreement. They were all thinking the same thing. Someone, likely the killer, had gone to great lengths to keep Everleigh in the hot seat.

"Payment was through an app," Clarke said. "I'm looking into it, but so far nothing helpful."

Melissa swallowed a curse. "They wouldn't have made a mistake at that point." She picked up a pen and drummed it against her palm, thinking.

"What happens to me?" Dunn asked, her voice small in the heavy silence.

Melissa exchanged a look with Troy. Her cousin shrugged. The decision on how to proceed was all hers. She pulled up Bowe's department headshot and showed it to Dunn, ignoring the raised eyebrows from her cousin and brother.

"Is this the man who bought your testimony?"

Dunn studied the image. "It could be. He was pretty average in height and build. He had on a hat and sunglasses the one time he spoke with me."

It would've been nice, but confirmation was a definite stretch. If she charged the woman, it would be public record and Stephanie could become a target of the person who actually killed Fritz Emerson. She wasn't willing to put anyone else in jeopardy.

"I won't press charges against you at this time," she said at last. Dunn sagged with relief. "And you haven't perjured yourself in the courtroom." The woman should send Hannah a thank-you card for that alone.

"However, we will document this meeting," she continued. "It sounds like you were targeted with deliberate intent. You will stay in town and I advise you *not* to discuss this with anyone else."

"Yes, ma'am."

"If you feel tempted to go against those two directives, I suggest you reach out to Clarke first."

"Okay. I will. Thank you, Chief."

Melissa held her breath, afraid to speak until Clarke led Dunn out of the office.

"You all right?" Troy asked.

"Are you?" She stood up, antsy and searching for the right direction. "This all but confirms Everleigh is innocent and there's a killer out there on the loose." In all her years on the force, she'd never expected to deal with something like this in Grave Gulch. "Has Ellie found anything?"

"She will," Troy said. "I'll spare you the techno-speak, but she's confident she can recover the files Bowe stole."

"Good." She'd had tough days on the job, but she'd never felt quite as ill-equipped as she did right now. Something was critically wrong with her forensics team. "I've only dealt with cases like this in a hypothetical ethics scenario." She paused to take a deep breath. "How is it we've missed the right killer in two cases?"

"We were deliberately misled," Troy said. "Now that we can see the facts and evidence clearly, we'll make progress in the right direction. On both cases."

"I hope you're right."

"What are you going to do?" Troy asked.

"The only thing I can do," she said. "Make the calls." He walked out and she closed her office door, keeping the blinds down for complete privacy. Her pulse pounded in her temples, but aspirin wouldn't help this headache. At her desk she rested her head on her folded arms, waiting for the pain to recede. An innocent woman might have been convicted without her grandmother's rash actions. What would it take to recover the community's trust?

When she was sure her stomach and head were settled, she picked up the handset and dialed the DA's number. The conversation with Parks was remarkably brief and, once more, a case was officially out of her hands. Next up, the mayor. No surprise that discussion ended in a summons to his home office for a private meeting. As she drove out to the mayor's house, a patrol tailing her as a precaution against Orr, she wondered if this would be her last act as the chief of police. Her foot eased off the gas pedal as the possibility of being removed from her post sunk in.

What would she do? Being chief of police had been her ultimate goal. Invested in the community and career, she'd never thought she might lose the job. Not like this. Unshed tears burned in the back of her throat and she continued to the meeting. Job first, emotions second.

When Antonio got the call that Melissa was finally on her way, he gave instructions for the staff to set up the dinner he'd ordered in the suite and open the wine.

Whatever had happened after they'd left her house, he wanted to pamper her a bit. He doubted she took enough time for herself in general, but definitely not when she had two killers on the loose in her city.

He refused to overthink it and simply followed his intuition about wanting to end the day on a happier note. They didn't know each other well on an emotional front, but he was looking forward to rectifying that tonight. He'd had a few hours to think it through, and he wanted to see where all these sparks led them.

He was downstairs in the lobby, eager as a kid on prom night, when her SUV pulled up in front of the main doors, followed by a patrol car. Good. He would've been frustrated if she'd put herself at risk.

Her smile for the valet was warm and a little weary when she handed off her keys. He thought that curve of her lips brightened a bit when she saw him. She walked straight to him, then seemed to catch herself, sticking out her gloved hand as if she was here for an official meeting. He couldn't stop the laughter. She was adorable.

"Is your long day over?" He guided her toward the elevators on the far side of the lobby, his hand barely touching the back of her coat. That wisp of contact sent a tingling hum of anticipation through his system.

"Finally."

"I can't wait to hear all about it," he said.

"Seriously?"

"As much as you want to share." Apparently that wasn't a common response. Good. He didn't have any intention of being a common occurrence in her world.

At the elevator reserved for his elite clientele, he pressed the button, helping her out of her coat while they waited. When the car arrived, they stepped in and he entered the code to access the secure suite on the top floor of the hotel.

With her hands full of her coat and purse, he brushed his lips across hers. "It's good to see you."

She stared up at him, her blue eyes a bit dazzled. He kissed her again, pleased that he could, savoring the easy connection.

The chime sounded, announcing their arrival at the suite. The doors parted to reveal a marble foyer and Melissa's gasp was a sweet reward to his ears. The staff had set out a vase of fresh flowers on the table by the door, giving the air a hint of spring.

"Welcome to your home away from home," he said, grinning. He threw open the door to the suite and she walked in ahead of him.

"This is…" She turned a slow circle as he closed the door. "Wow. It's wow."

Her eyes were huge and he took great pride in seeing her so impressed. "And completely secure." He took her coat and hung it in the front closet. "Make yourself at home. Your gun safe is right here," he said, pointing to the console table near the door. "I wasn't sure where you wanted to stow it."

"Thanks." She stowed her weapon and then didn't seem to know what to do with her hands. "Your office is stunning and completely you," she said. "This is just layer after layer of luxury." She ran her hand over the distressed leather sofa. "In a really comfortable way."

"That might be the best compliment I've ever received." Her cheeks turned rosy. "And this suite has the best view of the lake for miles."

"Seriously?"

He gestured toward the double French doors. "See for yourself." She dashed over, as delighted as a kid in a candy store. Her excitement gave him a rush of happiness he hadn't felt since…well, not since Karen.

The women he dated now expected the luxury, the indulgences of spending time in his world. Melissa seemed overwhelmed, as if every bit of polish, from the crown molding to the antique rug under her feet, was a miracle to be celebrated. Since when was refreshing so damn arousing?

While she delighted in the view outside, he knelt to start the fire. Gas logs, but the warmth and ambiance were real enough.

"Where did my suitcase wind up?" she asked, turning back to the room.

"Bedroom." He gestured toward the open door across the room. "Dinner is in the oven and the wine is breathing, but it'll keep if you aren't ready to eat."

"Oh, I'm starving," she admitted. "Just let me get out of these boots."

He'd noticed everything had its place in her house and she seemed to maintain that habit here, as she tucked her boots under the console table by the door.

She joined him at the table, where two places were set. A pitcher of water was within easy reach, as well as a basket of the hotel's famous rolls and a fresh salad. "I'm in trouble now," she said on a laugh. "Those rolls are addictive."

"You want the recipe?" he asked, with a heavy dose of flirting. "I know a guy."

"I bet you do." She sipped her wine and then filled the water glasses while he served up the spicy chicken casserole he'd requested for them tonight.

"This is amazing," she said after the first bite. "I don't recall seeing this before."

"Family recipe," he said. "Sometimes I just want the flavors I grew up with."

She hummed in agreement. They chatted about their favorite comfort foods as kids, promising to exchange a couple of recipes.

"More wine?" he asked when they'd had their fill of the food.

She covered her glass with that fine-boned hand. "On one condition."

"Name it."

"Tell me what we're doing. Please. I really enjoyed, um, earlier," she said, color suffusing her face. "And I appreciate the safe place, I do. It's just…I'm not sure what's going on with us."

He gathered her close and just held her for a moment. "I don't know if I have all the answers," he said, leading her toward the chairs in front of the fire. If he sat with her on the sofa, he wasn't sure he'd keep his hands to himself. That would only blur the lines when she wanted clarity. Returning to the table for the wine, he brought the glasses to the table tucked between the chairs.

"You surprise me," he admitted. "Yes, the suite is for our protection, but I want to spend time with you, apart from the crisis that brought us to this point. I want to give you a more normal evening. I think we could both enjoy more time together, if you're willing."

"This is so far from normal for me," she said with a light laugh. "But it's wonderful, too. Thank you. For the protection, and what seems to be a friendship with superb benefits."

He couldn't stop the grin. "If you'd be more comfortable with the whole thing, I can move downstairs to the office."

"No. I'd feel awful if you did that." She peered over his shoulder. "Worst case, I'll sleep on the couch."

"That's absurd."

She arched an auburn eyebrow in challenge. "Is it? Emergencies happen at the most inconvenient times."

"So I discovered this afternoon." He reached over and touched her hand. "Do you want to talk about it?"

She wrinkled her nose, pursed her lips and then nodded. "You're aware we found discrepancies in the evidence against Everleigh Emerson," she began. "I have a forensic scientist coming in to review our original findings. Troy called because of developments involving Randall Bowe, our forensic scientist. He signed off on the Paxton case *and* the Emerson case."

"Progress?"

"Not the direction I'd hoped for," she replied. "I believe in my people. I trusted Bowe, and he's run for the hills." She wound her sleek ponytail around her hand. "It's hard for me to accept that he's made unforgivable errors, or worse, been actively manipulating cases. That's caused you tremendous grief, and without Hannah, Everleigh might have wound up in jail."

His fingers tingled, ready to feel that glossy hair in his hands again. "Might have?"

"More developments," she said. "That's why I was so late. The DA and the mayor had to say their piece when I gave them the updates."

He fought the urge to bluster in her defense, but when she smiled he realized that wasn't what she needed.

"I expect the DA to release Everleigh tomorrow."

"And her grandmother?"

"No idea, though I hope they work it out soon. It's only a matter of time before me or someone else in the department bumps into one of those protestors."

"I heard she was moved to the prison infirmary." To his shock, her eyes welled with tears. "My mistake, I shouldn't have mentioned it."

"Of course, you should have. I caught the news on the drive over." He reached for her but she waved him off. "I'm okay. Really. The guilt just gets heavy. Everleigh was nearly convicted and her grandmother was only trying to help."

He clasped her hands. "Melissa, let me be a friend."

"None of my friends have all of this."

"I guarantee if they did, they'd share it with you."

Her blue eyes were wide and full of emotion when she lifted her gaze to his. "That's a lovely thing to say."

"Trust the expert observer." He stroked the back of her hand with his thumb. "You have the loyalty of your department."

Her gaze slipped to their joined hands. "We'll see if it lasts. Staying up here with you feels like hiding."

"To me it feels like hope." He heard the words, felt the rightness in them. "Come here." He drew her over to sit with him on the sofa, caving to his need to touch her. He traced the smooth line of her jaw, watched her lips part.

This time her lips tasted of wine and an essence that was uniquely hers. As she relaxed into the embrace, he eased back. "To me the police department in any town is a vague necessity. I valued the work and the officers, but it never clicked for me how much each of you do. When the GGPD let Orr walk, I was angry in part because his violent behavior proved I'd misjudged him. It was easier to lay all the blame on the police and not take any on myself.

"Seeing you in action these past days has opened my eyes. Not just to you, but to what you do." He tipped up her chin so he could look her in the eyes. "You don't change the rules to fit the person."

"Of course not."

He smiled. "You lead with knowledge and balance it with compassion. Up close, it makes you even more beautiful."

"Antonio."

This time when she kissed him, he didn't let her stop.

Chapter 12

Melissa had been a coward, waking early and slipping out of Antonio's arms, out of the suite, before he woke up. She'd left a note, claiming an urgent meeting and suggesting they meet for lunch, but now she wasn't sure that would be enough.

If there was a protocol for how to behave when a sexy man was going over and above to protect his latest romantic partner, no one had shared it with her. She hoped she wasn't giving him a reason to move on too soon.

It would be so easy to count on Antonio, to get used to conversations over wine and kisses in the dark and his body keeping her warm through the night. But she couldn't read too much into this interlude. He didn't do long-term and he hadn't made any promises.

"You're in early," Troy said, sticking his head into her office.

"Same to you. Any lead on Bowe?"

He shook his head. "His phone hasn't come back on. Probably ditched it by now."

"Have you found anything linking Bowe to the victims or any suspects in the Paxton or Emerson cases?"

"Not so far. I'm digging into his financials today and Ellie's been here all night reconstructing deleted files from the server. She says she'll have enough for the forensic guy from the state to start on soon."

"That's some progress," she said. They had to keep working the cases. "The DA's office will drop the charges against Everleigh soon. Today, probably," she told him. "I want to get through some paperwork before Parks gives me the go-ahead for the press conference. Then I'm going over to County."

Troy frowned at her. "You want to be there for her release?"

"Yes. We owe her an apology and if I can do that without a media circus, maybe she'll believe I'm sincere."

"Mel, come on," Troy protested. "We worked the case we were given."

"You think Bowe will show up and apologize for nearly destroying her life?" At Troy's grunt, she responded, "Exactly. I'm going. You don't have to like it. Go find Bowe."

"Yes, Chief."

She read through the summary of overnight calls and checked for updates on the search for the black car Orr had been driving the night he'd taken shots at Melissa and Antonio. So far, no one had spotted it, not even in her neighborhood. They'd just have to keep searching. If he was close enough to leave photos on her door, he was too close. And too cocky.

It was midmorning when Parks finally called, reporting the release paperwork for Everleigh was in progress and her family had been notified. "What about Hannah McPherson?" Melissa asked. "The protests are getting louder every day."

"I'm aware," Parks said. "I'll let you know when we make a decision on that one."

For several minutes, Melissa debated how to handle it. She wanted to apologize to Everleigh before the media swarm began, which meant the press conference had to wait.

She had her coat on and was nearly out the door when Desiree appeared, Danny on her hip. The little boy pushed away from his mother, reaching for Melissa. She happily accepted the sweet toddler hug.

"How is my little man today?"

"Happy and healthy as ever," Desiree replied.

"Good." Melissa looked at Desiree. "Did someone call you in?" The last thing she needed was a new case.

"No. I wanted to ask if there was anything I could do to help Hannah."

Melissa rolled her eyes and tickled Danny's tummy, making the boy giggle. "Your momma is silly."

"I can't imagine being so desperate for someone to listen," Desiree said.

"You wouldn't have resorted to kidnapping," Melissa stated. Melissa sympathized with both women and she couldn't say she knew what she would do in either situation since she wasn't a mother. She seemed to be locked into the role of doting aunt with her young cousin. That status wouldn't change as long as she was with Antonio. But what would a family with him be like…?

She handed Danny back to his mom. "I'm sorry I can't talk longer, but I'm on my way out. If you want my advice, write a letter to the DA on Hannah's behalf. As the victim's mother, that will carry the most weight."

"I'll write the letter," Desiree said, her voice sad as she kissed Danny's hair. "I just didn't want to cause trouble between us."

"Not a chance," Melissa said. "As a friend as well as your cousin, I think it's a great idea. You've got a big heart, Desiree, and I think Hannah is lucky to have a sympathetic mom in her corner."

"You're the best." Desiree gave her a big hug.

But Melissa didn't feel anywhere close to the best at anything as she drove out to the county jail with a patrol car behind her as protection. She gripped the steering wheel as another wave of frustration washed over her. Thanks to Bowe's betrayal, the GGPD's reputation might well be shattered and she didn't even understand why he'd tampered with evidence. On top of that, she was more than halfway in love with a man whose personal goals didn't line up with the commitment and family she craved.

She really should put an end to this fling before it dealt her heart a fatal blow.

But when her phone rang and his handsome, smiling face filled her screen, she knew she couldn't walk away from him. Not yet.

They spoke for a few minutes and made plans to have dinner together. Melissa felt as if she was glowing from the inside out every time she thought about Antonio. There was plenty going on around her, more than enough unpleasantness, but having something to look forward to in her personal life put all the rest into perspective.

With all the talk of work-life balance, maybe it was more about outlook and emotions than a true balance of actual hours on a calendar. It scared her more than a little that she enjoyed his company so much. Yet she didn't feel dependent on him. More like supported, encouraged. Of course, by their own agreement, whatever they were doing was more of a fling than the start of a lasting commitment.

Regardless, determined to enjoy the interlude, she was in a good mood when she reached the county jail. Thankfully, there seemed to be a distinct lack of media presence in the area surrounding the prison. She didn't want Everleigh to mistake this for some kind of feel-good publicity stunt.

Inside, she checked in with the guard and was told Everleigh was nearly through processing. A few minutes later the woman walked out wearing dark jeans, black ankle boots and a purple long-sleeved T-shirt with the Howlin' Eddie's logo from the bar where she'd worked. She had a coat over her arm and a simple, small black purse. Her short, blond hair had grown out and she had it tucked behind her ears.

Melissa wondered what she would do first now that her ordeal was over.

"Mrs. Emerson?" Melissa stepped up, her hand extended. "Chief Colton."

"I know who you are," Everleigh said, a wary edge in her hazel eyes. "My lawyer said he was sending a cab."

Melissa lowered her hand and refrained from sharing an opinion about the public defender. "I'm not here to harass you." She took a deep breath and squared her shoulders. "I wanted to see you and personally apologize on behalf of the GGPD."

"My lawyer said something about a problem with the evidence."

"Unfortunately, we didn't discover the issues earlier." Melissa opened the door for Everleigh. "Again, my apologies. I hope to regain your trust, in time."

Outside, Everleigh looked up to the sky. The door clanged shut behind them. Tears sparkled on her lashes when she turned to Melissa. "It's hard to care about what happened to me when Gram is still locked up. Is there anything you can do for her?"

"It's out of my hands." Melissa was getting tired of saying that. "The DA hasn't made any decisions about your grandmother's case, but I can assure you the community is rallying around her."

"Really?" Everleigh's eyes brightened for a moment and then her gaze fell to the pavement. "I can't believe she did that. Your family must be furious."

"Actually, no. The baby's mother wants Hannah released." She smiled a little. "Again, it's up to the DA." She watched the cab pull into the parking lot and walked over with Everleigh. "I won't keep you any longer. Take care of yourself."

What a mess, Melissa thought as she drove back toward town, followed by the patrol car. She hoped common sense would prevail in the DA's office and Everleigh's family would find a way to heal.

Her phone rang, interrupting her thoughts. She used the hands-free option to answer the call from the station.

"Chief, we found the black car."

Finally, a break. She flipped on her emergency lights. "Where?"

"In the employee parking lot at the hotel."

Her heart dropped to her stomach. Orr was after Antonio after all. She sped up and hit the siren. "I'm on the way."

The press conference would have to wait. Everything would have to wait—she needed to get to Antonio as soon as humanly possible.

Antonio headed downstairs and out into the courtyard he'd been working on recently. The day was bright, as sunlight danced across the snow-covered landscape. And the temperature was cold enough he really should've brought his coat and gloves. He didn't plan to stay long, he just wanted a moment to himself and a breath of air, no matter how cold.

He shoved his hands deep into his pockets and walked the narrow path the groundskeeper had cleared. In the summer, flowers bloomed within the circle of the low boxwood hedge. It was a knotted pattern he'd seen in an English garden on his honeymoon. He and Karen had decided they'd re-create the garden when they had a house and yard.

It had taken him years to work up the courage to build it here, but this was for her. A promise kept. When his mother had seen it, she'd asked why it was so easy to keep a promise to his dead wife and so impossible to make any kind of commitment to a new woman.

He'd given her some flippant reply about keeping dates and not breaking hearts. His mom, missing nothing, tapped a finger to his chest and told him that Karen would want him to find love again.

Loving again terrified him. The next right woman, if she was out there, would understand that he couldn't be open to that kind of pain again. Losing Karen and their growing family had all but destroyed him. If he took another chance and history repeated itself, he'd be no good to anyone in his family or his business interests. Too many people relied on him, on his ideas, his insights, and the jobs his hotels created. That's why he didn't cut corners and that's why he was happiest on his own. Until now…

He hunched his shoulders against a gust of wind and turned around, coming face-to-face with Orr.

The man was bundled up in a basic blue parka, his hair hidden by a knit cap and sunglasses over his eyes, a colorful scarf wrapped around the rest of his face. The outerwear didn't conceal the way he carried himself or the aggressive stance. This was definitely Orr.

No one else had cause to aim a gun at him. The threatening gun was no match for Antonio's rising fury. His mind raced, calculating how to put an end to this ordeal.

"I guess I'll tell my security team they can stop searching for you," Antonio said.

"They'll forget about me once they find your body. Everyone will want to know why the most eligible bachelor in Michigan killed himself."

Antonio's pulse hammered. "You can kill me, but that story won't fly."

"It will," Orr countered. "You're consumed with guilt for killing Wendy."

"*You* did that," he said, scrambling for a way out of this.

"No, you let your control issues and jealousy ruin a friendship and end her life."

Curses raced through Antonio's mind. His cell phone was in the office. He couldn't call for help. He'd chosen the most remote courtyard to wander through and his hands were stuffed in his pockets. No way to make a move without drawing notice.

He took a step, shifted one hand. "Let me call someone for you, Drew."

"Hold it." Orr aimed the gun at Antonio's chest.

"You're not making any calls. You'll sit right here in the snow and shoot yourself. With my help."

"Get out while you can," he said. "I've increased security across the property." He had to drag this out until the next patrol came through. "Everyone is looking for you now."

"Not everyone," Orr sneered. "And when I leave, they'll have all the evidence they need to pin two murders on your sorry ass. Wendy and your pretty cop friend."

Antonio's thoughts crystallized. He was not letting this maniac hurt Melissa or anyone else. "When exactly did you lose your mind?" he challenged, taking a step closer. Orr held his ground. "How can I do anything to the chief if I'm dead in this garden?"

"The elements will make it hard to determine time of death," Orr said. "I've done some homework. You set a trap for the chief, then came here and, full of remorse, shot yourself near the ashes of your wife and baby."

How did this useless, false friend even know about that? Antonio's vision hazed red. "You expect me to lie down and let you stage a suicide? No one will believe it. You need to turn yourself in."

Orr's lips twisted into a sick imitation of a smile. "Why? The world is about to know I'm innocent and you're the killer."

A big boom sounded nearby and a plume of black smoke pierced the clear day. "Huh. That was early," Orr said. "Should've watched that tutorial one more time."

The explosion gave Antonio the window he needed. He threw himself at Orr and took the man down into the hard, icy hedge. The gun flew out of his hand, landing out of reach and sliding across the cleared walk.

Antonio, with the advantage, punched at Orr's face.

He knocked away the sunglasses and reached for the scarf, planning to use it as restraint. Orr bucked Antonio off him and rolled, throwing elbows and fists in a wild attempt to get free. He got to his feet, but Antonio caught the hem of his jeans, and Orr went down, face-first this time.

With a scream, he rounded on Antonio, kicking as he scrambled backward, toward freedom. Antonio curled away from one kick aimed at his gut, taking another in the shoulder. He rolled up to his feet, but his shoes slipped on the icy ground and Orr got up and over the low wall. Antonio gave chase, shouting for help from anyone nearby, but Orr had planned his escape well. He jumped into an idling pickup truck and floored it, driving away on the service road. This time, Antonio had a clear view of the license plate. He repeated it over and over as he ran back toward the hotel.

One of the surveillance cameras should've caught a good view of Orr's face during the fight. If not, there was another one where the access road met the cross street. He looked around the courtyard, torn between picking up or leaving everything where it was.

He had to leave it, but he also needed to get someone out here in a hurry to bag the signs of the fight. What a time to forget his phone.

On the other side of the hotel, he could see that plume of smoke and he heard the sirens now. Was anyone even in the security office, monitoring the cameras? Antonio wanted to blame Orr for his clever tactics, but the only reason the bastard knew when and where to exploit the system was because Antonio had trusted him too quickly.

He blew into his hands and noticed the evidence of the fight. Maybe he had somehow gotten Orr's DNA on him, but he doubted it—he hadn't scratched his former associate with his nails. He picked his way across the cleared path to the door, relieved to see one of his security guards jogging toward him.

"Sir, are you okay?" Charles asked.

"Alive is better than just okay," Antonio said. "I don't have my phone on me, so can you please call the police?"

Charles pulled out his radio and made the call.

"Tell them my attacker was Drew Orr and he left in a dark green pickup with Illinois plates." Antonio recited the plate number, waiting for Charles to repeat it for the emergency dispatcher. "He threatened the chief of police."

"The chief is on-site, here," he assured Antonio before relaying the warning to the dispatcher. He lowered the radio. "What happened to you?"

"Orr was hoping to frame me for a bunch of crap and fake my suicide. What's that about?" He lifted his chin toward the black smoke.

"Car explosion," Charles said. "We noticed a black car matching a BOLO in the employee lot and reported it. The police were pretty sure it was the car you described during the drive-by shooting on Saturday night. Not sure why it blew up."

His blood chilled, and it had nothing to do with being outside in the January afternoon. "Was anyone hurt?"

"No, sir," Charles replied. "One of ours was in the car, unconscious but alive."

"One of ours," Antonio echoed. "He's okay?"

"Yes, sir." Charles shuffled his feet. "When they opened the door to check on him, a charge blew under the engine. Other than the smoke it was mostly noise."

"Hell of a diversion," Antonio muttered. Melissa had

asked him about Orr's skills, but there was no way he could've predicted something like this. "Let's block off the area and—"

The security guard's radio crackled a moment before he saw Melissa striding up. Emotions surged too fast and high for him to name them individually. The general theme was relief that she was safe and he was alive to appreciate it, underscored by a current of gratitude, desire and the softer sense that she was here. Right here, within reach.

Her face was pale, her gaze sharp, as she approached. All that motion and intensity came to a quick stop when she entered the courtyard. "Are you okay?"

"Nothing a bag of frozen peas won't cure."

Her gaze swept over the scene and he knew she saw it all. The gun, the scarf and sunglasses, the flattened snow from the fight, the footprints leading to the wall.

"He left in a green pickup truck. Got the plate number this time," he said.

Her eyes locked with his and he didn't know whether to step back or close the distance between them. He could sense the fire blazing under the calm exterior.

Much as she'd done at the wedding reception, she gave directions to everyone present, including him. "I'll take you to the hospital."

"I'm fine," he said, though it was obvious she wasn't interested in his opinion on his health.

"Come on." She turned, clearly expecting him to follow.

He didn't want to be anywhere else, so he obeyed without comment. It took all his willpower and focus to not wrap her up and kiss her in the sheer joy of being alive.

Chapter 13

Melissa didn't trust her voice, didn't believe the first questions out of her mouth would be the slightest bit professional. As they walked to her vehicle on the other side of the hotel, she called in the K-9 teams, giving orders for them to sweep the area for Orr. He'd been waiting out there somewhere and she wanted his hiding place. But she wanted to touch Antonio, to clean his battered knuckles and the cut over his eye herself. Now that he was warm, the swelling had set in. The bruising was sure to be colorful.

He was wet from the snow, his slacks plastered to his long legs, his sweater torn. Must've been one wild fight.

Time seemed to slow and everything snapped into sharp focus. She was in love with Antonio. This wasn't mere attraction or lust or a relationship she could explore after the crisis passed. She was in it, living it. Her breath backed up in her lungs. She loved him. Now she had to figure out how to deal with it.

At the intersection where the main hotel drive met the street, the light was red. She gripped the steering wheel tight in her gloved hands. "Tell me what happened," she said, tackling the official work first. "Why were you out there without a coat? It's January."

He reached over and covered her hand with his bare one. She stared at those raw scrapes, looked past them to admire his lean hands. It was all she could do to keep from lacing her fingers with his. The offered comfort and connection were so tempting, so dangerous to her peace of mind. She couldn't deny wanting to feel those hands gliding over her skin again.

"I was worried about you, too," he said. "That explosion, the smoke."

"Not a scratch on me." The light changed and he pulled back so she could drive. She missed his touch immediately. "Don't make me read this in a report, Antonio."

"I needed some air," he began. "Only meant to go out for a few minutes."

She listened, questions taking shape in her mind as he walked her through Orr's approach, his threats and the fight that ensued.

"Wait," she said as they pulled up at the emergency-room entrance. "You stepped closer to an armed man who has killed before."

"So you believe me now?"

She shook her head. "I've never really not believed you. We just couldn't prove his connection to the Paxton crime scene."

"Right."

"I'm not going to tell you how to run a hotel, so don't tell me how to be a cop."

"Right," he repeated.

"You need medical help."

"For agreeing with you?" Antonio had the audacity to chuckle. "This isn't a concussion talking," he said. "Orr is a serious threat."

"I'm aware." The GGPD had to get him into custody before anyone was seriously injured. She hopped out of the car and came around to open his door. "Let's get you checked out."

"This isn't necessary," he said, keeping his seat. "I can deal with it at the suite."

She leaned across him and unbuckled the seat belt, took his chilled hand and tugged him just enough to get out of the car. "It helps the case if we get your injuries, minor or otherwise, documented." She could rattle off the growing list of charges she planned to bring against Orr as soon as they found him.

Antonio and the security guard who had been trapped in the car when the explosion happened were the only patients in the ER at that time. Melissa didn't have a long wait, but it was enough time for her to start second-guessing their dinner plans and her presence in his secure suite.

Just when she was working out how to postpone and move to a different safe location, he was wheeled out into the waiting room, a mildly annoyed expression on his lean face and a trio of butterfly bandages over his eyebrow.

It hit her then, at the worst possible moment, that she might easily have found him dead in that courtyard. Only the combination of Orr's desire to trash Antonio's reputation and Antonio's quick thinking had saved him.

As a cop, she was no stranger to crime scenes or physical violence, but the idea of Antonio becoming a statistic made her stomach drop. Her hands went cold and she fought off a dizzy spell. If anything happened to him it would destroy her. One more good reason to put some distance between them, and fast, she thought.

Annoyance shifted to concern in his warm brown eyes when he saw her. "Melissa? You're pale."

"Just what every woman wants to hear," she said, exchanging a glance with the nurse. "Don't worry about me." She forced her lips into a bright smile. "Everything's good."

It was obvious he didn't believe her, so she spoke with the nurse. "Any precautions or follow-up?"

"Oh, you're together? I'm sorry, Chief." The nurse handed Melissa the paperwork. "You should've said something and we would've let you back with him."

She blanked at the nurse's assumption that they were a couple. Her heart gave a hopeful kick, but being in love with him didn't erase that they wanted different things. "It's okay. I had calls," she fibbed.

Beside her, Antonio collected the paperwork. "Thank you."

"Take care of yourself, Mr. Ruiz," the woman said with a starstruck smile. "Those butterfly bandages will itch in a day or two," she warned. "Don't pick at them."

"The chief will make sure I behave," he replied, urging Melissa toward the exit.

"I'm parked over here." A fact he surely knew since her marked vehicle stood out from the others.

"Don't," he said, stopping short and catching her arm. "Let me call a car from the hotel."

"You can't be serious."

"Have they found Orr yet?"

She sighed. "Not to my knowledge."

"I'm not taking any chances that he did a better job with a second explosive than he did with the first."

She tried to reason with him. "No one has been near the car."

"You can't be sure," he accused, backing away and tugging her along.

"I can be. The patrol is right there." She pointed to the police car parked at the end of the row with a clear view of the ER entrance and her SUV. She understood his hesitation, recognized the signs as the reality of what he'd escaped settled over him. "We're safe," she promised.

The temperature was dropping as the sun dipped lower on the horizon. "You need to get into warm clothes. A hot shower wouldn't hurt," she told him concernedly.

He glanced at his watch. "I guess I have time for that before our dinner date tonight."

She dropped her keys. He thought of it as a real date? What was between them was more than just friends who had great sex? Her blood simmered and she felt her cheeks color. She gave all her attention to backing out of the parking space.

"We should probably reschedule." There, now she sounded like herself. Reasonable, calm, steady.

"Why?" he asked.

"Because you're hurt and your brain needs to rest."

"I don't have a concussion."

"They put it on your discharge papers," she said. "Under signs and complications to watch for."

He unfolded the paper, gave a grunt. "Orr has snapped," he said. "Maybe the man I knew was the mask and this is the real him."

"Either way, we'll find him soon. Rest is probably the better choice for both of us tonight." They needed a break from the talk of Orr. It would be nice to sit in front of the fire with him and just relax…and back off any talk of real "dates."

She drove around to the side entrance of the hotel and parked, determined to walk him in and make sure he got inside safely.

He grumbled a little when he spotted one of her officers standing next to one of his security men at the door. "Team effort," she reminded him. "At least until we have Orr in custody."

"Smart," he reluctantly agreed. "You don't have to feel obligated to hold my hand."

She had a sudden wish that they were holding hands. "I'll be back around seven."

"You won't be alone, either?" He twisted around, looking for the car that followed them from the hospital.

"They have my back," she assured him.

"I suppose I have to trust that's enough."

"It would help if you did." She heard a vehicle behind them. The engine and tires sounded way too fast for the parking lot.

She turned to look, but everything blurred as Antonio grabbed her by the coat and spun her around, all but tossing her into the shrubs planted around one of the light poles.

She used the momentum to roll to her feet, then pulled her gun, but the truck careened around the end of the parking row and sped away.

The men near the door had pulled their weapons, too, and both fired. The rear window shattered and the tailgate bounced open as the driver hit a pothole, but the truck didn't stop.

Antonio caught her around the waist when she started after him. "You're not going anywhere," he declared. "Not until that maniac is under control."

"That was Orr?"

"Same ugly face. Same truck he escaped in earlier," Antonio confirmed.

She holstered the weapon she'd never had a chance to fire. "You saved my life," she said on a shaky breath. "Thanks." She pressed her fist to her pounding heart. Melissa sucked in another deep breath, afraid to close her eyes and see that truck bearing down on her. "Thank you," she said again.

He was holding her, giving her far more support than she should be asking for. But she couldn't get the image out of her head, just how close she'd come to being run down. A hard shiver ripped through her and he just held on, keeping her steady. Without Antonio's quick reaction she would be headed for a hospital at best.

The officer assigned to support the hotel staff jogged over, followed by one of Antonio's security guards. "I've called it in. We have a BOLO on the plates and driver."

"Should've had that earlier," Antonio grumbled.

"Easy," she said, automatically defensive. "They put out the order and everyone has been combing the streets." She looked around, though there wasn't anything to see. "To be this much of a pest, Orr is hiding somewhere close."

"Pest?" Antonio glared at her. "That's the second time he's tried to kill you. He's a menace."

She straightened her shoulders, pulling herself together. A jagged ache started in one shoulder and ran down her back to the opposite hip. She wasn't seriously hurt, but she'd feel this for a few days. She turned to Antonio's security guard. "Please make sure he gets upstairs safely. And have someone check on him periodically."

"Where are you going?" he snapped.

"Station," she replied, willing the quivering in her knees to stop. "Need to write this up. Keep the search rolling."

"You need a hospital."

"I do not." She tried another smile. "You made sure of that."

He stepped closer, lowered his voice. "Melissa. Take a minute for yourself."

"I'm okay. Really." She'd be better once she got back to the station. The familiar surroundings and the routine of the paperwork would be a comfort.

He touched her elbow and she hissed in pain. His eyes flared. "You're not. I hurt you."

"No." She rested her hand on his shoulder until he met her gaze. "I've taken worse in training classes. Please don't give it another thought."

Nothing she said eased the worry in his gaze. As she studied his face, her eyes lingered on his lips, and she wished she had the right to kiss him. This wasn't the time or place to stir up that kind of gossip. She tried to back away, to get to the safety of her car. A little distance would restore her sanity and put this all into perspective. "Thank you again," she said. "I'll call when I'm on my way back."

"Melissa."

She took another step and tripped over the curb, or possibly her own feet. But she didn't tumble. Antonio had caught her. How was it a man that was such a threat to her peace of mind could make her feel so safe?

"Humor me," he said. "Come inside."

"But there are reports to file."

"You're the chief of police. Surely we can handle all of it here," he insisted. "You want me to get into warm clothing? To rest?"

"Yes."

"Then come make sure I do."

"That's low," she said, despite being inexplicably charmed by the tactic.

"But it worked." He smiled.

His arm was still at her waist, but she couldn't pull herself away from that support, that persuasive warmth. He just kept guiding her. Into the hotel, down the hall, to the private elevator.

"Happy to be of service."

Antonio gave in to temptation and kissed her in the privacy of the elevator. To hell with shock, a possible concussion and his busted lip. He'd come too close to losing her out there. When he paused to breathe, her blue eyes, still appearing dazed from the near miss, landed on his lips like a touch and he had to start over.

He wasn't sure his heart rate would ever settle again and he doubted he'd get any sleep tonight. Every time he blinked, he saw that truck mowing her down.

But she was here. Alive and breathing, if pale. She was warm against his side. Thankfully, she wasn't shrugging off his touch. It was irrational, but he was afraid to let go, afraid if he did he'd discover Orr had succeeded after all.

First, they went to his office, where they could speak to her officers in person or by phone while he cleaned up and changed into dry clothes. He refused to allow *anyone* up to the suite where they would be staying until Orr was in custody.

At the knock, he opened the door to two of her officers. "Make yourselves comfortable," he said. "I'll just be a few minutes."

"Take your time," she said, giving his fingers a squeeze. "I can fill them in."

He shot her a look as he retreated to the small bedroom behind his office. "I'll be right back." A fast hot shower—he was mindful of the butterfly bandages—did wonders for him. And hearing her voice in the other room smoothed out the last rough edges.

He felt almost normal as he dressed in a pair of jeans and a thick cable sweater. He slipped his watch back over his wrist and sent an order for food and wine to be delivered to the suite. Opening the door, he paused, just taking in the sight of her in one piece. A weight lifted from his shoulders and a peacefulness he'd nearly forgotten swept through him. She was here, safe and alive, and they would find their way through this together.

"Please…" She motioned him in. "They're ready for your statement if you feel good enough to give it now," she said.

She wasn't at the table tucked into the bay window. She'd settled her team in the conversation area that was situated away from the glass. He didn't think she'd made the choice solely because there was more room. The two incidents had clearly left her on edge. Him, too.

"Better to do it while it's fresh in my mind." Maybe getting it out would clear the horror. He sat down next to her on the couch, keeping his hands to himself when he desperately wanted to reach for her.

She poured him a glass of water and he sipped gingerly around his busted lip as he answered each question. At last it was over, and the two officers got up to leave. "Do you still have a detail watching your house?" he asked.

All three of them nodded. "We'll keep it that way until Orr is caught," Melissa explained.

"Good." He didn't want her to suffer any more for his poor choice in associates. He added his thanks to hers.

When they were alone, he took her hands in his, staring into her pretty eyes. "How are you feeling?"

"Sore," she confessed. Her gaze swept over his face, lingering this time on the cut over his eye. She lifted a hand, caught herself. "May I?"

"Of course." He craved her touch, anywhere he could get it. "You can have your way with me."

Whoops, too far. She stopped, her fingertips a hairbreadth away. "Glad you have your sense of humor," she said, pressing gently at the edges of the bandages. "You shouldn't have gotten this wet so soon."

"Hard to avoid it when the rest of me needed cleaning up." Her lips were so close, peachy and full. He stole a quick kiss, happy to see it bring color into her cheeks. "Warm clothes do make a difference."

She smiled, but it was a faint imitation of her usually vibrant expression.

"Hell of a day," he said.

Her stomach rumbled and he chuckled. "I've ordered food and wine. It should be delivered upstairs soon."

Her gaze fell to their joined hands. "It sounds wonderful, but I should stick with water since I have to keep tabs on you and that concussion."

"I'm fine," he insisted. "A glass of wine will be good for both of us."

Her lips tipped up in a half smile. "I don't know whether to be impressed or intimidated around you."

"How about just pleased?"

She met his gaze and the half smile blossomed. "I think I can do that."

"Excellent."

Holding hands, they left the office behind for the safety of the suite upstairs. She went to clean up and change clothes, stepping out of the bedroom a few minutes later in faded jeans and a beautiful green turtleneck that hugged her curves and set off her red hair to perfection.

"I'm sorry about the mistakes we made last summer," she said as she joined him at the table. "They won't be repeated when we bring him in again."

"We've let Orr steal enough of our time." He wanted her to be able to relax and rest in the awareness that they were safe. "Let's talk about anything else. We could even not talk at all."

He stroked a hand along her spine, bringing her closer. How could a woman so trim be so strong? She was steel wrapped in supple silk. Her hair was down and he let the gleaming fire sift through his fingers. "You're beautiful."

Resting his lips gently on hers, he took his time with the kiss, enjoying the gentle torture of resisting the urge to drive and rush and plunder.

"Wow," she whispered into the charged air between them. "What was that?"

"Just about perfect," he said. "Should we try again?"

She gave a tiny shake of her head. "I think I need a minute."

He let her step away, though it cost him. "You're going to blame all of this between us on adrenaline or shock."

She cocked an eyebrow. "It has to factor."

He didn't believe in making excuses, but maybe she was right. Seeing the pickup bearing down on her, he hadn't thought, only reacted. Save *this* woman. He could do something to protect Melissa when he'd had no power to save his wife. He wasn't a monster; he would've done his best to help anyone in the same situation. But he wouldn't have needed the personal touch, the affirmation, afterward. He had no desire to replace his lost wife with this woman. Melissa was not Karen; she was a wonderful person in her own right.

"I suppose you're right. But recent events don't explain away everything between us."

"No?"

"No." He pulled out a chair for her, relieved when she sat down. Room service had delivered a cart full of food to the foyer, even popped the cork on a bottle of wine. He'd loaded the table with bowls and platters with a fresh green salad, stuffed mushrooms and pasta with two sauces, as well as traditional meatballs and grilled chicken. It was wonderful to care for someone again. To take these steps for Melissa. "I tried to cover all the bases," he explained as he poured the wine.

He raised his glass. "To our health."

She touched her glass to his and sipped. He'd ordered extra rolls, but tonight she didn't seem all that enthused.

"Do you remember the roofing project on the east side of town?" he asked.

Her gaze narrowed. "Last September, right?"

"That's it." He'd donated supplies for several homes in need of new roofs before winter set it. "You weren't afraid of any pitch, you said yes to every request."

"We were there to work," she said, finally cutting into her chicken.

"It sure contradicted my theory that you were lazy and less than invested in this city." He placed a roll on her plate. "I'd like to apologize."

She laughed, the sound tired and merry at the same time. "Accepted." She broke the roll in half. "You were right to be upset with the department." Those blue eyes locked with his. "With me."

One thing he'd learned in business was never to go into a discussion without having a clear outcome in mind. "I brought it up, the roofing project, because I think I owe you an apology."

"For what?"

"Ogling you. You have amazing legs." He wiggled his eyebrows. "And everything else."

The blush stealing across her face, the incredulity in her gaze—it was all worth admitting his less-than-honorable behavior that day.

"But it also proves that this amazing chemistry isn't just shock and adrenaline."

He wasn't sure why it mattered so much. He wasn't a long-term man. Not anymore. He didn't want anyone relying on him, didn't want to wind up devastated if something happened. And Orr coming after her today only illustrated his less-than-stellar track record with relationships. The last person he needed to care about was a woman who might rush into a dangerous crisis on any given day at work…the risk was too much. He couldn't lie to himself, he did have deep feelings for her, but he didn't dare admit it.

"All right." She leaned forward. "If we're exchanging confessions, I should tell you that we didn't run out of water right after lunch."

"No?"

Her hair swayed with the tiny shake of her head. "There were two cases in my trunk. But then you took off your shirt." She licked her lips, her gaze raking over his chest as if she could see through his sweater. "I knew I'd embarrass myself if I didn't get out of there for a minute."

"Lying about water is a serious offense," he said with a smile, tracing her fingertips.

"Just a misdemeanor," she corrected him. "And no one suffered from dehydration."

He laughed and she joined him, and then, somehow they were kissing and the meal was forgotten as they indulged in each other, proving that adrenaline had nothing to do with this undefinable, thoroughly wonderful chemistry between them.

Later, when they were reheating the food for a snack, she tasted the red sauce. "*Mmm.* That's good. My mom would be impressed."

"I'll take that as the highest compliment," he said.

"One hundred percent," Melissa said. "She is the best cook I know. Dad was on vacation in Italy and it was love at first sight. When it was time for him to return to the States, she came along with him."

"How romantic." It was the safest response. He'd felt that wild rush of love at first sight with Karen. And he could admit he'd been attracted to Melissa from the get-go, too. Was it happening again? He'd never expected his heart would heal enough for another true love. With Melissa, the thrill he remembered was brewing, along with a new sense of deep alignment.

"It's pretty much a family legend. They raised my brothers and me in a home full of laughter and love.

Lived the example of devotion, commitment and abiding love."

"Tough standard," he said.

She sighed. "The right partner is worth the wait," she said, her eyes on her plate. "Your parents are still married, right?"

He set down his fork, wondering how she knew that. Then it dawned on him. "How much digging did you do last summer when Orr suggested I killed his girlfriend?"

She wrinkled her nose. "Just the basic, standard rundown. Plus, you're local, so your family history is local, too. Grave Gulch isn't so big."

It certainly felt small right now. "My parents moved to Florida ten years ago. But you must know that, too."

She avoided his gaze, studiously creating a perfect bite of her salad greens. Reluctantly amused, he waited her out.

"There are trends in criminal justice," she said in a rush. "A basic history can reveal circumstances that might lead to delinquent or outright illegal behaviors."

"I've never broken the law." Though he wouldn't hesitate to take whatever action was necessary if he ever laid eyes on Orr again after today.

"I'm aware of that," she said, matching his level tone. "But Orr did throw suspicion on you and I did my due diligence. You can't run around town accusing me of being lazy and then get aggravated when you feel challenged because I'm good at my job."

"It's not about feeling challenged. And I already told you about the moment I realized you aren't lazy."

He felt too many things at that moment, and he wasn't eager to discuss any of them. If she knew about his parents and his lack of criminal activity, it was logical that she knew he'd been widowed. He couldn't decide if that was good or bad.

"So tell me about your stable home," she suggested, ending the awkward silence.

For a split second he thought of Karen and their house, which hadn't been too unlike Melissa's. The first piece of new furniture they'd purchased had been a rocking chair for the nursery.

"My mother's parents are originally from Cuba but she grew up in Florida," he began. "My father is from Puerto Rico. They met in college and followed his career as a commercial real-estate developer until they settled here, raised the family."

Should he mention his wife or would it be old news to her that he'd met Karen in college? How should he feel if she already knew? Did he want her to know? Antonio was unsure.

"Like your parents," he continued, "they're still wildly in love and happier on the beach than dealing with snowstorms." *Or killers*, he thought, grateful they were out of harm's way.

"I don't suppose you'd be willing to take a vacation and let someone else deal with Orr?" he asked.

"Not an option." He caught a flash of deep sadness in her eyes, though she tried to hide it by starting to clear the table. "I do take vacations," she said. "I know how to relax."

Was he supposed to gain some insight from that? Unsure, he loaded the room-service cart with the serving dishes and pushed it out to the foyer for the staff to pick up when they had a chance.

When he returned, she was on the phone, pacing in

front of the balcony windows. She moved with such a lithe grace, and his body responded to her with an intensity he hadn't experienced in a long time. Until she noticed him watching. Then her cheeks turned rosy and she forced herself to be still.

It was adorable.

Antonio felt the realization click like a lock opening. Melissa Colton had come to mean everything to him. She was part of his life now and he wanted her to stay that way, forever.

Chapter 14

While Antonio dealt with the cart, Melissa was debating another glass of wine when her cell phone rang. "Chief Colton," she said, picking up.

"It's Joseph. They found the truck Orr was driving."

"Where?" She darted into the bedroom, tucking the phone between her ear and shoulder while she gathered up her clothes. She could hardly answer a call in the plush hotel robe. "Did you call the others?"

"They're on the way."

"So am I."

Antonio, seeing her dressing, started to grab his clothing, too.

"I'd advise against that, Chief. Let us clear the scene. After what happened at the hotel, I think staying away is the smarter play."

"Sergeant," she began and stopped herself. He made a good point and if she ever wanted to find a balance, she had to be willing to step back and change up her patterns. "I don't like it, but you're right."

"I'll keep you in the loop."

"Every step of the way, please," she said. "We need to drop a net on this guy."

"Sure thing," Joseph promised.

Ending the call, she looked up at Antonio. "They found the pickup truck," she said. "No sign of Orr yet."

"Are you staying or are we going?"

That use of "we" sent butterflies swarming in her belly. "Staying."

He straightened his robe and crossed the room to her. "Good." He kissed her, his lips soft and sweet against hers. "I suggest more wine, in front of the fire." He bumped her nose with his. "I'll show you my pecs."

It was impossible to argue with a man who made her laugh.

"It's not forever," he said, his voice low as he nuzzled her neck. Was he talking about her staying up here, out of the way, or was he referring to their amazing sexual connection?

Her heart picked apart every syllable, searching for meaning and significance. The fact was, sex didn't make a relationship. Attraction and chemistry and some crazy near-death vibes could be all he wanted.

She wanted so much more from life. For her life. The thrill of hauling in bad guys wasn't enough anymore. When she went home, the house had a stagnant feel, as if it was merely holding its breath for a real family to walk in and liven up the place.

At one time, she'd dreamed of filling a home with children. One of four, she was used to the noise and camaraderie and sibling shenanigans. Then she just kept getting older, and while she was healthy and fit, her job wrecked every relationship.

Her mother had told her if the man was right, her career wouldn't matter. In Melissa's experience there wasn't a single man in Grave Gulch willing to play second fiddle to the police work. Except Antonio had said "we" as if he planned to accompany her to the call if needed.

How did she interpret that?

She shot him a sheepish smile, shaking free of her troubling thoughts. "Wine and pecs, it is."

She accepted the glass he handed her and took a sip. "That's smooth."

"One reason it's a favorite. It's from my brother's vineyard."

She felt her chin drop. "Your brother has a vineyard?"

"Up in Traverse City." He winked. "That didn't show up in the background check?"

"I'm a police officer, not a snoop," she said.

"You say tomato..."

She knew he was joking, but it was often close to the truth. "Come over here." He held out a hand. "Sit with me and enjoy the fire."

He pulled two chairs closer and moved an ottoman, urging her to prop up her feet and relax "You make it easy to put work away," she said with a sigh.

"Years of practice," he admitted. "At least a decade before I found any balance. You have a demanding career."

"The same could be said for you."

"Until Orr, the fatality risk was minimal."

She wanted to laugh, but it was a little too soon. "Is that why you built this suite? To manage risk?"

"It's good to be prepared. We cater to high-end clients and they can be paranoid."

"I've always admired people like you who can be casual, have fun and not hurt themselves or others."

He paused, staring at her. "Is that a compliment or a dig?"

"Compliment," she said in a rush as her cheeks heated with embarrassment. "I get accused of being too serious, too focused."

She rolled the wineglass between her palms, sipped again. "Sorry. I admire your balance. My personal and professional goals have been at odds lately," she blurted out. "It creeps up on me when I'm tired or stressed."

"And you've had plenty of stress these past days," he said.

"With more to come." But the wine and the fire and the man beside her were helping.

He leaned forward, elbows to knees, his wineglass held loosely in his hands. "Melissa?"

"Hmm?"

"What is it you really want, sweetheart?"

You. By some miracle, she managed not to blurt that out. "The balance you've found," she said after a moment. "From over here it looks fabulous."

"My balance isn't all that great." He sat back, scrubbing a hand through his hair. "You know why I was in the courtyard when Orr found me?"

She shook her head, half-afraid of the pain in his gaze.

"I go out there to think. It took me twenty years or so, but I built that garden last summer based on a plan I made with my wife. Her ashes, and the ashes of the child she carried, are scattered there. They died due to a complication with the pregnancy."

Her heart cracked for him. His choices suddenly made more sense. No commitments or emotional ties meant he couldn't be hurt like that again. "I'm so sorry." She set her wine on the table and just held his hand, offering comfort. Her love for him and her longing for a family might well be more of a burden than Antonio could bear.

"Some balance. When I lost her, I poured myself into work rather than face the empty house." He squeezed her hand, tried to smile. "Orr figured out that she inspired that garden. I should've said all of this to the officers earlier, but I couldn't. He said he would kill me and make it look like a suicide."

"No one would've believed that," she said. "We would never have let that story stand."

His smile was sad at the edges. "I told him the same thing." He pulled her up into his lap.

She ran her fingers over the soft bristles of his beard. "An empty house is a hard thing sometimes." They watched the fire for several quiet minutes as a contentment filled her. "Being here with you is nice."

"And more fun," he said.

She appreciated his attempt to lighten the mood. "And more fun," she agreed, her gaze on the fire. "You know what you want, what's important," she murmured. "I admire that. There are days I go home alone after a shift and the satisfaction I felt on the job fizzles when there's no one to share it with. Does that ever happen to you?"

"The views take the sting out of it," he said.

She started to get up, to leave the melancholy behind, but his arm around her waist held firm. "What is it you want, Melissa?"

With her fingers in his hair, the answer just tumbled

past her lips. "What my parents have. That partnership and closeness. Kids." She caught herself. "I don't mean to trample on a sore spot."

"You aren't trampling anything. Tell me more."

He was easy to talk to in this moment, with the darkness outside and the glow of the fire and warmth of the wine. "I want it all, and no one wants it with me. The police gig gets in the way."

"Wait." He brought her face around to meet her gaze. "Men have said that to you?"

"Yes. And I do understand no one wants to be the runner-up to a city all the time." She sighed, moved back to her own chair. "I had three years under my belt with the GGPD when I met the guy I thought was the one."

Antonio smiled. "I remember that feeling."

"That's the whole point, right?" she said, keeping it light though jealousy of the woman he'd loved prickled like a rash under her skin. "He was a contractor. He understood the ever-changing schedule. For over a year we managed the missed dates and cold dinners and had a great time.

"Then one morning I went into the bathroom, peed on a stick and while we were waiting for the results, he'd drafted my resignation. I wanted a husband and family. He wanted a wife and children. In his head, that meant I'd quit the force and stay home."

"That's not a partnership," he said.

Agreeing with him, she almost let out a cheer. "It does work for plenty of families."

"But you weren't done with your career."

"Not even close back then. I'm still not," she admitted. "It's probably time to stop wishing for the impossible and make a new dream."

"Were you pregnant?"

His question made her heart ache all over. "No." Although the negative result still stung some days. "Good thing, too, since those three minutes made our conflicting goals crystal clear."

She stretched her toes toward the fire. "I know we weren't expecting any of this to happen. I do understand it doesn't mean anything in the way of serious commitment."

"Melissa." He sat on the ottoman, stroking her leg from her ankle to her knee and back again. "I care for you, in and out of bed." The sparkle in his eyes was irresistible. "I enjoy spending time with you, though I wouldn't mind fewer crises. But I don't want to hurt you. I want to be clear that I'm not built for relationships anymore."

Melissa watched the fire reflected in Antonio's eyes. She caressed his jaw, the texture of his trimmed beard teasing her palm.

She should say no. A fling with Antonio would only delay and derail her goals of husband and family. Although…who was she kidding? There wasn't anyone on the horizon willing to compete with her career. She deliberately released those intangible dreams for the very real and present pleasure sitting right in front of her.

Whatever had brought her to this point, she couldn't resist the desire Antonio created. Tomorrow would have enough problems of its own.

She touched her lips to his, let herself go into his arms. Giving all she had to him, to this moment, she forgot goals and threats looming outside the suite. He was all she needed right now and she wanted to be all he needed, as well.

Taking things slow, as if they had nothing but time

in this safe cocoon, they made love in front of the fire, desire cresting in soft waves. Content and sated after, she cuddled close while he told her about purchasing the original Grave Gulch Hotel and turning it into this exquisite property that brought tourists to town. When she shivered, he carried her to the bedroom while she giggled at the two of them.

Laughter faded to sweet sighs as they snuggled under the covers, his strong body at her back, his arm heavy across her waist as she listened to his even breathing.

But she couldn't sleep. Her mind went round and round on why Bowe had manipulated evidence in at least two cases, the cycle interrupted only by ideas on how to catch Orr. This city relied on her to keep order and peace. She wouldn't let them down.

Antonio started to snore lightly. This time with him might be temporary, but it was good for her. Not just as a distraction. It was nice to have a friend, someone who knew her as she was right now. Someone with his own expectations and goals. Yes, they were wonderful together, not just in bed. She vowed she would stay his friend, even after they were done.

Their conversation gave her hope that if he could understand her career goals, someone else might, as well. Someday. Her heart wished for today to be the day and Antonio to be the man, but that was a dangerous wish that could bring this all crashing down on her head too soon.

Careful not to disturb Antonio, she slipped out of the bed. The plush hotel robe was cozy around her body as she left the bedroom. Her phone was charged and she checked her messages, finding two from Troy.

It was just past midnight, but only an hour had passed since his last attempt to reach her. He often worked as obsessively as she did when following a case. She called him back, prepared to leave a message.

Waiting for the phone to ring, she carried the empty wineglasses to the dishwasher in the kitchen. The space was so well-designed that a person really could be at home here for an extended period of time. If she dared to imagine life with Antonio, suites like this one would be a decadent perk, but she would want a true home to return to. Immediately the view from the deck of his lakeside home popped into her mind and she willed it away. Growing more attached would only make it harder when this ended.

"Melissa?"

"Did I wake you?" she asked.

"Not even close," he replied. "How are you doing?"

She felt remarkably refreshed, considering she couldn't sleep and had nearly been run over. Not that she could say any of that to her cousin. "About as well as you think," she hedged.

"I saw the other officers come back after they lost Orr's trail. Everyone wants this guy off the streets."

"He's clever, but unraveling. He'll make a mistake soon," she said with confidence.

She just hoped it wouldn't mean more pain or further injury to Antonio or his hotel. They needed to find the right draw to lure in Orr. Maybe it was time to use the press sticking close to the station for word about Hannah McPherson to prod Orr into acting before he was ready.

"So why did you call me earlier?" she asked.

"It's Bowe." He sighed. "The more we dig, the worse it looks for the GGPD's forensics department."

Goose bumps raced up her arms. "So Ellie found something."

"An understatement. Now that she has recovered the files, it confirms the evidence against Everleigh was both circumstantial and falsified."

Melissa swore.

"I said the same thing," Troy agreed. "The fibers Bowe reported finding on the murder weapon were originally from the apron used at the bar where she worked. Not anywhere close to something found on the bloody paperweight used to kill Fritz Emerson."

That matched Jillian's claim.

"The real issue is some of the evidence is right," Troy continued. "Only the pieces that tie Everleigh into the crime are not."

"What about the hairs they found on the paperweight?"

"Those were originally logged as 'potential suspect DNA.' An unspecified number of hairs appear to have been pulled from a hairbrush in the residence."

"I guess I'll get back with Jillian. She'll be relieved to know she didn't make a mistake."

"Already done," Troy said. "The hairbrush was collected to rule out or match other material at the scene."

"Standard procedure," Melissa mused, thinking out loud.

"Everything Ellie found backs up Jillian's work and report. Why in the hell would Bowe deliberately falsify those results? There is nothing I can find that connects him to anyone involved in this case."

"The same question is keeping me up at night," she admitted, pacing in front of the hearth. Bowe had manipulated evidence from the Emerson crime scene, which only lent more support to Ian's allegation that Bowe had smeared the fingerprint on Paxton's body.

"Mel," Troy began, "what if this is only—"

"Don't you dare finish that sentence," she snapped. "Yes, it's a safe bet that Emerson and Orr weren't the only cases Bowe tampered with, but let's keep a lid on that can of worms for now. If we learn *why* he manipulated evidence in these two cases, we can narrow down our search to similar incidents."

It tested her confidence in her own judgment that Bowe had done this right under her nose. The entire GGPD would be dealing with the fallout, likely for years to come. Attorneys would be filing appeals left and right, and soon the lawsuits would roll in against the department. Her officers hadn't specifically done anything wrong, but Bowe's actions would blow back on them, anyway. Most citizens lumped all the aspects of law enforcement together…not to mention however many miscarriages of justice had been perpetrated as a result of his misconduct.

"Do we have any leads on where he's hiding?" It might take five minutes or five days, but she would make Bowe talk when they caught him.

"He's in the wind," Troy said. "The last time he used his credit card, it was to fill up with gas just outside the city, on the south side. Not a trace of him since that transaction.

"Assuming he's outside the city, maybe we should put Clarke on this. I'll give him a call in the morning. Go get some rest."

"Is that an order?"

She heard the smile in his voice. "For both of us."

Antonio walked out of the bedroom, thrilled to find Melissa hadn't disappeared early on him this morning. She was sipping coffee and watching the local news. He went straight to her for a kiss, refusing to dwell on why that was more important than anything else.

Then she smiled and his heart soared.

Love was the reason.

He'd known his feelings for her were growing deeper than the remarkable physical intimacy between them. And he'd already decided he wanted to find a way to keep her in his life. But love? He didn't expect it to feel so wonderful.

More than a little bewildered, he poured coffee, considering how he wanted to proceed now that he knew for sure. Should he tell her? No, he should wait. He knew his reputation and it would take time to overcome it. Besides, there was too much going on. When he told her, he wanted it to be special. Memorable. *That was it.* He wanted to start creating new memories with Melissa that they would cherish for years to come.

She made an incomprehensible sound. "If I see one more 'free Granny' hashtag I might start writing citations."

He glanced at the television and winced. Sure enough, they were reporting on the protests all over the city on behalf of Hannah. "You can do that?"

"No," she admitted. "But it's a nice fantasy."

"At least they're showing the crowd in front of city hall, too, instead of just the police station."

"True." She carried her empty coffee to the sink. "Given the choice, I'd let her go," she said, rinsing the mug and loading it into the dishwasher.

He wondered how long it would take her to get used to Housekeeping handling those chores. Then again, Melissa likely wouldn't drop a good habit.

"You can't recommend that to the DA?"

"I have." She turned to look at him and her red ponytail spilled over her shoulder.

The sunlight from the French doors caught that fiery silk, striking some strands gold, others deep copper. He wished he could just take her right back to bed.

"You don't have to look so surprised." Her scolding brought him back to the moment. "I know the woman only did the unthinkable under duress. And it worked," she said with another grumble.

Her gaze clouded over and he wondered what else was on her mind. "She kidnapped a toddler. Sent the entire town into a panic," he said. "There should be consequences."

"And we got him back right away, thanks in part to you." She smiled and walked to his side of the counter and hugged his shoulders.

"Most people are stuck on the image of you arresting her," he said, wishing he could erase all her distress. "It'll pass eventually."

She checked her phone and dropped it into her purse, pulling out her keys. "I have to hope the story that blots out 'Free Granny' is good news, but the odds aren't in my favor. It seems the city is suddenly rife with killers."

"Rife?" he echoed.

"Orr is at large. Whoever really killed Fritz Emerson is out there, too. Bowe's actions have eroded the public's trust and I'm not sure how long it will take to pull things back together." She wrinkled her nose. "Sorry to dump on you first thing in the morning."

"I don't mind." Another sweet wave of emotion toward her coursed through his system. For all the times he'd been frustrated with her and her department, he understood now just how hard she'd tried to find justice for Wendy last summer.

Antonio topped off his coffee, smiling to himself. He could see mornings like this tomorrow, a week from now, next year, setting up for the day in the familiar peace of each other. After avoiding this kind of intimacy for so many years, he wanted it all. With her.

"I have a hotel in Chicago that I need to visit soon," he said. "Why not come with me?" It would be the perfect place for romancing her, and over champagne and strawberries he could tell her how he felt. "A few days away might be the break that reveals the solution." And he'd consider it a happy coincidence that the trip would take her out of Orr's reach for a little while.

"The department is already working on a solution," she said absently, lacing up her boots. "This morning we're officially reopening the Paxton case and moving Drew Orr to the top of the most wanted list."

"You are?"

Her auburn eyebrows knitted and she frowned. "I promised you I would."

"Well, yes, but you've had your hands full." And she'd nearly been run over. It had been six months since Orr had killed Wendy; surely a few more days wouldn't matter now.

"The department is in agreement that we have to be deliberate and provoke a reaction to put an end to his harassment. I can't be effective if he's taking shots at me at will."

Antonio's pulse stuttered. "Deliberate how?" She couldn't mean to make herself a target. He couldn't let her even think about it. To lose her now, after realizing what she meant to him—life couldn't be that cruel.

She walked over and kissed him. "We're still working on the details," she said. "I'll check in with you later, okay? Have a good day."

He trailed her to the door, pulling her in for one more kiss. "Be safe," he said, too shocked by his roiling emotions to add anything more.

"Don't worry." She squeezed his shoulders. "The GGPD isn't nearly as inept as recent events suggest."

"I wasn't thinking that," he began.

The small huff of skepticism was followed by a quick laugh. "That wasn't aimed at you," she said. "Bowe's actions have put a spotlight on the GGPD. It hasn't been our finest hour. We need to close a case, the right way, and soon."

He couldn't argue with the logic of starting with Orr. The man was a clear and present threat to her. "Use me," he said as she opened the door to leave. "I can lure him out, lure him here." It was the perfect plan and it kept her out of danger. "Then your officers can haul him away."

She paused in the foyer, her blue eyes full of affection. "Antonio, you've done more than your share already." She rested a hand on his chest for just a moment. "There's no way I'm using you or any other civilian for this. Leave it to the GGPD."

If only he could. Leaving it to her meant relinquishing control and sitting on the sidelines while she took all the risks. Not happening. He squeezed her hand, feeling the strength, yes, but also the fragility. To lose her would destroy him. Orr was a liar, a cheat and a killer. He'd nearly succeeded in killing Melissa twice already. Antonio would not give his former associate another chance.

"I can't do that," he murmured.

Her body stiffened and her hand fell away. There was a sudden chill in the foyer.

"Of course, that's too much to ask." Melissa's voice

was as brittle as the winter ice edging the lake. "I'm sorry, Antonio. For all of it." She punched the button for the elevator. "If I could, I would fix the past."

"What?" He'd made a misstep, but wasn't sure just where he'd gone wrong.

"And I can't rewrite procedure to suit you," she snapped. The elevator arrived and she stepped farther away from him.

"Melissa, wait." He stuck out his hand, keeping the doors open. "Talk to me."

She shook her head. "I'm already late. I'll stay at the station tonight. It's safe enough."

"Like hell it is."

Her face went pale, her eyes full of a pain that he couldn't put into context. He would suffer if something went wrong, too, not just her.

"Safe enough," she repeated. "I'm the chief of police. An entire community counts on me."

"I know that." What did that have to do with anything? "People count on me, too. I understand obligations. I'm trying to help you with yours."

"No need." Her mouth set into a flat line. "That's outside your scope now, but the GGPD appreciates your offer."

What was he missing?

The elevator chimed, an alert that the door had been open too long. "Thank you for your hospitality. Please have my things delivered to the station." Her voice cracked as she pushed his hand out of the way. "Someone will be in touch if we need the hotel for the Orr capture."

The doors closed between them and he struggled to make sense of it. She'd left him. No, it didn't make sense. What had set her off? He replayed the conversation in his head, struggling to identify his mistake so he could fix things.

He would not accept that he'd lost her just when he'd figured out she was the woman he wanted with him forever.

Chapter 15

Melissa was almost grateful for Drew Orr. With her heart caught in an ever-tightening vise after walking away from Antonio, setting a trap for a criminal was the perfect distraction.

She wasn't looking forward to spending another awful, lonely night on a cot in her office, even if it was the right move. The station was the safest place in town with Orr on the loose. *Second* safest, she amended. But she couldn't have stayed in that suite a minute longer, loving a man who doubted her work. She'd thought he had started to come around, that at the very least she'd earned some respect. Her heart felt pinched and she ached from the inside out. Even focused on her work, she knew loving Antonio had changed her.

Bowe was a bad apple—he'd deceived everyone around him—but that didn't make the entire department irredeemable. She couldn't go around arresting people without evidence, even if the witness was the man she loved. There were rules, laws, procedures that kept the entire community safe.

Melissa looked at the others gathered around the table helping her plan an operation to take down Orr. Yesterday, she'd given another press conference to announce the reopening of the Paxton case. Everyone had been on their toes, but Orr hadn't yet responded. As much as she'd like to hope he'd left town, she couldn't count on it.

"What else can we do to get him to make a move on me?" she asked the room at large.

The easiest path was to offer herself as bait. A year ago, even a month ago, she might've done it, taking the chance to minimize any risk to her officers. But after refusing to allow Antonio to pull the same stunt, she couldn't expose herself on purpose. They might not have a future, but he'd suffered enough. She wouldn't pile on.

"Why not leak the detail about the fingerprint?" Troy asked.

"I think the victim's family would be impossible for Orr to resist," Officer Coleman said. He and Bear were taking more walks around the station and the hotel, under the guise of training, while searching for any sign of Orr. "We could float the news that they're coming to meet with you and discuss new evidence found in their daughter's effects."

Melissa nodded, turning that over in her mind. "Yes. That has potential." And it meant less risk to the community. She tapped her pen against her palm. She looked at the others one by one. "I want eyes at the hotel and regular updates. I'm aware Mr. Ruiz has his own security team, but I want to know if Orr goes directly at him again."

"Yes, ma'am."

"All right, let's get the word out. Who wants to pose as the parents?" She thanked the volunteers with a nod as soon as the hands shot up. With the right outerwear for the winter weather, the officers would be able to pass as the Paxtons from a distance. "The rest of us need to eliminate the places he can lie in wait." It bothered her to no end that they hadn't yet found Orr's hideout.

Troy arched an eyebrow. "We can put officers in place posing as repairmen over in city hall, up on rooftops, that kind of thing."

She walked closer to the city map projected on the screen at one end of the room. Using the remote, she zoomed in on the blocks around the station, pointing out where she wanted undercover officers stationed in anticipation of Orr's response. When she was confident they had every possible approach covered, she sent a statement to the local networks and instructed the GGPD social-media liaison to post an update online.

"Chief—" Officer Warren came skidding into the room "—we just got a silent alarm from the hotel. Orr forced Mr. Ruiz out at gunpoint."

The words hung in the air, an incomprehensible shock to her system. Her heart stalled out and she couldn't get a full breath. "Which direction—"

But there was no time to finish the question as screams erupted from the ever-present protestors out front. She swore and stormed to the front of the station, assessing the scene from just inside the bullet-proof glass doors.

Heedless of pedestrians, Orr had driven right up onto the sidewalk and was shouting for the chief of police.

The bastard was using Antonio as a shield. Fear and fury lashed at her. She couldn't give in to the emotions, couldn't look at Antonio as the man she loved. Yes, *loved*, despite all her best attempts to resist it. All of that had to wait until they were clear.

"Get an ambulance over here," she ordered. "No sirens. Tell them to hold back out of sight." Someone got on the radio and was speaking in hushed tones.

"Warren, I want the street blocked."

"On it," he said, rushing off.

She faced her department, steel in her voice. "I want everyone out of harm's way. One hostage is all he gets today." On the street, Orr fired into the air and bellowed for her again. She ignored him. "Troy, get someone on a roof with a clear shot. I want teams of two, but no one moves without my order. I'll keep him distracted."

Everyone leaped into motion as she stepped outside, hand resting casually on her gun. For the first time in days the steps were clear of protestors and she resented Orr for ruining the moment.

She desperately wanted to give Antonio some kind of reassurance, but she couldn't. If she looked at him, at the danger he was in, she might break. That would put them all in jeopardy and no doubt raise the body count.

"Mr. Orr, thanks for coming over," she said, as if they'd been lifelong friends. "We've been wanting to speak with you."

"I'm not in the mood to talk, bitch." He shoved Antonio forward with his gun. "I'm making a special delivery."

"That so?" In her periphery, she saw her officers drawing away the bystanders a few at a time. "Please turn over your weapon," she said. "It's unlawful to fire a gun inside city limits."

"Come on down and take him," Orr shouted. "Wendy Paxton's killer, ready to confess."

"You can't mean Mr. Ruiz." She caught sight of Troy across the street, escorting one of their best marksmen, armed with a rifle, into city hall. She couldn't let it get that far. "We have his prints on file and they are not a match to the evidence on Wendy Paxton's body."

"He did it." He gave Antonio another little shove.

"Lower your weapon," she directed, pulling her own gun. "Let Mr. Ruiz go. We can get to the bottom of this together." She had a shot, as did several of her officers by now. "This is no way to resolve anything."

"He's been spreading lies about me. He killed Wendy and ran me out of town."

"Okay. That's upsetting." She tilted her head. "Hey, is that the gun you used to fire at me on Saturday night?"

The tactic worked. Orr shifted to look at the weapon in his hand and she used the distraction to advance. He recovered quickly, though, raising the gun and taking aim at her.

Everyone moved at the same time. In a blink, Orr pulled the trigger while Antonio slammed into him and the bullet went wide, missing her and the glass doors, and lodging in the stone facade. He and Antonio were twisting around in the snow and the gun slid out of reach. Her officers closed in from both sides of the street, separating the men and guiding Antonio away.

Her heart had stalled during the scramble and seeing Antonio safe, she felt it beating again. The surge of relief would have brought her to her knees if she didn't have unfinished business with Orr.

Someone collected the gun while others brought Orr under control. She walked over and snapped the cuffs on his wrists herself. "You are done."

He screamed in outrage, making vile threats and promises of vengeance.

She let his anger roll over her, squeezed the cuffs another notch tighter as she stared him down. "Did you fire a weapon at me and Mr. Ruiz on Saturday night?"

"I was shooting at *him*," he snarled, looking around for Antonio.

"Good start." She stepped back, hands on her hips. "Did you try to run me over with a stolen truck?"

"Would've been two for one," he said. "Ruiz and a cop for a spare."

The spittle gathered at the corners of his mouth had her taking a half step back. "Did you kill Wendy Paxton?"

"Hell yes!" Orr shrieked.

"Take him to County," she said.

The officers aimed him toward the patrol car that had just pulled up.

"She had it coming!" Orr did everything in his power to shake off the officers to no avail. "Cheating on me like that. She didn't know anything."

"County," she repeated, turning away.

"You can't hold me," he screamed. "I have great lawyers. I'll be out by dinner." Orr laughed, and the maniacal sound slithered down her spine.

Why wreck his fantasy? They had him dead to rights for attempted murder today, and they would pile on with the other attempts he'd made on her life and Antonio's. Wendy's parents would have justice at last.

She started up the steps, baffled by the horror on the faces in front of her, when the sounds of a fight registered behind her. A grunt, a shouted warning and another gunshot.

Whirling around, Melissa saw one officer down,

clutching his thigh, and Orr, hands cuffed, with a service weapon in his grasp, taking aim at her again. She fired, twice, center mass.

In slow motion, she watched the gun fall from his hand, watched the man crumple to the ground. Blood pooled under the lifeless body, following the bumpy pavement and staining the snow along the way.

Then, abruptly, the world snapped back to reality. She handed over her weapon, then let the paramedics confirm Orr's demise and tend to her injured officer.

Orr was dead.

Given a choice, she would rather have Orr behind bars. She looked down at her empty hands, feeling utterly disconnected and slightly out of step with everyone around her. She'd shot him in self-defense, but it was more to protect her community than herself.

Reeling with a strange sadness, she instinctively looked for Antonio, but he was gone.

Antonio's heart pounded against his ribs and his only coherent thought was to go to Melissa. He wanted to hold her until he was certain she was safe and whole. But she was surrounded by GGPD personnel and was being ushered away for whatever had to happen after an officer fired a gun.

In a fatality.

"Take it easy." Troy guided him away from the scene, around the corner of city hall. "You'll be able to see her soon," the detective said.

"Should I give a statement?" He craned his neck, hoping to get a glimpse of Melissa. Surely with so many witnesses she wouldn't be in trouble for taking lethal action. "She didn't do anything wrong."

"That's why I'm here. For your statement. Relax, Antonio. Walk me through it."

It took another few hard heartbeats to absorb the words, the meaning. He cleared his throat and explained how Orr had traded one hostage for Antonio at the hotel. "I saw Chief Colton do what was necessary to prevent further loss of life," he said to finish. "Can I see her now?"

But he had to fill in more details as Troy questioned him, until finally the interview was complete.

"We appreciate your help," Troy said. "You've been an asset to the department, to the chief in particular, and that helps all of us. Thank you again for helping us rescue my nephew."

Antonio gave a nod, but trailed after Troy. "What happens next? For Melissa, I mean. They won't force her out, will they?"

"Every officer-involved shooting is investigated and she'll have to speak with a psychologist before she can return to duty."

"But she'll return?" Antonio couldn't bear it if Orr killed her career. Melissa lived for the job, for the opportunity to serve the city and people she loved.

"I can't just say yes, because we have to follow protocol," Troy explained. "But the takedown was a group effort and there were plenty of witnesses to her necessary actions."

Nothing he could do. The helplessness burned through him. He needed a minute with her; that was all. Just enough time to make sure she was all right, but they'd led her somewhere he couldn't follow.

Returning to the hotel, he went straight to his office, making it clear Melissa was the only interruption he would allow. It seemed to take forever for his heart to find a normal rhythm again. He pressed his fingers lightly to the tender spot on his jaw where he'd taken another punch from Orr. It was begging for ice.

Would've been nice to sit beside Melissa, watch the fire together while the ice relieved the ache. Would anyone take care of her tonight or would she be dealing with all of this alone?

Their last conversation hadn't gone well and she hadn't returned his calls. Still, she had to know she could come to him, that he would be a friend, even if she didn't return his feelings. More than anything else right now he regretted that she'd gone up against Orr, unsure of how much Antonio believed in her and the GGPD. And she had no idea how much he loved her.

Chapter 16

The next morning, her coffee in hand, Melissa tucked herself into her office. She wasn't in the mood for much chatter today, but she needed to be here. The department psychologist had helped her through the immediate turmoil of the shooting. Together they decided her officers and detectives needed to see the normal routine, as close as she could manage anyway, despite the questions that remained unanswered.

Studying her desktop, she searched for a silver lining amid the stacked-up files and overflowing email inbox waiting for her attention. Well, she was still the chief of police, still had her dream job, even if she had to ride a desk after firing her weapon and ending a man's life.

That hadn't been her ideal outcome, taking a life never was, although in this instance she didn't harbor any regrets.

Orr would've killed Antonio and anyone else within reach if she hadn't taken swift, decisive action.

She shied away from thoughts of Antonio. Last night, alone in her own bed at home, had been unbearably lonely. That scared her more than a little, since the beautiful peace she'd found with him had to be over. Her house had felt awkward rather than welcoming and it went beyond the differences in decor, food options and security. How many times had she started to call him last night, only to change her mind?

She wanted something he couldn't give. A clean break was for the best. Look at that, she'd found a silver lining.

She sipped her coffee and picked up a file, only to toss it back down, unread, as her concentration fractured. What was truly regrettable was that Bowe's actions had left Orr free for too long. She supposed the subsequent desk duty gave her plenty of time to review Bowe's old cases for any other signs of manipulation. What messes would they be cleaning up next?

And maybe not so silvery, but riding a desk gave her ample time to think about the next steps. For herself. Though she loved her work, she was tired of settling for only professional satisfaction. Being chief was demanding and definitely unpredictable, but her heart yearned for balance.

Swiveling in her chair, she picked up the framed photo of Desiree and Danny, a gift her cousin had dropped off after the kidnapping ordeal. Desiree was raising a child alone and doing it well. That little boy had Melissa wrapped around his tiny finger. Her heart ached in her chest as she imagined raising a child of her own. Maybe it was time to take that leap, even without a husband and partner in place. She couldn't stop the fantasy of playdates with Danny and Desiree, trips to the park, family traditions, as she and her cousin raised the next generation of Coltons.

In her mind, though, her little one had Antonio's dark eyes and mischievous grin. On a shaky breath, she returned the picture to its place of honor on her desk. Desiree's path wasn't for her. She wanted it all. Husband and children and a career. She craved that balance, but no longer with a faceless partner.

With Antonio. The man who didn't trust her department. The man who'd vowed—with good reason—not to travel a family path again.

There were some things "I love you" couldn't cure. Her career. His past. Her obligations. His doubts.

Swiping a tear from her cheek, she turned her attention to the slew of emails she'd been ignoring during the recent chaos and set to work. She had no idea she'd left her desk to stare out her office window until someone knocked on her door.

Turning, she saw Antonio. It took every ounce of willpower not to rush forward, expecting him to catch her in that warm embrace.

"Can I come in?" he asked. "I've been worried."

"Of course." She tried to smile and gave up. "Close the door." Just in case she lost it, no sense upsetting the entire department.

He did as she asked, but didn't sit down in one of the chairs facing her desk. With his hands in his pockets, he stood there and studied her.

She assumed he saw it all. The dark circles under her eyes, the tension in her jaw, the badge that represented a system he didn't trust.

"Are you all right?" he asked.

That smooth, deep voice was a balm to her frayed nerves and she shamelessly soaked it in. "I am. It won't take them long to confirm the shooting was justified." Her gaze locked with his. Until right now she hadn't thought that maybe he disapproved of what she'd done.

"You were remarkable out there," he said, pride radiating from his eyes. "The whole department was absolutely remarkable."

She bit her lip. It was hard to accept his praise, after killing a man he'd once considered a friend.

"What do you do while waiting for the process and protocols?" he asked.

She gestured to her desk. "Plenty of work and enough time to get it done for a change."

"I see." He tipped his head. "No time off?"

She resisted the urge to fold her arms over her chest to shelter her heart from him. "Not really. We are looking into all of Bowe's cases. It will take time, but we'll figure out why he did what he did. And where he's hiding."

"That's good."

There was an awkward silence that she couldn't bear. "Antonio…" Then the words started tumbling out. "I love you. I want more time with you. But I can't settle." Her pulse steadied as the words resonated. "I want my career *and* everything else that makes a life full." He was going to walk out any second and she braced for the pain even as she rushed on. "I want a husband and children. I want family chaos and jammed-up schedules." She sucked in a breath. She wanted it all with him, despite the furrow pleating his brow. "I'm not going to be completely me, not completely happy, until I'm on that track." She stopped just short of apologizing for her dreams.

"You love me," he said.

"Yes." For all the good it did either of them.

"Do you see that love for me changing? Fading out with a fling? Maybe you'll get tired of me and the demands of my work."

No. That was the worst piece of this entire situation. She'd fallen in love with the wrong man. "No." She wouldn't lie. "Never. But that doesn't change that everything I want is at odds with what you need."

She wished she could be the one to leave, but she wasn't about to run out of her office, an emotional wreck, in front of the officers who looked up to her as the example.

Unable to read him, she turned back to the window. Just because he would leave, didn't mean she had to watch him go. She listened for the squeak of the doorknob so she knew when it would be safe to let the tears fall.

He stared at the elegant line of her back and realized just how far he'd come. She expected him to walk out. He'd given her every reason to come to that conclusion.

"I'm not leaving, Melissa."

She didn't turn around.

"I love you, too." He stepped up behind her, resting his hands lightly on her shoulders. When she didn't shrug him off, he wrapped his arms around her, holding her close. Their image was a faint reflection in the window, but it was enough to confirm he was doing the right thing. For himself. For her. For their future.

"I've been scared for years. Two decades, really. Until you." He brushed a soft kiss to her cheek. "Although I suspect I'll have more reason to be scared for you in the years ahead, I am absolutely terrified of the years ahead if you're not in my world." He shifted so she was facing him. "I'm done running from a full life, 'ong as you're in it." He dropped to one knee, smiling when she gasped at the ring he held for her. "Melissa Colton, will you marry me and help me fill the hotel with beautiful redheaded children?"

"You can't be serious." A slow smile illuminated her face, lit up the room like a sunrise. "It's a big hotel." She caught her lip between her teeth. "Are you sure? I know what this—"

He cut her off. "I've never been more certain of anything. Marry me, Melissa." He watched her face as he pushed the ring into place on her finger. She bounced on her toes and tugged him to his feet. His heart was bursting with happiness when she wrapped her arms around him. "Is that a yes?"

She leaned back, her smile filling him with a joy he hadn't allowed himself in far too long.

"Yes." Her hands trembled as she touched his face, pulled him close for a kiss. "You're everything I've always wanted and so much more than I dared to hope for."

He felt weightless and full of light as he held her close. She was his future, his heart. He didn't want to let go, but they both had work. "I'll have the champagne on ice in the suite," he said, kissing her once more.

She beamed, her eyes sparkling brighter than the diamond on her hand. "I'll call when I'm on the way over."

And there it was, he thought—the first day of the rest of their lives.

* * * * *

Don't miss the next book in
The Coltons of Grave Gulch miniseries

Colton's Killer Pursuit *by Tara Taylor Quinn*

Available February 2021 from
Harlequin Romantic Suspense!

WE HOPE YOU ENJOYED
THIS BOOK FROM

H HARLEQUIN
ROMANTIC
SUSPENSE

Danger. Passion. Drama.

These heart-racing page-turners will keep you guessing to the very end. Experience the thrill of unexpected plot twists and irresistible chemistry.

4 NEW BOOKS AVAILABLE EVERY MONTH!

She shivered next to him, clearly upset as she spoke. He put his arm around her and pressed a kiss to the top of her head.

"It's okay," he soothed, stroking her upper arm. "I'm here now. I won't let anyone hurt you or Ben."

"I think he has a key."

That got his attention. He paused midstroke, digesting this bit of news. "What makes you say that?"

She told him about Jake Porter, the man who claimed to be Will's grandson. The way he'd visited her earlier, his displeasure at finding her in the house.

"We'll change all the locks," Carter declared. "I'll go first thing in the morning, as soon as the hardware stores open. We can even put some extra locks on, as additional deterrent. And I want you and Ben to stay with me until he's apprehended." His apartment wasn't large, but they would make it work. She could have his bed and he'd take the couch. The discomfort was a small price to pay for knowing she and the baby were safe.

"Oh, no," she said. "We can't do that."

Carter drew back and stared at her, blinking in confusion. This was a no-brainer. Someone was out there with an agenda, and it was clear they were after something inside this house. Changing the locks was a good first step, but he doubted the intruder was going to be put off so easily. Unless he missed his guess, this guy was going to come back. And the next time, he might not be content to simply ransack a few rooms.

Carter took her hand. "I'm not trying to be alarmist here, but he's probably going to try again."

"But the locks," she said weakly.

"I doubt he'll let new locks stop him," Carter replied. "And given the way he acted with you before, it's probably only going to escalate. If he finds you here, he might hurt you."

Don't miss
Ranger's Family in Danger *by Lara Lacombe,*
available February 2021 wherever
Harlequin Romantic Suspense
books and ebooks are sold.

Harlequin.com

Get 4 FREE REWARDS!

We'll send you 2 FREE Books plus 2 FREE Mystery Gifts.

Harlequin Romantic Suspense books are heart-racing page-turners with unexpected plot twists and irresistible chemistry that will keep you guessing to the very end.

FREE
Value Over
$20

Love Harlequin romance?

DISCOVER.

Be the first to find out about promotions, news and exclusive content!

Facebook.com/HarlequinBooks

Twitter.com/HarlequinBooks

Instagram.com/HarlequinBooks

Pinterest.com/HarlequinBooks

ReaderService.com

EXPLORE.

Sign up for the Harlequin e-newsletter and download a free book from any series at **TryHarlequin.com**

CONNECT.

Join our Harlequin community to share your thoughts and connect with other romance readers!
Facebook.com/groups/HarlequinConnection

HSOCIAL2020